THE
DETAIL

DANA WAYNE

Book Liftoff
1209 South Main Street
PMB 126
Lindale, Texas 75771

Book design by Champagne Book Design
Cover design by Just Write.Creations

Library of Congress Control Number Data
Wayne, Dana
The Detail / Dana Wayne.
1. Suspense—Romance—Fiction.
2. General—Romance—Fiction.

BISAC:
FIC 027110 FICTION / Romance / Suspense.
FIC 027000 FICTION / Romance / General.

2021919516

ISBN: 978-1-947946-77-4 (Amazon/Kindle Direct)

www.danawayne.com
www.bookliftoff.com

BOOKS BY
DANA WAYNE

PRAISE FOR DANA WAYNE BOOKS

"Dana Wayne's characters don't live on the printed page. They live in your heart for a long time." Caleb Pirtle, III award-winning author

Unveiling Beulah

"Breathtakingly beautiful read"—Amazon reader

"…emotional, well-laced and kept me engaged with intriguing characters, humor and plot twists."—Amazon Reader

"Beautifully written love story." Amazon Reader

"Absolutely heartwarming…the perfect book for romance lovers who want characters who are can overcome anything."—5* with Crowned Heart for Excellence InD'tale Magazine

Chasing Hope

"A feel-good romance at its finest!"—KayBees Bookshelf

"My kind of romance!"—Readers Favorite

"A truly special book that deserves a place of honor on your bookshelf."—InD'tale Magazine

"Strong characters, a sweet romance, and a hopeful examination of real-world issues."—BookLife Prize

"…(can) draw out a plot that is predictable in all the right places yet still offers twists that surprise, delight and keep the story moving."—Ruthie Jones Reviews

Whispers on The Wind

"Excellent mix for chilling read!"—InD'tale Magazine

"Truly a joy to read!"—Readers Favorite

"...both sizzles and gives you chills."—Book Chick Blog

"...crafted a story that weaves ghosts, romance, Southern hospitality, a couple of murders and mystery that kept me guessing."—Amazon reader

"...perfect blend of a love story and suspense!"—Amazon Reader

Mail Order Groom

"...brings the characters to life in a way that has you leaning against the fence post watching it all unfold. Five Stars!"—Coffee in The Morning Blog

"...well written, romantic and suspenseful!"—Books and Benches Magazine

"A gripping story that cannot be ignored for a second!"—Readers Favorite

"Intricately crafted story with many curves along the trail that the reader never anticipates!"—InD'tale Magazine

"...exceptional piece of literature from a well-accomplished writer who is now one of my favorite writers of all time!" Redheaded Book Blog

Secrets of the Heart

"...a good romance, storyline with substance, and very interesting well-developed characters." Linda Thompson, The Author Show

"...stands out for originality...characters are strong and the work well-written." Kevin Cooper

"...she blends heartbreak and despair with love and hope." Coffee In The Morning Blog

"...a romantic winner that touches all the emotions and touches them with love and compassion."—The Book Editor

"For all lovers of romance, get this book!"—Amazon Reader

"One of the few books in my life I can't wait to read again!"— Amazon Reader

THE
DETAIL

CHAPTER ONE

"I'LL ONLY BE GONE A COUPLE OF DAYS, MOM. I'LL DROP BY when I get back. I know. I'll think about it."

Detective Jessie Foster heard the click when her mother ended the call without a goodbye. Again. She paused, then slapped the receiver in its cradle. Two seconds later, she flung a pencil across the room where it ricocheted off a corner of the cushioned cubical wall before it landed on the other desk.

Her mom could turn a good day into a bad one in a heartbeat.

"Whoa, there, Texas. What's got your panties in a wad this time?"

The question from Seth Hamilton, her partner and co-habitant of this padded cell, reminded her she wasn't alone. "Can it, Hammer. I'm not in the mood." She sighed and tugged the red scrunchy from her ponytail, tossed it on the desk, then leaned back and raked slender fingers through dark, shoulder-length curls. A tension headache crept up the back of her neck. *Perfect. Just damn perfect.* "And stop calling me Texas. And Tex."

"I would, but I hear bitch isn't politically correct these days."

Despite her anger, she snorted. "You're such an ass."

"Says you." He sauntered over and rested his hip on the corner of her desk. "She still after you to take that job with the feds?"

Before she could reply, he continued. "And in Dallas, no less. You hate the traffic."

"A desk job is a place to start." Even as the lie slid off her tongue, her inner voice chided, 'Coward,' and she caught herself before she blurted out the hard truth. *It's killing me to work side-by-side with you every day and not tell you how I feel.*

"You like working in the field, Tex. A desk job isn't for you, and you know it. So, what gives?"

She didn't address his comment. She also knew he wouldn't let it go. "I'm a damn good cop whether I'm behind a desk or out in the field."

She ignored the teasing snicker from Seth. He delighted in getting her riled. Today, she refused to take the bait.

"I have my last interview with them next week." She stood and scanned her work area. Small, crowded, and noisy, it was nonetheless a decent space. The police force in Walker, a quiet town southeast of Dallas, was a small, tight-knit group. Granted, most called her names behind her back, mainly because she refused to take any crap from them, but if push came to shove, they'd be there for her. Did she really want to start over somewhere else?

Or was she simply running away?

"They don't deserve you," said Seth. "And we'd miss you here."

She grunted. "Yeah. Right."

He had the audacity to laugh. The throaty, masculine sound made her stomach quiver. *Aw, hell. I've worked side-by-side with him for over a fricking year, and now my stomach flutters when he laughs. Or winks.*

Or breathes.

Just shoot me.

If she were honest with herself—which she always tried to be—he was nice-looking, handsome even. Five years older than her at thirty-eight, he carried his age well. Cognac-colored eyes framed by long, dark lashes she silently envied, and heavy brows were the first thing she noticed about him.

The second was his mouth—those lips. Women paid a fortune to fake what God gave him free gratis. Even a slight overbite and crooked nose didn't detract from his rugged good looks. From the top of his military cut, salt and pepper head to the souls of his cowboy boots, he was six feet three inches of blatant masculinity coupled with a compelling sex appeal hard to ignore, but she managed.

Well, most of the time.

Lately, not so much.

One whiff of his cologne, coupled with a provocative man-smell, was enough to send rational thought straight to the gutter.

It took determination to get her wayward mind back on track. "You're just playing nice cause you think you'll get lucky."

"Yeah, right. I relish the idea of sex with a buzz saw."

She flinched and buried the hurt his comment elicited; defensive walls shored and braced. She knew him so well and knew he liked to tease, but still, it gave her pause. Had the job finally robbed her of all femininity? Desirability?

Is that how he saw her?

Suck it up, buttercup. It is what it is. "Time to rock and roll," she snapped and gave herself a mental shake. Focus on their detail—pick up Jack Walls in Denver and bring him back to Walker to stand trial. Suspected of killing two of his former girlfriends, Jess couldn't prove the first one, and by the time they got the evidence needed to arrest him for the second, he vanished without a trace. Until now.

"With any luck," continued Jess, "we can get there before midnight tonight and be back late tomorrow night."

The grueling fourteen-hour drive was just another part of the job. Hours alone with her partner presented issues she did not want to dwell on.

Seth smirked. "What's your hurry, Tex? Hot date?"

"The sooner this is over with, the better."

He stood, grabbed his jacket off the rack, and draped it over one arm. "Personally, I can't wait to spend the next three days trapped in a car with Miss Congeniality and a deranged sociopath."

She lifted the paperwork and her purse off the desk, grabbed her go-bag, and headed for the hallway. "Wonder why you got stuck with me for a partner."

"Obviously, somewhere along the way, I spit in someone's Cheerios."

Jess shook her head. An anomaly, Seth always spoke his mind. She liked that about him, though he sometimes goaded her to no end. For whatever reason, they clicked from the start, probably because they were more alike than different. Neither of them liked all the hoops they jumped through daily to get the bad guys, and both sported a wicked sense of humor not everyone could handle. Plus, they each tended to call a spade a spade without apology.

Unable to curb the impulse, she cast him a quick sideways glance. Immediately, butterflies the size of a roadrunner took flight in her stomach.

Probably some kind of hormonal-biological-clock thing. I am thirty-three now. It will pass. Probably like a kidney stone, but it will pass.

Disgusted with her wandering mind, she strode toward the elevator, Seth following a few steps behind. She barely managed to smother the temptation to strut a bit. *What the hell is wrong with me?* She gave the elevator dial a harder-than-necessary push. *I don't care what he thinks of my ass in these slacks.*

The doors opened, and she walked in, pressing the garage button as she turned.

Seth met her gaze, sensuous mouth curved up in a Cheshire-cat smile. "I appreciate the show."

"Shut up."

He winked.

It was going to be a long three days.

♂♀

Seth knew he skated a fine line with Jess. The department's stand on sexual harassment left no room for doubt. One word from her, and his ass was in a sling.

But he was just vain enough to believe she enjoyed their suggestive banter. And she gave as good as she got, too. He liked a woman who spoke her mind and didn't get all ticked off when a man did the same.

His transfer to Walker coincided with her last partner's move to Austin. He didn't miss the snickers drifting among his fellow officers after the announcement of their partnership. Later, he discovered most didn't like working with her, calling her testy, hardheaded, and bitchy. But he never saw that side of her personality. Instead, he saw a first-rate detective, intensely dedicated to the job, with a warped sense of humor to match his own.

She was also a beautiful, fascinating woman who worked hard to hide that fact from the rest of the world. And it was the woman behind the badge who captivated his thoughts these days.

Granted, he sometimes took things a bit too far, like the buzz-saw comment. The brief flash of pain he saw in her eyes tore at his conscience. Filters he found so easy to employ around others failed him completely around Jess. From day one, she took whatever he dished out and gave it back in spades. So much so, he inched further and further across that invisible line just to see how she would respond.

Lately, though, something was different. *She* was different. An occasional look in her eye that quickly disappeared made him wonder. What if she saw him as more than her irritating partner with a propensity for spouting out useless trivia?

What if she saw *him*?

Finally.

That *what-if* kept him awake most of last night, and he vowed to use this trip to explore the prospect in depth.

After she got over being mad, of course.

Man, she was something when riled—like now. Her cheeks were a flattering shade of red, and that sexy, sassy mouth formed a tight line across her face. Her anger never lasted, so he'd just wait her out.

And try not to think about other things that could put such an enticing flush on her cheeks.

The door slid open, and she started to exit ahead of him, then stopped and scowled.

He grinned and strolled out. "How about I take the first turn at the wheel. Your driving makes me nervous."

"Since when?"

"Since you go into a cussing rampage in traffic, and we'll hit the start of rush hour through Dallas."

"Whatever. Drive." She pitched him the keys and walked to the passenger side, throwing her bag into the back seat before buckling in.

He placed his go-bag beside hers and climbed behind the wheel of the older model SUV.

Jess dug through the paperwork and pulled out a map. "The GPS is on the fritz again, and cell service may be iffy."

He glared at the map in her hand. "I don't need a map."

"Need I remind you of the last time we had this conversation?"

"That was then. This is now. I don't need the map."

"I swear, Hammer, you will sincerely regret it if you get us lost and drag this trip out any more than necessary."

"Duly noted."

He put the car in gear and headed out of the garage toward the interstate through Dallas. Traffic would be horrible, the drive exhausting, but he looked forward to the hours of proximity with his feisty partner, who of late pressed every male button he possessed.

It was time he located a few of her female ones.

CHAPTER TWO

JESS PEERED OUT THE WINDOW AND HUFFED AS BOREDOM CREPT in. The Panhandle of Texas was a treat at first since she'd never been this far north, but monotony converted minutes into hours when all you had to look at was mile after mile of scrub brush, sand, and rocks.

At first, the time flew by. They discussed the assignment, the scenery and planned where they would stop on the return trip. By Wichita Falls, they were out of what she considered safe subjects, and conversation lagged. Seth appeared unusually preoccupied, and she found herself repeating things to him. Since he'd voiced no response to her last question, she tried another conversation starter. "I officially don't like this part of Texas. Not enough green."

He gave a half-hearted shrug. "It's all in what you get used to, I guess."

"Well, I'm used to pine trees and lakes."

"Hmmm."

She cut her eyes toward him and immediately recognized his deep-in-thought expression.

Head tilted to one side, forehead creased into a frown, as one finger tapped out a staccato on the steering wheel.

Definitely something on his mind. Not the job. Something else?

She hesitated, then tried again. "That's the third jet I've seen in the last half hour."

The frown deepened, and his voice lacked any trace of interest. "Sheppard Air Force Base is in Wichita Falls."

What is up with him? She fiddled with her tablet, then cut her eyes toward him. Cheeks like carved granite, darkened by five o'clock shadow, the bump in his aquiline nose was more pronounced from this angle but did nothing to diminish his formidable appeal. If anything, it enhanced an already striking profile. He flexed his fingers on the steering wheel, and she forced her eyes forward. Strong hands, too. She chewed her lower lip, fighting to pull her thoughts from his hands and how they might feel on her skin.

"A crocodile can't stick his tongue out."

After the extended silence, it took a moment for his unexpected blast of trivia to connect to her brain, still preoccupied with his hands. "A pregnant goldfish is called a twit."

He grinned. "The glue on Israeli postage stamps is certified kosher."

She dug through her memory for a decent counter. "It's impossible to sneeze with your eyes open."

"A pig's orgasm lasts thirty minutes."

Jess snorted and shook her head. "Fine. You win. Can't top that one."

His low laugh sent a delicate hum flowing through her body.

"Come on, Tex, don't give up so easy."

"How do you remember all this stuff?" she grumbled. "I do good to remember what I read yesterday."

He tapped the side of his head with one long finger. "Storehouse of totally useless knowledge."

"Useless being the operative phrase."

"You gotta admit it helps pass the time."

She opened her tablet. "So does playing games on this."

"Put that away and talk to me."

"Talk? About what?"

"Anything."

He glanced at her, but she couldn't see his eyes for the aviator shades he wore.

"We've never really talked before. Except for work stuff. And we have a lot of time to kill."

"Like what's my favorite food or how I like my coffee?"

"Nah, I know that already."

Surprised, she blinked. "You do?"

He shrugged. "I'm a detective. I detect things."

"Like what?"

His lips puckered and moved side to side.

The hum infusing her body kicked up a notch, along with her heart rate. *Holy mother of pearl.* She forced a relaxed expression and tried to concentrate on his words.

"Let's see...your favorite foods are Mexican, but only from Tele's over on Bowie Street, and Chinese takeout from that new place downtown. You prefer wine over hard liquor, strong coffee with a little cream, don't like beer unless it's ice cold. You work out like a fiend almost every day to maintain that tight body of yours; you love chocolate-filled donuts and hate cottage cheese."

"Tight body?" She was sure he mentioned other stuff, but her brain chose to single out that remark.

He nodded, eyes straight ahead. "Yep."

She faced forward and tried to neutralize her body's tingly response to his comment. "You love to fish, hate broccoli, and could live on greasy-spoon burgers." She paused. "And work out often to...stay in shape."

His smile was positively lethal. "So, you noticed my tight body, too, huh?"

A quick intake of air carried his distinctive scent, scattering her thoughts. How could she not notice? Heat rushed to her cheeks, and she swallowed hard. "It's forbidden to call a pig Napoleon in France."

He glanced her way, then back to the road again. "Tell me about your family."

Uneasy, she shifted in her seat. *How many ways can you say dysfunctional?* "Not much to tell. An accident took my biological dad right after I was born. Mom married Frank Cantrell when I was three. They divorced when I was ten, remarried each other two years later." *Then proceeded to make everyone miserable for the next fifteen years.* "What about you?"

"Folks live in Weatherford when they aren't checking off another place on their bucket list. Two sisters, both younger and one brother, older."

"They live in Weatherford, too?"

"Just the girls. Jason is a Marshall in Tyler." He tilted his head in her direction. "Your turn."

She pulled the phone's charging cable from her purse and plugged it in. Family was not a comfortable topic of conversation. "In Vermont, a woman has to have her husband's permission to get false teeth."

He remained silent for a heartbeat. "A dentist invented the electric chair."

σ♭

Seth pulled into the massive truck stop across the Texas-New Mexico border and killed the engine, desperate for hot coffee and a pit stop. He knew Texas was big but never dreamed he'd drive eight hours before crossing the state line.

He peeked at Jess, who fell asleep an hour or so ago, her head lolled toward him. Gone were the tight lines that gave her face a perpetual scowl; her impertinent mouth gaped a little, and a soft snore made him grin. Her lack of desire to talk about herself or her family was minor and not unexpected. Besides, he already knew most of it. Like the fact her stepfather Frank Cantrell was a drunk and small-time hood with a rap sheet covering decades, who fled town several years ago, one step ahead of an arrest warrant. He didn't know much about her younger sister, Tina, but her mother, Ivy, was emotionally needy and made Jess feel like an ungrateful daughter at every opportunity. He could only wonder about her childhood with Frank and Ivy as role models, which probably explained why she shied away from permanent relationships.

He ran the back of one finger against her cheek because he couldn't help himself. *Petal soft. Just like I thought.* His knuckle grazed her lower lip, and he jerked his hand back.

Holy hell.

He took a deep breath and nudged her shoulder. "Wake up, Tex. Potty stop."

She jerked up and glanced around. "Where are we? Why didn't you wake me sooner? How long have we been on the road?"

The last question preceded an extended yawn and a long stretch.

It took immense willpower not to watch. Sleek as a cat with long, shapely legs, Jess sported a trim body and full, firm breasts. His body did what any normal red-blooded one would, and he swallowed a groan. "New Mexico. I didn't need to. Eight hours." He pushed open the door and got out, not surprised at the chilled air.

He rounded the front of the car where she joined him, arms folded across her middle. "Dang, it's cold. I didn't expect this."

"I checked the weather before we left. Upper-thirties for lows the next couple of days." He took in her appearance and frowned. "Didn't you bring a jacket?"

"It's April. It's not supposed to be cold in April."

He shook his head, opened the rear door, and pulled his bag from the back. A moment later, he tossed a heavy hoodie her way. "Higher elevation means colder temps. Put this on before you freeze."

"I have my suit coat in the back." She slipped on the hoodie and zipped it up. "But this is warmer. Thanks."

Jess stood five-eight, but still, the garment swallowed her, making her look more diminutive and, for whatever reason, more feminine. The bottom hung past her hips and the arms six inches below her hands. She said nothing about the fit as she rolled up the sleeves and walked toward the entrance.

He held the door as she entered, making a beeline for the restrooms.

When he came out a few minutes later, he found her in the check-out line with what he hoped was a large cup of coffee in each hand, a sweatshirt draped over one arm, a bag of chips and other junk food cradled in the crook.

"There's a fast-food place at the other end of this monstrosity." Jess passed him a cup. "We could grab a quick bite to eat."

He took a careful sip and all but swooned in contentment. Truck stops knew how to make good coffee. And she didn't have to ask how he took it. No sugar, a little cream. Just like hers. "Works for me."

Thirty minutes later, they were headed back to the car.

"Let me drive a while," reasoned Jess. "You're exhausted."

He started to object but knew she'd pitch a hissy fit. Much as he would like to see her provoked, he was too tired to appreciate the show. Besides, he needed a break. He handed her the keys before sliding in the passenger side. "Give me an hour to regroup."

"Two."

"One."

"We'll see."

Her silence lasted less than a mile.

"I still think he killed the Potter woman, too."

Seth knew she referred to Walls. The man had a history of violence against women, mainly prostitutes, who were less likely to press charges.

Angie Potter was the first homicide he worked with Jess, and Walls was the prime suspect. Unfortunately, there wasn't enough evidence to get an arrest warrant. But Jess refused to give up and dogged him at every opportunity. When he and Lottie Moore hooked up, Jess tried to warn her off, but the woman refused to believe her, even after two trips to the local ER. Consequently, Lottie's death hit her hard. "I agree. He's a sick, twisted bastard." He turned to face her. "But we got him, Tex. You got him."

"Yeah."

Seth sighed and leaned back against the headrest. "Shrink thinks he has issues with women."

"Duh."

"Probably hates his mother, too."

"A lot of people dislike their mothers, Hammer, but they don't go around killing other women."

"Big difference between hate and dislike, Tex. Walls *hates* women." He closed his eyes and saw Lottie's crime scene photos. Jaw tight, he slowly relaxed. "Death is too good for him."

"Roger that."

He angled the seat back a little where he could stretch out. "Wake me in an hour."

"Two."

"No wonder you're still single. You're too bossy." Immediately, he regretted the comment but couldn't take it back.

"And you're a macho pain in the ass. And single to boot. I wonder why?"

He exhaled and closed his eyes. *Damn. If I can't choose my words better, I'll never hit those female buttons of hers, besides the one for ticked off bitch, of course, which is no problem at all.*

Confident his internal alarm would wake him in an hour, he stretched out and closed his eyes. They had reservations at a motel in town and could grab a few hours of sleep in a real bed before the return trip.

Tomorrow would be one long-ass day.

Thoughts of sharing a warm bed with Jess lulled him into a deep sleep.

CHAPTER THREE

JESS STOPPED UNDER THE CANOPY OF THE CHAIN MOTEL AND killed the engine. Weather conditions steadily declined, starting with rain, then light sleet, and dropping temperatures. Even though intermittent snow made for tricky driving, she refused to wake Seth. He'd driven for eight hours straight without complaint. If she could navigate Dallas during rush hour, she could handle a few snowflakes.

Muted light from the motel's sign highlighted his features, emphasizing dark beard stubble and the chiseled plane of his jaw, giving him a mysterious, rakish aura. He sighed and rolled his head toward her. His tongue slid across his lower lip, and breath lodged in her throat.

Holy mother of pearl. No man has the right to be so damned sexy sound asleep.

She reached over and punched the solid muscle of his shoulder. Dark eyes snapped open and focused like a laser beam.

"Why the hell didn't you wake me?"

Sarcasm hid his unsettling effect on her. "Because, unlike your usual woman, I'm not a helpless bimbo."

He sat up and scrubbed his face with both hands. "Didn't realize I was so beat."

"Yeah, well, even Superman has to rest."

Those hypnotic eyes made her stomach lurch.

"Thanks for letting me sleep, Jess."

She blinked twice. "We've worked together for over a year, and I can count on one hand the times you've called me by my name."

He opened the door. "Well, technically, I didn't call you by your name."

She joined him in front of the car. "You called me Jess."

"True." He opened the door to the lobby. "But I didn't call you Jessica Louise Foster."

Unsettled, she stumbled over the threshold, and he grabbed her against him. Her heart slammed so hard she expected it to burst through the chest wall as she caught a whiff of cologne and man. Desire hit like a tsunami. *Oh my God. What have you done to me?*

"You were supposed to wake me in an hour," scolded Seth. "You're dead on your feet."

"I'm fine." She stepped out of his embrace and headed for the desk on shaky legs. "Just been sitting too long."

Ten minutes later, they walked up to the set of adjoining rooms.

"PD expects us by o-nine-hundred," instructed Jess, "so we need to hit it early."

One dark brow kicked up, as did a corner of that sexy mouth. "I can hit it anytime you're ready."

She refused to suck in a breath when her mind drifted off into the gutter. Again. "Just knock on my door when you're

17

ready." She held up her hand when he opened his mouth. "Not another word, Hammer. Not. One. Word."

His light chuckle followed her inside.

Jess set the alarm on her phone and fell across the bed. As motel rooms went, this one wasn't bad. At least it smelled clean, and the heat worked. *Just a short rest, then I'll shower and get ready for bed.*

Her short rest ended with Van Halen's *Jump* blaring from the phone at six-thirty a.m.

When Seth knocked on the door twenty minutes later, her hair was still wet from the shower.

He stared at her head. "I never realized your hair was so curly."

Self-conscious, she raked her fingers through the mess of swirls. "Yeah, well, the blow dryer wouldn't work, and I don't have any clips with me."

"Curls look good on you."

Wait. Did he just compliment me?

Before she could react, Seth spoke again. "There's a diner a couple of blocks away. We can grab breakfast and hopefully be back on the road before noon."

Fifteen minutes later, they sat across from each other in a red vinyl-covered booth near the back. Tendrils of steam rose from coffee cups in front of them.

Despite the early hour, the place bustled with activity. An old country and western song blared from speakers in the ceiling, and an odd menagerie of tables and chairs as diverse in size and shape as a jigsaw puzzle filled the large room. Three busy servers scurried about carrying refills of coffee or trays burdened down with food. A Formica-covered counter to the right of the front entrance boasted six tall, swivel stools occupied by an eclectic mix of patrons.

Jess caught one man blatantly checking her out, but not in a sexual way. It was more wary, concerned. Something about him struck a familiar chord, but she couldn't nail it down.

Expression cautious, he shifted his gaze to Seth then back to her.

Cop Spidey-sense kicked into gear, and the hair on the back of her neck prickled.

"I bet this place hasn't changed a bit in the last fifty years," asserted Seth.

She picked up the menu and made a show of reading the contents, though she kept an eye on the man at the counter.

"I wonder if *The Fonz* ever ate here."

She heard Seth's comment but concentrated on figuring out why the stranger made her uneasy.

"I'm not wearing underwear."

She lowered the menu and gaped at him.

"You're ignoring me."

"You said you weren't wearing underwear."

"I said several things, but that's all you heard." Dark eyes twinkled as he watched her. "I wonder why?"

Unwilling to go down that rabbit hole, she sipped her coffee. "White male, last stool on the far end. Dark blue jacket."

"You mean the one who's been checking you out since we walked in?"

Not surprised he noticed, she nodded. "There's something about him."

Seth added cream to his coffee. "Like what?"

She shook her head and picked up the menu. "Can't put my finger on it. The way he looked at me, then you. Like what he saw bothered him."

"Probably unhappy to see he's got competition for your attention."

She heaved a sigh and dropped the menu on the table. "Seth—"

"What bothers you about him?"

"Not sure, but something's off."

When the server walked up to take their order, the man dropped money on the counter and left without a backward glance.

She started to get up and see if she could find out what he was driving, but Seth beat her to it. "Order for me, Babe, while I powder my nose."

He winked and made his way past the counter and down the hall toward the restrooms.

"Your husband is hot."

The not-so-subtle comment from the waitress jerked her back to the present. "Yes. And he's mine." The words were out before she could stop them. Flustered, she placed their order and sat there fuming until Seth returned.

"He made a call outside and left in a dark Jeep Wrangler. The hood is in red primer." He sipped his lukewarm coffee. "Texas plates."

"Babe? Wait...Texas plates?"

His lopsided grin made nerve endings tingle and stir.

"Didn't want Flo to think I was available." He picked up his cup. "Majority of the cars out there have out-of-state tags. And most are Texas." He shrugged and sipped his coffee. "Mountains are a big draw though not much to hunt this time of year. Except for maybe snow bunnies."

She ignored the last comment. "Walls has me imagining things."

"Never doubt your instinct, Tex. It doesn't lie."

She met his steady gaze, and her stomach flipped over like on the downhill ride of a giant roller coaster. Thankfully, their food arrived and saved her from having to speak.

Seth looked at his plate and grinned. "Over easy, crisp hash browns and sausage. You detect, too, I see."

"Hush and eat before it gets cold."

By the time they reached the local police department an hour later, thoughts of the man in the diner had faded, replaced by trepidation at seeing Jack Walls in person again. For months he was an elusive shadow who haunted her dreams and remained just out of reach. The carnage he left behind, though, was all too real and terrifying in its brutality.

Game face on, she walked into the holding room.

Walls waited behind a barred metal door, hands and feet shackled to the chain around his waist. Disheveled dirt-colored hair stuck out at odd angles as he stood with head bowed and shoulders stooped. The faded orange jumpsuit was a size too large, the legs pooling around his ankles.

Jess knew that behind that innocuous harmless-man-mask existed a vicious killer with a history of violence against women. Prostitutes were his victim of choice because they seldom pressed charges. But Annie Potter did. Twice. And paid for it with her life. The evidence wasn't substantial enough for the DA to prosecute, and he walked.

Another woman ended up in the hospital and refused to press charges before he hooked up with Lottie Moore. Even after two domestic disturbance calls to their place, Lottie declined to press charges, claiming he loved her, and she had no reason to fear him.

She was dead wrong.

One step ahead of them, he skipped town before they could arrest him.

Four months of beating herself up for not moving fast enough ended two days ago, thanks to a broken taillight.

The door's lock clicked, bringing her back to the present with an unpleasant jolt. She resisted the sudden urge to take a step back when Walls entered the room and stopped six feet away.

His posture didn't change as he slowly lifted his head and stared directly at her.

Gone was the precisely orchestrated façade he showed the world. In its place stood evil personified.

Eyes black as volcanic rock telegraphed anger and hatred like a physical blow. His nostrils flared when he drew in a breath. The muscles in his cheek worked as he clamped his jaw tight, then released it before lowering his head.

Heart racing, she glanced at Seth. His attention was on the jailer and the paperwork. If he saw Walls' display, he gave no sign.

"No way in hell would I want to be in your shoes right now." The man behind the desk spoke to Seth as he reached for the paperwork transferring the prisoner to their custody. "He's bat shit crazy."

Seth passed the signed paperwork to him. "Thanks for taking care of this so quickly."

"No problem. Glad to have him out of here." The man hesitated, and his eyes flicked from Seth to Walls. "Weather's tricky this time of year. More snow headed our way. Weatherman says another six to eight inches is possible today. Up this high, though, it's likely to be more. Hope you have snow chains." Brows furrowed, he squinted from Jess to the prisoner.

Jess's hair prickled on the nape of her neck. She didn't relish the idea of a delay of any kind with Walls in the car. Before she voiced her concern, Seth spoke up.

"A couple of your men are working on the chains. With any luck, we can be through the worst of the weather in a couple of hours."

"Maybe. But more's on the way." He scratched his chin and shuffled the papers. "Where's your first stop?"

"Colorado City."

He shook his head. "I-25's congested on a slow day. You can plan on at least three to four hours in this weather."

"We've got a Plan B," offered Seth.

Jess kept her expression neutral. If they had a Plan B, he was the only one who knew it.

The jailer and two officers escorted them from the small processing room to the sally port, where their vehicle waited.

"Snow chains are ready to go, Detective," said one of the men installing them. "You know how to take them off?"

"Been a while," Seth offered. "But, yeah, I can do it."

Once Walls was safely ensconced in the back, Seth got behind the wheel.

The killer's anger was an almost tangible thing. "It's a long way to Walker," he pronounced at last. "A lot can happen."

Jess's skin crawled, and her fingers trembled as she buckled her seat belt. His words, though softly spoken, carried the threat of danger loud and clear.

CHAPTER FOUR

HALF AN HOUR FROM COLORADO CITY, TRAFFIC CAME TO A dead stop. Again. Seth sighed. Two hours of stop-and-go traffic, intermittent snow, and complaints from Walls had him grinding his teeth for patience.

"I thought these people knew how to drive in this crap," groused Jess.

He swallowed the sarcastic reply that popped into his head and did another mental ten-count as he shoved the gear into park. "Probably another fender-bender." *And now we're over an hour behind schedule.*

"How much longer?" snapped Walls, "I gotta piss."

Seth took a breath. "Depends on how long it takes them to clear whatever's blocking the road."

Chains rattled, and Seth checked the rearview mirror and found their prisoner looking behind them.

Seth looked at Jess, who watched him with narrowed eyes.

"So, what's this fabulous Plan B you mentioned back there?"

"I'll let you know when it forms."

Hazelnut eyes flashed fire his way. "Crap." She crossed her arms and stared out the window. "Another fine mess you've gotten me into."

She leaned over and scrutinized the side mirror before casually sitting up straight, picking invisible lint from her pant leg, then smoothed it down. She met his gaze, and one dark brow arched up, a silent question in her eyes. *Did you see the Jeep three cars back?*

Her intuitiveness no longer surprised him. He gave a light nod.

"Just flipping great. How much further in the toilet can this day go?"

"You need to teach her some manners, Detective." Low and sinister, Walls' tone resonated malice. "I could give you some pointers."

"Shut up, Jack," snapped Seth. Tension cramped his shoulders, and he willed himself to relax. Without warning, the crime scene photos flashed through his brain, a gruesome reminder of how the man taught manners. He sucked in a breath and forced the images back to their darkened corner.

Chains jangled again as their cargo shifted in his seat. "A real man wouldn't let her get away with talking to him like that."

Jaw clamped tight, Seth ignored the jibe. Walls wasn't the first criminal to use that tactic nor the last.

"He's more of a man than you'll ever be."

Jess's unexpected comment surprised Seth. It wasn't like her to respond to such taunts. He watched her from the corner of his eye. Hands clasped tight in her lap, cheeks bright red, she stared straight ahead.

"You think he's a man, do you?" Walls' voice dropped to an ominous whisper. "Trust me, sweetheart. I can show you what a real man is."

"Enough, Jack," snapped Seth. "Or I'll add a gag to your wardrobe."

The prisoner's harsh laugh sent a chill down Seth's spine, and gooseflesh pricked his arms. He gripped the wheel tighter and imagined planting a fist in the middle of Walls' arrogant face, then quickly changed the image to a bullet. Right between the eyes. Double-tap. Problem solved.

The sharp ping of his cell phone ended the fantasy. He checked caller-ID. "It's Sarge," he told Jess, then answered. "Hamilton. Yes, sir. We're at a dead stop again. Not sure. Maybe half an hour. Longer if traffic continues to crawl. No. Any side road would be worse than the interstate. It looks like we have movement up ahead. Hopefully, we'll be on our way again. Yes, sir. I'll check in as soon as we get there. Roger that. Overnight would be the last resort."

For once, no one spoke as cars inched forward. Snow continued to fall in slow waves. Sometimes huge, cottony flakes, others light as dandelion fluff. The swirling mess was hell on his vision, and a headache pulsed in his temples. *Oh, goody. I was hoping for something else to screw up my day.*

He concentrated on the traffic and ignored the tension vibrating inside the SUV like sound waves from a boom-box. No stranger to touchy situations, this one was different somehow. He checked on Walls again.

The prisoner's depraved glance shifted from Seth to Jess and back. Then he smiled. A slow, cunning one that proclaimed, *I like what I see.*

Seth's inner voice shouted *Danger*, and cop instinct jumped to high alert, and he checked the side mirror for the Jeep. Still there. Coincidence or something else?

Somewhere in the parade, a diesel horn blared, and he jerked his attention back to the road just as the car in front braked suddenly and slid to the right. Thankfully, the distressed driver maintained control, but Seth couldn't shake a sense of impending peril.

Walls, on the other hand, didn't appear at all concerned for his current situation. A guilty verdict meant the death penalty. Occasional taunts aside, he behaved as though on a Sunday drive.

Seth rechecked the prisoner.

His expression remained fixed on the back of Jess's head. Nostrils flared slightly as his eyes closed. He inhaled and licked his lips as though savoring the taste of something delightful.

Or anticipating it.

☾☽

Jess remained quiet as they handed Walls over to Colorado City Police for their first official break. Heat climbed up her neck as she remembered her reaction to Walls' earlier remark. Why she found it necessary to respond to his blatant attempt to provoke was beyond her. A rookie mistake, and Seth was sure to give her hell about it. No way would he let it slide. Not just because it sounded like she defended him, which was bad enough, but because she allowed Walls to get to her. Cop 101—never let a suspect's jibes get to you. And she did.

She avoided eye contact with Seth as they secured the prisoner in a holding cell where his lunch waited. There would be ample time for him to eat, address his personal needs, and chill for a while before they hit the road again.

"We'll be back in an hour," Seth spoke to the jailer who escorted them out. "You got my cell number if you need me. We'll be across the street at the burger joint."

"Whatever. He ain't going anywhere."

A receptionist stopped them in the lobby. "Detective Hamilton?"

He turned to the perky blond woman behind the desk.

"If you're going to be around a while, I'd be glad to give you the ten-cent tour."

"I'm afraid we have to get back on the road as soon as we eat."

She tilted her head and gave him a sideways glance through lowered lashes. "Too bad. I give excellent tours."

"I'm sure you do." He leaned around and glimpsed the name-plate centered on the desk. "Miss Thomas. Perhaps another time."

"Bethany." A dazzling smile accompanied a slight move forward. "But my friends call me Bets."

Jess clenched her teeth. *Good grief! If she'd flopped over the desk and shouted, 'Come here, big boy,' she could not be more obvious. And the jerk's eating it up.*

"Maybe another time, Bets." Seth's amiable smile removed any sting from the rejection.

"I hope so."

They exited the building and headed across the parking lot.

Jess held her tongue as long as she could manage, then made no effort to temper the sarcasm in her voice. "So sorry you're gonna miss Bets' tour."

"Yeah. Me, too." He grinned and placed his hand in the small of her back. "Careful. There's a layer of ice under the snow, and the parking lot is slippery. Wouldn't want you to fall."

All ire dissipated with his touch. The warmth of his hand penetrated layers of clothing directly to her core and forced her to accept the sad truth.

She was crazy about her partner.

And there isn't a bloody thing I can do about it.

She wished she were one of those women who knew how to flirt, how to appeal to a man like Seth. Someone like Bets who could flutter her lashes and shift her body to show just enough cleavage to entice without being slutty.

But you aren't, Sunshine, and you never will be, so just accept things the way they are and get on with it.

Fifteen minutes later, orders placed, they sat opposite each other in a corner booth. She fiddled with her napkin, moved her drink around in circles, and acted out how she felt. Nervous. Trapped. On edge. Waiting for the other shoe to drop. Yet, Seth didn't mention it.

"All right. All right. I shouldn't have reacted to Walls' comment. It was a rookie mistake, and I shouldn't have done it." *There.*

Someone finally addressed the elephant in the room. She blew out a breath and waited.

"No. You shouldn't have." A slow, sexy grin tempered the rebuke. "But at least now I know you think I'm a man."

She blinked a couple of times. "Why would I think otherwise?"

A red-headed young man walked up about then and slapped their food tray on the table. He grabbed the numbered tent and left without saying a word.

Jess watched him lumber off and shook her head. *What is wrong with this generation?*

She turned back to her partner, who took his food and passed her the tray.

"You didn't answer my question."

He popped three fries in his mouth at once and dusted his fingers on a napkin. "What question?"

She sighed. "Why would I question your man-card?"

For the first time in their acquaintance, Seth blushed. Like, he really blushed. His mouth momentarily stopped working on the fries, and he sat motionless for a heartbeat.

She couldn't decide which shocked her more, the fact that he blushed or that he appeared at a loss for words. That didn't happen. Ever.

He swallowed and slurped a long drink of soda before he met her gaze.

So fast she almost missed it, something fired in the depths of those whiskey-colored eyes, and her breath caught.

She may be woefully out of practice, but she recognized the brief flash of desire in those mysterious depths.

Or did she? Because, just like that, it vanished, leaving her to question if she saw it at all.

"We need to get back on the road as soon as possible," he declared at last. "That creep is getting on my last nerve, and we have a long way to go." He popped another fry in his mouth, followed by a large bite of his burger.

It's not like him to leave something hanging. What gives? For a moment, she considered pressing the issue but nixed the idea. If he answered her questions, he would expect her to return the favor.

She decided to stick to business, at least for now, and pulled a folded sheet of paper from her pocket. "Our next check-in is Raton Pass, New Mexico. About two hours from here." She dug out her phone and checked the weather app, thankful they had a decent signal this time. "With any luck, we should be out of the snow by then. But there's another front on the way."

Conversation during the rest of the meal consisted of trip logistics. To avoid fatigue, they would take turns at the wheel in three-hour segments. Stops for the prisoner would take place in Amarillo and Wichita Falls, Texas. Pit stops for them would be as needed.

"Hopefully, once out of the snow, we can make up some time." He glanced at his watch. "At this rate, we can probably make Walker by midnight."

This all-business Seth was no fun at all. Jess wanted the old Seth back. The one who joked and teased and made her feel like she was more than his partner.

The meal over, they headed back to the station. Seth made no move to put his hand on her back as they started across the parking lot. A definite bummer.

On a whim, she pretended to slip, ignoring the part of her brain shouting *foolish woman.*

Immediately, his arm circled her waist.

"Are you all right?" His breath, warm against her cheek, smelled of ketchup and fries.

Her heart skipped a beat, and she peeked at her shoes. "Yeah. I probably should have changed to my sneakers. These aren't exactly ideal for trekking through the snow."

He studied the black, mid-heeled shoes she always wore as though he didn't realize she had them on.

Just then, she glimpsed Bets walk out of the station and did another little skid for good measure.

He tightened his hold. "I better hang on to you till we get back."

Her insides did a little happy dance. "Thanks. We should stop at the car, and I'll change shoes."

"Okay."

Later, she may anguish over her childish attempt at flirting, but for now, she relished the warmth coming from the man beside her.

Scarlett had the right idea. I'll worry about that tomorrow.

They were almost to the car when she saw the Jeep parked down the block from the station.

CHAPTER FIVE

STILL SHAKEN BY THE NEAR SLIP-UP IN THE RESTAURANT, SETH remained silent as he kept Jess pinned to his side. A little voice in his head argued the stumble didn't appear natural, but he dismissed it. *Why would she fake it?*

He glanced to the side and noted the high color on her cheek. Was that from the cold or something else?

He gave himself a mental kick. *Jess is my partner. My work partner.* No matter how much he wanted more, it wasn't. He needed to accept it and move on.

Deep in thought, her sudden stop caught him off-guard.

"One o'clock," she murmured and resumed walking.

He looked up and mumbled a curse. He needed to get his head out of his ass and pay attention. "He wasn't there when we left the station."

She slid her arm through his. "I don't see anyone inside. Let's get closer; see if we can make out the plates."

Like two lovers out for a mid-day stroll, they turned toward the Jeep. Two minutes later, Seth had the plate memorized.

"No such thing as coincidence," noted Jess.

"Yeah. I'll have Baker run it while you change shoes."

He turned around and led them toward the car.

She nodded and made no move to pull her arm from his even though the sidewalk was clear of ice and snow.

He allowed himself a moment to savor the normalcy of walking arm-in-arm with her. *One of these days...*

When they reached the SUV, he opened the back and stepped aside to call Baker.

Jess hummed an unrecognizable tune as she bent over and rummaged in her bag, tight derriere a scant two feet from his left hand. All thoughts of license plates and unlikely coincidences evaporated, replaced by a yearning so intense it verged on physical pain. From the first moment he met her, he knew she was different. Sometimes volatile as a summer storm, she radiated a deep intelligence and vitality that drew him like a magnet. Everything about her appealed to him, from her off-beat sense of humor to her steadfast dedication to the job.

Dreams of stripping away her protective barriers to the woman underneath kept him awake most nights these days, and the latest one chose now to re-emerge in his mind's eye.

The relentless ring of his cell stopped him a split second before he did something stupid, like tell her how he felt.

Angered with himself for his lack of control, he turned his back on Jess and answered the phone. "Hamilton. What? Are you sure, Baker? Okay. Look, I need you to run a plate for me." He rattled it off from memory. "Yeah. I'll wait."

Jess finished changing shoes and stood beside him. "What's going on?"

He held up a finger when Baker came back on the line. "Okay. Thanks. Keep digging. Something's off; we can feel it. On our way back to get him now. Yeah. We'll need to stop and take off the snow chains at some point, likely just over the border in New Mexico. The next break for him will be Amarillo, then Wichita Falls. Roger that."

"Well?"

"Jeep's registered to Walter Koslow of Midland. No known connection to Walls, but Baker's still checking." He started toward the entrance to the station. "And we might run into some nasty weather later. And to add icing to the misery cake, brass wants half-hour check-in's going forward, and we'll have a state trooper escort from here on."

"Holy crap. That's three different states."

"Yep."

She shook her head. "So much for keeping a low profile."

The exasperation in her voice matched his own.

"You said something was familiar about the guy at the diner." Seth studied her face. "And he seemed troubled by our presence. Now the Jeep shows up here. I don't like it."

She cocked her head toward him. "You told Baker, '*We* can feel it.'"

Confused, he stared and waited for clarification.

"Just now when you were talking to Baker. You said, 'Something's off; *we* can feel it.'"

"Well, don't you? Feel like something is off, I mean?"

She joined him, and they walked toward the door. "Yeah. I just didn't know you noticed."

He opened the door for her. "I notice everything about you." *Hell of a time to test the waters, Hamilton.* "You're interesting to watch."

"I am?"

She sounded surprised.

He stood aside for her to enter. "Yes ma'am."

Bets was back at her desk and jumped up when she saw them enter. "Detective Hamilton." She moved to the corner and leaned one hip on the edge. "Enjoy your lunch? Can I do anything for you?"

Beside him, Jess stiffened.

Is it too much to hope she's a tiny bit jealous?

He briefly considered egging her on but nixed the idea. He still hoped to find those female buttons of hers, and a sure-fire way to ensure failure was to make her mad.

So, he went one hundred and eighty degrees the other way.

"Thanks, Bets, but I'm good." He slipped his arm around Jess's waist in a not-to-be-misunderstood gesture of possession.

Braced for indignation over his chest-thumping move, he was pleasantly surprised when she studied him and arched one brow.

"What?" He attempted an innocent expression. "I didn't want to give her any false hope."

She huffed and shook her head.

But didn't pull away.

The moment they entered the secure area, all thoughts of buttons and an actual life faded as they waited for Walls to be remanded back into their custody.

Once the prisoner was secured in the back seat of the SUV, they were ready to hit the road again with a state trooper escort. The jeep's presence here was too much of a coincidence, and they weren't taking any chances.

"I rechecked the weather at the station," said Jess as she placed the road map behind the sun visor. "We should be out of the snow in an hour or so. But there's another cold front behind us." She sighed and sat back in the seat. "By the time we get to Texas, it's gonna be stormy as all get out." She turned to him. "I can drive a while if you want."

He found a country station on the radio and checked his mirrors before backing out. "I don't mind driving. It keeps me awake."

He scanned the empty Jeep as they drove past. There were two eating establishments nearby, so one could assume he stopped to eat. If one believed in chance and wasn't hauling a murder suspect nine-hundred miles to stand trial, that is.

Jess buckled her seat belt. "Once we're out of this mess, I'll drive."

"Okay."

Thankfully, the snow was back to small Dandelion puffs and made driving less nerve-racking. Still, the icy conditions were less than ideal, and once again, Seth was thankful for the snow chains.

Walls dozed in the back, and the next ninety minutes passed with little conversation beyond the dark clouds building behind them and occasional remarks on the rugged beauty of the mountains. Traffic thinned, and they were able to make up a small amount of the time they lost.

He glanced back at Walls and noted the man appeared to be asleep. "In Ohio, it's against the law to get a fish drunk."

She snorted but didn't look up from her tablet. "One can only wonder why such a law was even needed." She made a couple of moves on her game. "In Boulder, it's illegal for people to own pets."

"Huh?"

"Yep. The citizens there are merely pet minders."

"Any month that starts on a Sunday will have a Friday the thirteenth in it." He slowed when the truck in front of him signaled a turn.

When she made no reply, he asked, "Are you all right? You're unusually quiet."

She shifted in the seat. "Yeah. Fine. Just tired." She closed the tablet and stuffed it in her purse. "When's the next stop?"

"There's a truck stop just past Raton Pass. Another fifteen minutes or so. I'll take the chains off there. After that, won't be another full stop till Amarillo, another three, four hours depending on traffic and weather." He passed a slow-moving car, then moved back to the right lane, trooper escort close behind. "Work for you?"

"Yeah."

"You could grab us some coffee while I remove the chains, then take over driving to Amarillo."

"Sounds like a plan."

When she stretched and yawned, he bit back a groan. *She is, without a doubt, the sexiest woman I've ever known.*

He used the rearview mirror to check on Walls.

The man watched him closely. His thin lips curled up in a sleazy smirk. "I like my coffee hot and strong," he purred, "just like my women."

Jess stiffened but didn't respond to his taunt.

Seth gripped the wheel tighter. *Only nine hours to go.*

A short pit stop later, their little convoy was back on the road.

"I wanted hot coffee," whined Walls. "Not bottled water and cupcakes."

"Then don't eat it." Seth settled into the passenger seat. Hot coffee in the face could incapacitate. Only a fool would give the man a potential weapon. And Seth was no fool.

A Texas State Trooper met them at Texline to continue the escort. Just past Dalhart, the trooper flashed his lights and gave a short siren blast. Per their agreement, Seth called the trooper's cell phone and listened in silence.

When the call ended without Seth saying a word, Jess cut worried eyes toward him. "What's going on?"

"Bad wreck." He turned around and observed the once roiling gray clouds were now a mocha tinged brown. And it was gaining on them. Not an encouraging sign. "And there's a dust storm headed this way. We should hold up in Dumas and wait for it to pass."

"A dust storm?" She gave him a skeptical look. "Here?"

"Yeah. I went through my share in Iraq. Can get pretty nasty." He shifted in the seat. "Storm fronts can cause them to pop up out of nowhere, especially in dry, flat areas like this."

She checked the side mirror. "I see a difference in the clouds now. They were dark gray. Now they have these different shades of brown to them." She inched up her speed. "How long do they last?"

He shrugged. "Depends. They form ahead of a front, so the

actual storm won't last but about fifteen or twenty minutes." He paused. "But it won't be pretty. Depending on the speed of the storm, we could have high winds, hail, and dust so thick you can't see your hand in front of your face." He took a breath. "After the rains come, it all turns to mud."

"Well, aren't you just a bundle of cheerful news?"

He shrugged. "You asked."

She pressed down on the accelerator. "So, what do we do?"

"Don't you worry your pretty little head, sweetheart," sneered Walls, "It'll be over soon."

Seth studied their prisoner, who sat grinning like he didn't have a care in the world. "Something on your mind, Walls?"

"In due time, Detective," he whispered. "In due time."

"Seth?"

Jess's worried voice drew his attention. "Yeah?"

"What do you do in a dust storm?"

He searched the semi-barren landscape, finding little to slow the storm's progress. "Well, I hoped we could make it to Dumas, but it doesn't look like that's a possibility now. Shelter would be nice, but I think we're just going to have to stop and wait it out."

Walls rattled his chains. "You can't leave me tied up like this when the storm hits."

"I'll do whatever I damn well please," snapped Seth, "so shut the hell up."

"What about our escort?" asked Jess.

"He'll pick us up in Dumas."

She sighed and focused on the road.

Seth dug his phone from the console. "I better call it in."

Jess shook her head. "It's so flat out here; very few trees scattered around."

"That's why dust storms gather so much speed. Nothing to slow them down."

"If it weren't for the occasional gulley or washout, there would be no break in the land at all." Jess glanced back and stiffened. "Holy mother of pearl."

The fear in her voice got his attention. "What?"

"It's gaining on us."

He glimpsed in the side mirror, then rolled the window down for a better look. "It's a big one." He rolled the window up and scanned the road ahead, noting the big rig coming toward them had pulled off the road. "We need to find some kind of cover."

"Yeah, well, which pebble do you suggest?" Her sarcastic tone didn't hide her concern. "There's hardly a dip in the road. What about that eighteen-wheeler who's pulling over? Would we be safe behind it?"

He squinted at the approaching storm. "Too dangerous. Winds on those things can hit sixty to eighty miles an hour." He didn't bother to hide his apprehension. "Catches him just right, it will flip it like a toy."

She surveyed the area through the side window. "Looks like a gulley or ravine of some sort just off the road on this side. Would that work?"

Eyes on the approaching storm, he didn't answer as he waited for his call to go through.

"Dammit."

Jess's whispered expletive got his attention.

She tilted her head backward.

When he looked behind them, a surge of adrenaline made his head swim.

The Jeep raced in front of the rolling wall of dust.

Seth pulled his weapon and held it against his right thigh.

Jess kept her hands on the wheel as the speedometer edged past eighty, the storm and the Jeep gaining on them.

He checked on Walls, and the look on the prisoner's face turned his blood to ice.

Lips parted in a snarl, his cold, dead eyes gleamed with malice.

He gripped the shoulder harness and pushed back as though bracing for an accident. "I win," he sneered.

Seth heard the gunshot a split second before the left rear tire blew, sending the SUV in a deadly fish-tailspin.

"Shit!" shouted Jess as she fought to control the vehicle. "I can't hold it."

A second shot and the right tire blew as the dust cloud reached them. The last thing he heard was Jess's terrified scream as she lost control, and they rolled over.

CHAPTER SIX

SETH STRUGGLED TO BRING HIMSELF OUT OF THE FOG AND process the situation. Powder from the airbag mingled with dirt and filled his nose and mouth. He tried to push away from it but couldn't lift his arms. He struggled for a clear breath, then blew out through his nose. His head hurt like hell, and he tasted bloody dirt.

Gunshots. We crashed. Jess.

He turned his head toward her and swallowed a grunt of pain.

"Not without the woman."

"She's pinned in. We ain't got time to get her out."

The angry voices penetrated the cloud in Seth's head.

"We make time."

Walls. Who was the other one? Koslow?

"You're out of your fricking mind, Walls," shouted another man. "And the storm's getting worse."

A different voice. Shit. Two accomplices?

The car rocked when someone tugged on Jess's door.

"Not without her."

"We ain't got time, Jack. Come on!"

Darkness crept up on Seth, and he struggled to push it back. *Jess. Save Jess.*

Someone pounded on the roof of the car. "I want the woman!"

Seth tried again to rouse himself, but darkness won the battle.

☌

Pain mingled with worried voices ebbed and flowed as Seth's consciousness played hide-and-seek.

Time held no meaning in the void. It could have been a day, a week, or a month before pain lessened and the murk faded. He tried to speak, but his tongue stuck to the roof of his bone-dry mouth and distorted his words. "Wa…ther."

"He's coming around."

The anxious voice was familiar, but his confused brain could not attach a name.

"Seth? Seth? Can you hear me?"

The voice grew insistent, agitated.

"Take it easy. Give him time."

A new voice. Unfamiliar.

But he recognized the command in the first one.

"Nod if you can hear me."

It took a ton of effort, but he managed to follow the command.

"Okay. Don't try to talk. Just listen."

Seth focused on the voice when the gloom threatened to take him under again.

"There was an accident. You're in a hospital in Amarillo."

Pain pulsed in his temples as he struggled to speak. "Jess?" He couldn't decide if the next pause was real or imagined, and his stomach churned with equal parts anxiety and alarm as he forced one eye open, then the other.

Sergeant Phillips stood beside his bed along with an older man in a lab coat, stethoscope around his neck. A third man, Drake

Sampson, a Texas Ranger he met after he transferred to Walker, waited at the foot of the bed.

"Can you tell me what happened?" Sergeant Phillips's voice radiated distress.

The man in the lab coat placed a hand on Phillips' arm and addressed Seth. "Would you like some water, Detective?"

Seth didn't take his eyes off Phillips. "Pleeshe."

The doctor lifted a pitcher from the bedside table, poured water in a plastic glass, and added the bendable straw. He raised the angle of the bed so Seth could drink. "Take it slow, son," said the man. "Easy."

Seth took a cautious sip and asked again. "Jess?" His gaze shifted to Drake. "Where is she? Is she all right?"

His agonized face gave voice to Seth's greatest fear.

She didn't make it.

Anguish tore at his heart. *Oh, God. Jess.*

"She wasn't in the car when EMS got there." Phillips paused. "Neither was Walls."

It took his sluggish brain several seconds to process the words. When it did, his breath caught. "Wh…what?" *Oh, God. Did Walls take her?*

"They weren't in the car, Seth." Sergeant Phillips's hands gripped the bed railing as he leaned forward. "Your call kept the line open, and we pinged your location, but the storms hampered response time." He gripped the rails harder. "The seat belts for her and Walls were cut. We found blood on the airbag and driver's side window." He took a deep breath. "That was two days ago."

The beep from the monitor beside the bed kept time with his accelerated heart rate.

Two days. With a deadly psycho who hates women.

Especially Jess.

Seth didn't realize he'd tried to get up until Sergeant Phillips laid a hand on his chest and pushed him back on the bed.

"Easy, son, easy."

Drake spoke up. "We put out a BOLO (be on the lookout) for the Jeep, and every LEO (law enforcement officer) in the state is looking for them. Koslow's place is under surveillance, too, but I need what you know."

Hand trembling, Seth reached for the water glass, and the doctor helped him drink again. Then, he took a deep breath and talked, slowly at first, pausing often to gather strength and keep his words coherent as his scrambled brain cleared, and the mother of all headaches pounded his brain to mush.

Exhausted from the effort, he closed his eyes and sighed. "The last thing I heard was Walls say he wouldn't leave without her."

"And you didn't recognize the other voices?" asked Drake. "Didn't see them?"

"No. But it was the same Jeep we saw in Colorado. Can only assume one of the other two voices was Koslow."

Phillips stood back and spoke to Drake. "Anything else right now?"

"Not at the moment."

A forty-something career lawman, Drake was sharp, dedicated, and personable. They met soon after he transferred to Walker and formed a quick friendship based on mutual respect.

"I'll catch up to you back in Walker." With that, Drake turned and left.

Tom planted both hands on his hips. "Okay." He turned to the other man. "Dr. Hennessey? How soon can he be released?"

"He needs to remain under observation at least another twenty-four to forty-eight hours. He's been out for two days."

Seth tried to push himself up. "No." It ticked him off to discover he was too weak to finish the task. Not to mention it hurt like hell. He fell back on the bed.

"The concussion notwithstanding, your injuries are not too severe," stated the doctor. "A couple of bruised ribs, your right shoulder has a mild sprain and several cuts and abrasions. You were lucky." Pain radiated from world-weary eyes. "My son was a police officer, too."

Seth caught the *was* but didn't comment. "I need to get out of here, Sarge."

"You need to take care of yourself," insisted Phillips. "You'll be no good to any of us, especially Jess, otherwise."

He hated to admit defeat but knew Tom was right. His beautiful, courageous Jess was in the hands of a deranged sociopath.

And he was helpless to do anything about it.

ᓂ

Pain. Thirst. Cold.

Jess tried to separate herself from the discomfort and concentrate. *Where am I?*

Rocks grated against her left cheek, and dirt filled her mouth. Thunder rolled, and lightning flashed around her. Rain pelted her back, and cold leached into her bones. *I'm in a ditch.*

She vaguely remembered the fall that saved her from a fate worse than death. While the ravine provided no shelter from the rain or cold, it protected her from the brunt of the dust storm's formidable wind.

Blinded by torrential rain, she couldn't accurately judge the gulley's dimensions but guessed about fifteen feet across and ten feet deep. Storm-fed water rushed through the bottom of the ravine. She shifted, then grimaced as pain shot through her left knee. More misery followed when she tried to move her head.

It took a moment to realize the water now reached her knees. *I must get higher.* Despite the pain, she clawed her way up the slippery slope, inch by agonizing inch, until her head touched the underside of a jagged rock jutting out from the wall near the top. The small projection deflected the rain enough for her to see the surrounding area. Intermittent lightning flashes revealed the silhouette of a tree and scattered brush along the edge of the gully to her right, and a minuscule assortment of roots dangled from the dirt wall. Teeth gritted against the pain, she edged closer to the nearest tuber and looped an arm through it, crying out in pain. Water now tugged at her hips, and she held on tighter. The storm raged as she clung to the meager lifeline, the pain in her body almost unbearable.

Debris in the water brushed against her legs, and she held on tighter.

Walls.

Walls and someone else pulled her from the wreckage, intent on taking her with them. Ironically, the storm rescued her. One minute they dragged her toward the Jeep. The next, she rolled along the ground like a tumbleweed, battered by wind and dust.

Her teeth chattered, and her body trembled as frigid air swirled through the ravine. Afraid to fall asleep, she spoke aloud to stay focused. "We were almost to Dumas when all hell broke loose. Decent traffic, so someone is likely to come by at some point." Her arm cramped with the exertion of hanging on, but she ignored it. "Unless that someone is Walls, in which case, not so good." Shiver after shiver racked her body. "God, I'll never be warm again." She sucked in a ragged breath. "Seth had his phone out so they can find us, but not until the storm passes." A new realization made her heart jump. "Oh, no. They will think Walls took me."

She shifted, pushing up with her legs to test the pain in her knee, but stopped when it became too intense. "Walking is out." She took a calming breath. "But I'll crawl if I have to."

The storm raged for hours, and by the time it ended, water reached her chest, and the temperature dropped drastically. Exhaustion threatened to loosen her grip on the root, and she prayed for the strength to hold on. "Just till morning. I just need to stay awake until morning. Someone will find me then."

CHAPTER SEVEN

"**A** COUPLE HEADED TO DALHART FOUND HER LATE YESTER-
day and brought her in."

Jess heard a compassionate female voice and struggled
to open her eyes. *Thank God someone found me.*

"All things considered, she's pretty lucky."

Right. Lucky. But where am I? A hospital?

"No ID?" A second voice, male, older, sounded impatient.

"None that we found."

The man huffed out a breath. "How soon can I talk to her?"

Jess flinched when cold fingers brushed against her arm and
adjusted something attached to her hand.

"Between hypothermia, exhaustion, and pain meds, she's in
and out. Someone will call you when she wakes up."

"Can't you wake her? I ain't got all day." The male's voice we
from aggravated whisper to angry hiss.

Jess moaned and squinted against the bright light in the ro
"Where am I?"

"About time," snapped the male voice. "I'm Deputy Wallace. I need to ask you some questions."

She blinked until her vision cleared, then scanned the room.

A woman in blue scrubs stood beside the head of the bed, a stethoscope around her neck. An older man in a deputy sheriff's uniform stood next to her.

"Water…please." Her dry tongue rasped like sandpaper against the roof of her mouth, but she was warm, and the pain remained bearable.

The woman in blue put a straw to her lips. "Easy. A little at a time."

Jess followed instructions and swished each drink to coat her parched mouth. "Thanks."

"Who are you?" snipped the portly deputy. "What happened to you?"

"Where am I?"

"Moore County Hospital," answered the nurse.

The deputy interrupted her. "I ask the questions here." Brusque and impatient, he stepped closer to the bed. "What's your name?"

"Call Sergeant Phillips."

He scowled. "Sergeant Phillips?"

She nodded. "My boss. Walker PD. We, my partner and I, were transporting a prisoner to Walker."

His eyes widened, and he straightened. "You're Detective ster?" His voice edged up a notch. "The woman every cop in tate is looking for?" He tapped the small notebook in his hand the bedrail. "And I found you."

be not every cop but for sure Sergeant Philips and Seth arching for her. "My partner. Seth Hamilton. How is he?"

se spoke up. "I don't know his exact injuries, but they im to Amarillo."

d back the tears burning her eyelids. Walls escaped, kay. "I need to make a call."

Wallace scowled. "Not until I have the information I need." He straightened and glared at her, notebook in hand. "What happened out there?"

Jess stared at the rude man. She was a victim, for cripes sake, and he treated her like a suspect. Jess decided he could get his answers somewhere else. She had nothing to say until she talked with Phillips. And Seth. Besides, the Rangers and possibly the FBI were already involved, and he could deal with them. "I'm not sure. The storm came up so fast. One minute, things were fine. The next, I lost control. I think we rolled, but I'm not sure. I honestly don't remember much after that." She inhaled. "I need to call my boss."

"In a minute." He leaned forward. "The bulletin we got said Walls took you with him when he escaped." His beady eyes narrowed, and one bushy brow kicked up. "How did you get away from him?"

He had the personality of a pit viper, and her dislike shot up several degrees. "I don't remember anything after they pulled me from the wreck until I woke up in a ditch."

He stared at her for a long moment before he snapped his notebook shut, his displeasure showing in the sharp tone of his voice when he spoke over his shoulder to the nurse. "Nobody comes in here without my okay." He pointed toward the door, intense gaze now on Jess. "For your own protection, Detective, I'll have a guard posted outside."

"My sergeant?"

"I'll make the necessary notifications when I get back to th office."

He rushed out before Jess could protest further.

A light tap on the door preceded the entrance of a yo woman bearing a food tray. She placed it on the hospital table left as silently as she walked in.

The nurse pushed the tray table over the bed. "Do you help eating?"

Distracted by the cell phone peeking out of the nurse's scrub pocket, Jess glanced at her name tag. "Please, Janet. I need to call my sergeant. Or my partner. They'll be worried sick."

Janet cut her eyes toward the door. "He said he'd call."

"This can't wait. If you don't want to lend me your phone, I'll give you the number, and you can call."

She chewed her bottom lip. "...I don't know."

"Please. They think I'm in the hands of a sadistic killer. I have to tell them I'm okay."

She hesitated, then pulled the phone from her pocket and passed it over. "One minute. That's all. And if you say I let you do this, I'll deny it."

Jess reached for the phone and punched in Tom Phillips' number.

♂♀

"They'll release you today, but you have to take it easy for a while."

"Any other news?" Seth sat on the side of the bed and halfway listened to Phillips, more concerned with how he was supposed to get dressed with his arm in a sling. His gut tightened at the thought of what Jess may be going through.

"We caught the Jeep on a surveillance camera this morning." ʼillips straddled a chair across from Seth, his arms crossed over ʼack. "Some truck stop on the outskirts of Childress."

ʼhildress?" He shrugged his shoulders, trying to ease the muscles. "How many people in the car?" *Was Jess with them?*

ʼok his head. "Bad angle on it. We identified the guy who dlow but couldn't tell how many others were inside."

ng
and

Seth pushed up from the bed, ignoring the flash of ured shoulder, then sat back down when dizziness

need

ss comes if you move too fast."

50

Seth inhaled slowly, wincing when his sore ribs protested. "What's our next move?"

"Get you home."

Seth shook his head. "Not till I find Jess. And Walls."

Phillips sat up straight. "Lieutenant's orders. You're going home. End of discussion."

Tom never used ten words when three would do, and his clipped answers grated on Seth's frayed nerves. He glared at the man he respected and admired but didn't like very much right now.

"I mean it, Seth. You do nothing until medical releases you."

He opened his mouth to argue but stopped when Tom's cell phone rang.

"Phillips." He jumped up from his chair, mouth gaping. "Where are you? Are you all right? Don't worry about it. I'll take care of everything. He's being discharged today." He grinned at Seth. "We'll be on our way within the hour. Thank God you're all right. Yes. I will. See you soon."

Seth didn't realize he held his breath until Tom clamped a hand on his uninjured shoulder and grinned.

"She's in the hospital in Dumas."

"How bad?"

"Didn't say. No time to talk." Tom tossed Seth the bag he brought with him from Walker. "Get dressed. Let's find out."

A long agonizing hour later, they were on the road to Dumas.

"How did she get away from Walls? How did we miss her?"

"I don't know."

Seth's mind raced with all kinds of scenarios, each more horrific than the last. By the time they pulled into the hospital parking lot, white-hot pain pulsed through his temples with each beat of his heart.

By sheer force of will, he managed to exit the car without help. But when he stood, a wave of dizziness joined with the headache and forced him to lean against the door or hit the ground. Teeth clamped tight against nausea roiling through his stomach, Seth hissed in a breath.

"Want a wheelchair?"

Tom's clipped question got him a snarl. "Just give me a minute."

Shoulder throbbing, head pounding, he took a cautious step forward. Then another. Every step brought new pain to life, but he pushed it aside.

He had to see her for himself.

Tom knew her room number, and they made a beeline for it. A deputy lounged in a chair outside the door. He jumped up when they approached and barred their way. "No visitors."

Tom pulled his credentials. "She's my detective. I'm going in."

Before the man could voice an argument, Seth stepped around them and into the room. Tom could deal with the deputy. He had to see Jess.

At the sight of her lying in the bed, breath lodged in his throat, and unfamiliar tears threatened. Jaw clamped tight, he braced one hand against the wall and studied her. Scrapes and cuts marred both arms, and dark bruises peeked over the top edge of her hospital gown. Both eyes were swollen and spotted with color. A stark white bandage covered the left side of her forehead. Various shades of black and purple trailed down her left cheek and neck. Pillows elevated her left knee, and her right hand hid beneath a large bandage. Her fingernails were all ragged and broken. A small cut marred her lower lip.

She'd never looked more beautiful.

As though sensing his presence, her eyes sluggishly opened and locked with his. Neither spoke for several moments.

"Hey," she murmured.

"Hey." He took a cautious step forward. Knees weak with relief and still a bit dizzy, he stumbled and grabbed the foot of the bed.

Alarm flashed across her face. "Dammit, Seth. Sit before you fall."

He eyed a chair across the room but knew he'd never make it. "I'm good."

"No. You're not," she scolded and patted the space beside her. "Sit."

Mindful of her elevated leg, he eased himself onto the bed.

Her eyes scanned his face, studied the raised lump above his right eye and the sling on his right arm. "How bad?"

He shook his head and immediately regretted the quick move when pulsing pain followed by a surge of nausea resulted. Ignoring the discomfort, he focused on Jess's face. "Concussion, bumps, and bruises." He edged up his left shoulder and managed not to wince. "I've had worse." He focused on her. "How about you?"

"Mild hypothermia. Sprained knee. Feel like I went two rounds with a heavyweight prize fighter but could be worse."

His heart jerked at the knowledge of just how much worse it could have been.

The cloud across her face said she knew it, too.

Jess shivered and met his steady gaze. "I was so scared," she whispered. "When I realized who pulled me out of the car."

Her hand gripped the sheet near his hip, and he covered it with his own. This fragile Jess was someone he'd never seen before and sprang his protective instincts to life. "Don't think about it. You're safe now."

She shook her head. "We had him, Seth. And let him escape."

"We didn't *let* him escape. There was nothing we could have done."

"But what—"

"We got him once. We'll get him again."

Tom walked in about that time. "How are you doing, Jess?"

She made no attempt to pull her hand from Seth's comforting grasp. "I've been better, Sir, but at least I'm alive."

Phillips pulled up the chair, sat on the opposite side of the bed from Seth, and got straight to the point. "What happened?"

Seth listened in silence as Jess related the sequence of events after the crash. Weak and tired sounding at first, her energy picked up the more she talked.

"At first, I didn't know who pulled me out. Everything was so surreal. The dust picked up, and I couldn't see. Then Walls spoke to me."

"What did he say?"

Tom's question mirrored the one in Seth's mind.

She swallowed hard, closed her eyes a moment. "He said, 'You're mine, now.'"

Tom nodded. "What happened next?"

"I couldn't walk, so they dragged me toward the Jeep."

"Who?" asked Seth, unable to keep quiet.

"Walls and some other man. I assume it was Koslow, but I can't be sure. The dust got worse by the second. All I thought was *don't get in the Jeep.*" She drew a shaky breath. "And then the wind just slammed into us. It was like being hit by a car."

Her voice cracked, and Seth lightly squeezed her hand in support.

"Take your time, Jess," urged Tom. "You're doing fine."

She rolled her head side to side, lips compressed into a tight line. "One minute I'm near the door of the Jeep, then I'm rolling along the ground like a tumbleweed. Next thing I know, I'm in a ravine knee-deep in water."

Tom bobbed his head up and down. "Reports say straight-line winds hit eighty miles an hour when it blew through. What happened next?"

"I faded in and out. It was dark and the storm—the storm was awful, so much lightning. When the water reached my waist, I pulled myself up near the edge and wrapped my arm around a root, and just held on. I guess I passed out because the next thing I knew, it was daytime, maybe mid-afternoon. Hard to tell. Anyway, the water was chest-deep by then. I've never been so cold in my life." A shiver racked her body, and she lifted her bandaged hand. "The root cut into my hand, but I hung on."

Seth squeezed her arm. "Go on."

"I don't remember anything after I pulled myself out. I found out earlier an elderly couple found me beside the road. No idea how I got there." She paused. "A nurse told me that judging by the scrapes and stuff on my arms and legs, I must have dragged myself to the highway. Anyway, they, the ones who found me, didn't have a cell phone, so they just put me in their car and drove here."

"Did you recognize anyone, Jess," asked Tom. "Other than Walls?"

"No. But by then, the dust storm was on us, and I couldn't see much of anything."

"The other man, the one who helped pull you to the Jeep. Did he say anything?" asked Seth.

Face strained, she nodded. "Something like 'This is a damn fool idea.'"

"Are you sure it was Koslow?" asked Seth.

"I couldn't swear to it. A decent lawyer would argue I assumed it was Koslow because of the vehicle registration."

"What about the other man? Did you get a look at him?"

"What other man?"

"I'm sure I heard three distinct voices," Seth insisted. "Walls and two others before I passed out."

"I only saw Walls and someone I assumed to be Koslow."

Further conversation halted as Deputy Wallace barged into the room. "What the hell are you doing here?"

Tom pointed toward Seth. "I'll be right back." He turned to Wallace and introduced himself. "Why don't we take this conversation outside and let her get some rest."

Before Wallace could argue, he took him by the arm and led him out the door.

Seth ignored the raised voices coming from the hall and squeezed her arm again. "Sure you're okay?"

A strained smile graced her face. "No permanent damage. A couple of weeks, and I'll be like new."

"Sarge called your mother on the way here."

The color drained from her face. "I wish he hadn't done that."

"The media is having a field day with this whole affair. He wanted her to know you were all right."

"I understand, but...Mom doesn't handle stress well." She closed her eyes.

Since Tom used the speakerphone to call because he was driving, Seth got an earful when Mrs. Cantrell had a meltdown. It took a solid ten minutes for the hysterics to pass. Telling Jess about it would only add to the stress, so he remained silent.

"Thank you," she whispered as she opened her eyes.

Tightness in his throat made speech difficult. He slid his tongue over too-dry lips. "You'd do the same for me." There was so much more he wanted to say, but now was not the time or place.

She gave him a weak smile. "The color blue attracts twice as many mosquitos as other colors."

"...Jack the Ripper committed his crimes only on weekends." She frowned.

"It's true. I read it on the internet."

She snuffled, and her eyes closed.

He watched her in silence, thanked God she was alive, and he vowed to make Walls pay. She sighed and nestled into her pillow. He knew she'd been through an exhausting two days and needed rest, but he couldn't leave. He looked around and spotted the chair Tom vacated. Not the most comfortable, but he'd manage, so he eased off the bed.

Immediately, she grabbed for his hand, blinking rapidly. "Where are you going?" The anxiety in her voice pulled at him.

"To the chair so you can sleep."

"You won't leave me?"

Common sense told him it was probably the pain meds causing her defenses to drop and expose this vulnerable side she worked hard to hide. Call him a fool, but he chose not to believe it was the meds alone.

He stood and brushed a knuckle over her cheek. "No. I won't leave you, Jess. I'll be here when you wake up."

CHAPTER EIGHT

J ESS WOKE TO THE COLD TOUCH OF A STETHOSCOPE ON HER chest.

"Sorry," murmured the young nurse beside the bed, "didn't mean to wake you."

Before Jess could ask why she whispered, she heard the soft snore coming from the other side of the bed.

She turned to find Seth sound asleep in a straight back chair, his feet propped on another, their fingers firmly linked together.

Emotions flooded through her as she drank in his strong profile, cheeks darkened by a two-day-old beard. A chemical gel ice pack on his shoulder replaced the sling. His chest rose and fell in slow, measured breaths.

The knowledge of how close they came to death chilled her to the bone. But he was alive. They both were, and she vowed not to waste this chance.

The young nurse heaved a blissful sigh. "Your husband stayed there all night, just holding your hand."

Jess blinked. *My what?*

The nurse looped the stethoscope around her neck, one hand resting over her heart. "That's so romantic." She straightened and faced Jess. "You had a bad dream earlier. I thought he was going to climb in there with you, but he just held your hand and whispered in your ear until you calmed down."

Memories of the nightmare flashed in her head. Fear, stark and brutal, made her cringe.

Immediately, Seth's eyes opened, fixed on her. "Are you all right?"

She blinked rapidly and bobbed her head.

He didn't even glance at the nurse watching them. "No more bad dreams?"

"No." She glanced down at their clasped hands.

"How's the pain?"

"Better than yesterday. You?"

He squeezed her hand. "Better now."

A sense of calm washed over her. "You didn't have to stay... but I'm glad you did."

"Someone should be in shortly with breakfast," advised the nurse, "Would you like me to order a tray for your husband, too?"

Seth spoke up. "I'd be happy with some coffee."

She grinned and left the room.

Cheeks hot, Jess chose not to address the husband remark. "I feel bad about your having to sleep in that chair. You couldn't have gotten any rest at all."

He grinned, and her heart flipped over.

"Well, your *husband* has slept in worse places."

Heat rushed to her cheeks. Before she could muster a reply, a light tap on the door preceded the entrance of an older woman bearing a food tray.

"Please tell me there's coffee in there," begged Jess.

"Yes, but only one cup. Sarah just told me your husband was here." She smiled at Seth. "I'll bring in another tray in a few minutes."

Jess refused to look at Seth, who still held her hand.

She heard the contentment in his voice when he spoke to the woman.

"I need coffee more than food if you can tell me where to find it."

She placed the tray on the rolling table and pushed it into place. She noted their clasped hands. "I'll bring it to you in a few minutes." She left the room and eased the door closed.

Seth released her hand and pushed himself up from the chair. "I'll get a wet rag from the bathroom for you."

This thoughtful, tender side of Seth made the ache in her heart grow. He was just being nice. It meant nothing. Did it?

He returned and raised the head of the bed so she could freshen up while he finished adding creamer to her coffee.

"That scruffy look works for you." As soon as the words were out, she flushed. *I shouldn't have said that out loud.*

"I didn't think you liked beards."

"Well, that's not a full beard."

He placed her cup where she could reach it and grinned. "So, you're saying you like how I look first thing in the morning with no shave, no shower, and bed head?"

A knock on the door saved her from answering. "Come in."

The woman returned with a tray carrying three cups of coffee. "I thought y'all might need a little extra." She scanned around for a place to put it.

"Here's fine." Seth placed the cups on Jess's tray table. "We'll share."

The woman pulled sugar and creamer packets from her pocket, handed them to Seth, then faced Jess. "You're a lucky woman."

Seth chuckled. "I tell her that all the time, but I don't think she believes me."

"Oh, I think she does," said the woman, "I see it in her face when she looks at you." She patted Jess's arm. "Very lucky indeed."

Jess couldn't catch her breath as she watched the woman leave the room. *Seth encouraged her to think we were married.*

He placed her food within reach, grabbed a cup of coffee, and settled back in the chair, stretching his back and shoulders. "Eat before your food gets cold."

She stared at him.

"What?"

"You let her think we're married."

"I didn't want to embarrass her." He pointed toward the tray. "Eat. Tom told me they're releasing you today, and we have a long drive ahead of us."

He fiddled with the TV remote and tuned to a program about a guy who worked on old cars.

She shook her head and reached for the coffee cup. Her stomach felt a bit queasy, so she ate the oatmeal and toast, passing the eggs and bacon to Seth.

They just finished their coffee when Tom walked in.

"Y'all look like hell."

"Thanks," mumbled Seth, "we love you, too."

Tom turned to Jess. "How are you today?"

"Better than yesterday for sure."

He ducked his head, then met her gaze. "I'm sorry we didn't do a better job of searching the area for you, Jess."

Any ire she harbored disappeared at Tom's downcast expression. "Seth saw him take me. You had no way of knowing the rest." She shifted in the bed and stifled a groan as sore muscles protested. "Anything new on Walls?"

"We've had two sightings. One in Childress and another outside Wichita Falls. By the time locals got the word, they were long gone."

"Dammit." Jess didn't bother to temper her impatience. "We need to find him."

"The only thing either of you are going to do," snapped Tom, as his searing gaze skipped from one to the other, "is go home until you're released to work."

Jess opened her mouth to protest, but Seth beat her to the punch.

"You need all hands on deck, Sarge."

"Both of you barely got out of this fiasco alive. And neither one of you will set foot in the office until medical gives the okay." His ruddy complexion grew redder as his voice hardened. "That's an order."

Jess knew better than to argue now and changed the subject. "How soon before I can get out of here?" She looked forward to sleeping in her comfortable bed tonight even though the six-hour drive to Walker loomed like a storm cloud.

"They're processing the paperwork now," advised Tom. "A Ranger will be in shortly to talk to Jess. After that, we should be free to go."

One hour crawled into three as the Ranger, Drake Sampson, accompanied by the obnoxious deputy, took her statement. The deputy seemed intent on taking charge of the conversation, but Sampson maneuvered around him.

Later, an aide helped her shower and don borrowed scrubs and socks. Her sneakers were filthy but dry, so, with Seth's help, she donned them as well and waited.

Noon came and went before they finally hit the road. The following six hours were nothing short of torture. The pain medicine the doctor insisted she down before they left made her nauseous. Thankfully, it also made her sleepy, and she managed to at least doze most of the way home.

However, awake, she was miserable. There wasn't a spot on her body that didn't hurt, itch, or throb, and there was no way to get comfortable in the back seat of Tom's car. By the time they reached her home on the outskirts of Walker, she was beyond irritable, sulky, and bitchy.

"Are you sure you don't want me to call someone for you? Your mother, maybe?" asked Tom as they negotiated the three steps to her front door. "Or your sister?"

Jess nearly laughed at the suggestion. She would end up taking care of them. "I'm fine, Sarge. Thanks." All she wanted right now was a hot shower and to sleep for a week. But the bath would have to wait until her friend, Esther, arrived. She'd left her a message and knew she'd come as soon as she could. Sleep, she could manage on the couch.

"You need someone here with you," insisted Seth, "at least until you can get around without the crutches."

Although she agreed with his assessment, she kept silent. Besides, she could take care of herself. More or less. "I left word for Esther. She'll be here anytime. I'll be fine until then." *Unless I need to pee again, of course.*

Heat burned her cheeks as she recalled the two times Seth helped her to the restroom on the ride home.

To his credit, he didn't tease about it once. In fact, he acted as though he indeed cared and wanted to help.

Like a husband would. She tossed aside the thought. He was her partner. Nothing more. Just because he let those ladies at the hospital think they were married meant nothing.

But her crazy heart clung to the hope that one day, things might change.

He spent the night beside me holding my hand, and I didn't imagine him tenderly touching my face. Or did I?

"I'll stay until she gets here," insisted Seth, "and grab a taxi later."

Patience dwindling, Jess snipped. "Don't be silly. You're dead on your feet. I'll be fine." She hobbled toward the sofa, gritting her teeth against the pain. "Go home."

"No." He limped toward the kitchen. "I need some ice for my shoulder. Got anything here to eat?"

Tom dropped her purse and go bag beside her feet. "You two

can slug it out. I'm going home. Mavis is holding dinner for me." He straightened and placed both hands on his hips. "I hate leaving y'all here like this."

She pointed to the items he'd dropped on the floor. "Thanks for hanging on to my stuff, Sarge, and for bringing me home." Suddenly fighting back tears, she swallowed hard. "I really appreciate it."

He shook his head. "Sure I can't call someone for you?"

"No sir. Thank you."

He walked out the door as Seth lumbered in from the kitchen. He groaned and dropped onto the couch beside her, an ice pack on his shoulder. "Coffee's on," he sighed and leaned back.

"You don't have to stay. I can—"

"I'm staying, so don't argue." He rested his head on the back of the couch and closed his eyes. "Give me a minute, and I'll fix you something to eat."

She eyeballed him when he didn't quite stifle a groan. *He must be in agony.* "Did you take something for the pain?"

"Uh-huh. Should kick in soon."

"Seth," she reasoned, "You're exhausted. You slept in a freaking chair last night. You need to be in bed."

That sexy mouth kicked up in a heart-stopping smile though he didn't open his eyes. "You offering yours?"

Unwanted images of Seth in bed—with her lying beside him, invaded her mind and prevented the formation of a coherent comeback.

His light chuckle pulled her mind from the bedroom.

"Does silence mean you're giving the idea some thought?"

She leaned back against the couch and grunted. "It means I can't believe that even half-dead you can't keep from provoking me."

He turned to face her, his gaze intent. "Is that what I'm doing?"

Something in his expression made her heart lurch and filled her with a longing so intense it bordered on physical pain. "Isn't it?"

"Is that what you want it to be?"

The sharp ring of her cell phone saved her from a reply. "Hello? Hey. Yeah, I just got home. No, Seth is with me. Oh…I'm sorry. No, no, that's fine. Thanks for calling. I hope things are better tomorrow. Yes. I will. Bye."

She ended the call and peered at Seth, whose gaze hadn't left her face. "Esther can't come over until tomorrow night."

"No problem. I'll be here."

CHAPTER NINE

SETH COULDN'T REMEMBER THE LAST TIME EXHAUSTION CONsumed him to this extent. Thanks to ibuprofen and the ice pack, his shoulder pain now bordered on bad toothache versus rusty-knife amputation. But there wasn't an inch on his body that didn't hurt.

He watched Jess's expression go from relieved to concern as she talked on the phone. By the time she ended the call, he'd figured out Esther couldn't make it tonight. Just as well because he wasn't ready to leave yet.

They had issues to resolve.

He didn't miss the quick flash of desire in those coffee-colored eyes before they shuttered once again. Something scared her. Maybe a commitment issue, could be him or something else entirely. One thing was certain: God gave him a second chance. He wasn't going to waste it. Just thinking about how close he came to losing her turned his blood to ice.

"What's Bitsy's deal?"

Seth nicknamed Esther Bitsy on their first meeting, short for

Lil Bit, due to her five-foot-nothing height. She returned the favor by calling him Studly. Neither seemed to mind the labels.

"Something at the nursing home with her mother."

He shifted to see her face better. "Nothing serious, I hope."

"Her Alzheimer's is pretty advanced. She has bad days and worse ones. Today is one of the worse ones."

"That's gotta be tough on her."

A grimace crossed her face when she leaned back.

"Do you need a pain pill?"

She closed her eyes and exhaled. "Not unless you have one for I-hurt-all-over-more-than-anywhere-else pain."

He clamped his jaw and forced himself to stand. "Ibuprofen might help if you don't want the pain pill. I left it in the kitchen."

"Thank you," she murmured after a moment, "for everything."

He turned to look her way. The bruises were lighter now, but distinct shades of black and purple with yellow-tinged edges still marred her flawless skin. Fatigue added dark circles under both eyes. The bandage on her forehead concealed four stitches. A crusty scab covered the cut on her lip.

"I look like hell, don't I?" she asked with a frown.

"You're beautiful."

She closed her eyes, and one corner of her mouth curled up. "Liar."

He barely stifled a groan as he sat back down and covered her hand with his. "You're beautiful because you're alive."

She opened her eyes and met his focused gaze.

"I thought I'd lost you, Jess," he whispered, voice choked with emotion. "I never want to have that feeling again."

Her chest rose, then halted as she held her breath.

"But it made me realize something I've denied for months. There's something between us. Something special."

She gulped and skimmed her tongue over chapped lips.

He leaned toward her. "One day. Soon. I aim to find out what that *something* is."

Breathing faster, she waited.

"But not tonight."

She blinked twice and swallowed.

"Tonight, we both need to sleep." Seth grunted and pulled himself up from the couch, then reached for her uninjured hand. "Come on. Let's get you to bed."

At her shocked expression, he grinned. "Alone, Texas. I think it's safe to say neither of us is at our best right now."

Her gaze ping-ponged from his outstretched hand to his face.

He wiggled his fingers, and she offered no resistance as he helped her stand.

"But we are going to discuss this again. Soon."

A light flush of red joined the multi-hued colors on her face. "We can't…you don't…."

He ignored her protest. "I've only seen this part of the house. Where's your bedroom?"

The color on her cheeks increased to bright red. Not wanting to add to her discomfort, Seth suppressed a smile.

"The master is down that hall," she mumbled.

Together, they limped down the corridor, and he sat her on the edge of a queen-size bed.

The very feminine room surprised him. He didn't know much about decorating but thought the space could easily grace the pages of any designer magazine. The muted shades of green and blue instilled peace and tranquility. He caught a whiff of something that made him think of tropical drinks on the beach.

The dark mahogany headboard contrasted with the muted green paint on the wall. Photographs of beach and ocean sunsets hung around the room, and all the lamps resembled shells. A ceiling fan caused the lacey blue window curtains to ripple like waves on the ocean. A comfortable-looking chair with a matching footstool in front of one window announced this was her haven.

Even I could live in this room. He regarded Jess with a carefully veiled expression. "I wondered where she lived."

"Who?"

"The woman behind the badge."

She chewed her lower lip and didn't speak.

"It's a nice room." He glanced around again. "Makes me think of the ocean. Did you take those photos?"

"Yes. My last vacation. Well, my only vacation. Right before you came on board."

He surveyed the bed, tried not to envision her—and him, in it. "What do I do with all those little pillows?"

"Throw pillows."

"What?"

"They're called throw pillows, and you can put them on the settee."

He looked around.

"The bench at the foot of the bed," she offered. "Just put them there."

He scooped them off the bed. "What are they for?"

"To look at."

He shook his head. "I guess it's a woman thing."

This time she smiled. "Yes, it is."

He stood in front of her. "Do you want to sleep in those scrubs or what?"

The flush returned to her cheeks, and she studied her feet. "In the bathroom, through that door." She pointed to the right. "There's a robe and a sleep shirt on a hook behind the door."

He found the robe, and underneath it hung a long cotton sleep shirt boasting, *I don't do mornings.* He threw the shirt over his shoulder and limped back to the bedroom.

She sucked in a breath as she reached for the shirt. "Thanks.

You, um, you can go now." The confines of the space amplified her jerky breaths, and her gaze skittered around the room.

"Can you manage by yourself?" He grinned and wiggled his fingers. "We're at your disposal."

"I'm not helpless," she snapped.

"Claws in, Jess. I never said you were. But if you need any help, I'll be out in the hall."

Tired as he was, her grunts and moans tested his resolve to leave her alone and sent his over-active imagination into hyperdrive. His solemn word was the only thing that kept his back turned as he waited outside her door.

Exhausted, body wracked with pain, he rotated his shoulders to loosen muscles. *When's that ibuprofen gonna kick in?*

"Dammit," she mumbled. "I can't lift my arm high enough."

"Take your good arm out first," he suggested, "then you can slide it off."

She huffed out a frustrated breath. "Just rip the damn thing off."

He chuckled. He couldn't help it. "Any other time, Texas, I'd love to hear those words."

"In your dreams, Hammer."

"How did you know?"

"Seth." Her theatrical groan drew his name out an extra syllable or two.

Maybe frustration will reduce her embarrassment. He entered the room.

"What are you doing?"

"I'm gonna help." He stood in front of her and assessed the situation.

"Then close your eyes."

Her discomfort this time amused him. "I don't think so. Although I have done some of my best work in the dark."

She mumbled something under her breath.

"What was that?" he teased.

"You can't—"

He barely managed not to groan when he squatted down in front of her. "Do you trust me, Jess?"

"Yes."

At least she didn't hesitate to answer. "I give you my word. No funny business."

Eyes wary, she hesitated. "Okay. Just the top. I had hell getting the sports bra on at the hospital. I'll save it until tomorrow."

Resolve in place, he skimmed his hands down her arm to the edge of the sleeve, doing his best not to think about the entire process. "Can you shimmy your arm out if I hold the shirt?"

"I'm not sure. It doesn't have much give to it." A minute later, she snapped, "This isn't working, either."

"Okay. If I pull up the bottom, do you think you can slide it out then?"

There was a slight pause before she answered. "Can't we just cut the damn thing off?"

"How much fun would that be?"

"You're enjoying this way too much," she grumbled.

You have no idea. Seth was smart enough not to say that out loud. He gathered the bottom edge of the shirt. "I'll go slow and easy. Stop me if it hurts."

Her snort made him grin. The sudden catch in her breathing when his fingers skimmed over bare skin made him falter. *Think about something else. Anything else. Taxes, grocery shopping, skin, silky skin. Crap.*

"Seth?"

Her gentle question penetrated the fog of desire that coursed through him and did what he couldn't do on his own—shamed him under control.

"Sorry," he mumbled. "Can you get your arm out now?"

Several fevered moments later, the top lay on the floor.

Seth stared at cuts and bruises previously hidden by her clothes.

"Damn." He inspected the damage to her body. "No wonder you're so sore. I don't have that many bruises."

She kept her head down and didn't meet his gaze, the deep flush on her cheeks warring with the bruises.

"Okay. Ready to try and put the other one on?"

She nodded, and he soon had it in place.

She blew out a long breath. "I can't even kick off my shoes."

The mortification in her voice got to him. *I need to make her think of something else.* "Next time, you can help me undress."

"You're incorrigible."

He squatted down again, praying he could pull himself up, and removed her socks and shoes. "Part of my charm." When he was finally upright again, he took a breath. "Ready for the pants?"

Gaze averted, she huffed. "They have a drawstring. Just help me stand, then untie it. They should just slide off."

It was more than fatigue making his hands tremble as he helped her stand. Using his shoulders for balance, she waited for him to finish the task. Just the thought of what he was doing was enough to test his resolve to remain unaffected. He might feel like death warmed over, but he wasn't a eunuch. He was, however, an honorable man, or at least, he tried hard to be. He swallowed his discomfort and forced his mind to think of anything other than what he was doing.

She clung to his biceps with shaky fingers, and he tried not to breathe in her scent. But she was right in front of him, her head touching his chin, her firm breasts inches from his chest. It took all his control to redirect his thoughts and counter his body's reaction to her proximity.

And it worked until he pulled the cotton strings and discovered he would have to insert his thumbs in the waistband to loosen the pants. Her skin was soft and warm and damn near fried what remained of his brain. He grit his teeth so hard his jaw ached, but he managed to ensure her sleep shirt dropped into place as the pants slid to the floor. He pulled in a ragged breath and stepped toward the head of the bed, transferring her grip to his left arm. "Hang on while I turn the covers back. You should be able to just step out of the pants."

Her breath convulsed in and out several times in the process of lying down, but she never complained.

Seth knew she must hurt as bad or worse than him, and his admiration edged up a notch. "Almost done, Jess, almost done."

Pillows adjusted, covers in place, he turned to go. "I'll be back in a minute with your pain meds. You need to take one."

Silent, lips rolled in, and eyes tightly closed, she jiggled her head in agreement.

It took every ounce of energy reserves he owned to walk to the kitchen and back. "I brought the crutches, too." He placed them against the end table, "in case you need them."

Jess took the pain medication without argument, which told him how bad she hurt.

"I turned off the coffee pot. I'll make fresh in the morning."

"Seth?" She opened her eyes. "Thank you…for all of this."

"You're welcome…*wifey*." He turned toward the door. "I'll leave the door open. Just call out if you need me."

"Seth?"

"Yeah?"

"Stay with me a while?"

"Stay with you?" He stumbled and grabbed the footboard. "In the bed?

She whooshed out a long breath. "Just till I go to sleep. The nightmare…"

He moved to the other side of the bed, then carefully positioned himself on top of the covers beside her.

Exhaustion claimed him the moment his head hit the pillow.

CHAPTER TEN

WALLS TAPPED THE STEERING WHEEL WITH HIS INDEX FINger and glanced at his watch. Ten o'clock at night. *What the hell is taking so long?* He examined the abandoned parking lot where a single security light cast eerie shadows along the side of the empty gas station.

"Let it go, Jack," grumbled Koslow. "you're gonna get us caught."

"My party," snapped Walls, "my rules."

Koslow fidgeted in the passenger seat of the stolen sedan. "The whole damn state is looking for us. We gotta lay low until things calm down."

Jack snarled at his cousin. "Sometimes I wonder why I even bother with you."

Koslow sat up straight in the seat. "You'd be in jail right now if it wasn't for me."

Walls banged his fist on the wheel. "Yeah, well, it's your stupid ass that got me caught in the first place."

"I didn't know the taillight was busted."

Jack tuned out his cousin's bluster. Family or not, he'd outlived his usefulness. The minute that smart-ass detective was back in his grasp, Kos was a dead man.

Jack had never killed a man before. Women were easier to control. A little slap, a threat or two, and, bingo, instant cooperation.

He rubbed a fist on his thigh, remembering the last one. She had a smart mouth, too, like that detective. She didn't like being bossed around, either. Unfortunately for her, she never accepted her place and her death took a while. He smiled. *Most fun I've had in a while.*

Kos belched several times in a row, and Jack's fingers wrapped around the wheel, easily imagining it was Kos's neck. Now that the idea of killing him took root, he found himself looking forward to the time. *I'll make it quick. After all, he is family and did help me escape.*

"You're acting crazy, Jack. This is a bad idea," griped Koslow. "Real bad."

Then again, maybe I won't make it quick.

Jack checked his watch. "Where is he?" he snapped. "He should have called by now."

"Well, it's not like he can just walk up and ask somebody where she lives."

Jack ground his teeth together. *I may not wait until I have the woman.* "Shut the hell up, Kos. I'm tired of listening to you."

His companion slumped down in the seat. "Why her? She's not even pretty. And she's a cop."

Jack inhaled and did a mental ten-count. "Because I want her, that's why."

Five minutes later, his burner phone chimed. Only one person had this number. "What the hell took you so long? Yeah, yeah, whatever. Give it to me." He scribbled down the information on a fast-food napkin found in the glove box. "Is he still there?" He jotted on the makeshift notepad. "Don't you start on me, too. I'm not leaving town without her. Don't give me any crap. Be ready when I call or be sorry."

Jack ended the call and snickered in anticipation. He needed time to decide just how he would teach that smart-mouthed bitch a much-needed lesson.

ᛜ

Jess woke to the warmth of Seth's chest against her cheek and the steady *thump* of his heart under her palm. Her injured knee rested comfortably on his bare thigh. The weight of his hand on the curve of her hip sent warm shivers through her.

When did he take off his sweatpants and get under the covers?

Brain still foggy from the pain medicine, it took a moment to put the pieces together. The nightmare returned, more frightening than before. And then Seth was there. He pulled her chilled body into the circle of his arms, whispering words of comfort that chased away the demons and allowed blissful sleep.

She inhaled his spicy, masculine scent, exhaled slowly, and allowed herself a moment of indulgence. There was something so very intimate about waking up in a man's embrace. She racked her brain, without success, for the last time it happened. *Never in this bed, for sure.*

His hand slid up to rest over her midriff, and breath caught in her throat.

Holy mother of pearl.

She took another slow, steady breath and conducted a pain inventory. Knee, stiff, hurts to move. Shoulder, bearable, hand, aching, but flexible. Numerous sore spots all over.

Now what? Common sense urged her to get up, but the part of her brain governing action appeared content to remain in this happy place.

Unable to resist the temptation, she eased her hand over the muscled plane of his chest, down to his six-pack abs and back up.

The steady pace of his heart under her palm increased in speed.

"Just to be clear...." Seth's sleep-roughened voice made her jump, and she craned her head to meet his gaze.

"I may be all banged up, but parts of me are working just fine." Dark eyes bored into hers in silent expectation. "If you want to know which parts, keep doing that."

She couldn't move if her life depended on it. "I—I didn't...."

The smoldering flame in his eyes held her captive. The very air in the room crackled with electricity as the stare-down continued.

I want this. I've always wanted this. But...

"There are a gazillion reasons why this is a bad idea," she babbled.

The warmth of his hand as it slid down her hip and back up scrambled her thoughts.

"Name one."

She struggled for an answer. "We're partners."

Whisper-soft, his hand slid down her hip and up again, bringing the hem of her sleep shirt with it. "Want me to stop?"

Not one of the gazillion reasons she knew existed materialized. "No," she purred.

Before she had time to consider the repercussions, she moved up and lightly brushed her sore lips over his. Once. Twice.

His hand slid up her back to cup her neck and brought them together for a deep, lingering kiss. Fire flooded her veins even as her sore mouth protested, but the pain was nothing compared to the pleasure of his lips on hers.

At last.

Seth shifted to pull her on top. The sudden movement made them both grunt in pain and freeze mid-kiss.

Neither moved for a heartbeat, then Seth laughed, a smooth, throaty sound that tickled her lips. "Great idea. Bad timing."

Jess eased off his chest and maneuvered down onto her pillow, helpless to stop the flood of embarrassment to her cheeks. The movement brought a flash of pain in her knee, and she groaned. The pain was less severe if kept slightly bent, so she reached around for a pillow to put under it.

Seth pulled the one out from under his head and slipped it under her knee. "I think yours is on the floor."

He paused, and she heard the self-satisfied humor in his voice. "Although I do think you liked my thigh better."

She couldn't make herself look at him. "I'm sorry. I shouldn't have done that."

"Why not?"

No suitable reply made it through her jumbled brain.

"Jess? Look at me."

When she didn't comply, he tilted her face toward him. "Please."

Face aflame, she met his steady gaze.

He lay on his side, propped up on his elbow, and ran the tip of his finger across her lips. "Don't apologize for beating me to the kiss." He gently touched the swollen curve of her lower lip. "Even though I'm sure it hurt like hell."

Stomach tight with anxiety, she barely breathed.

His voice grew thoughtful, reserved. "I've wanted to do that for months."

The shock of discovery hit her full force, and air shot from her lungs. "You have?"

He nodded. "I meant what I said last night." His voice rang with command. "I aim to find out what this is between us because we both know it's more than being partners." His finger retraced her lips. "More than friends."

She was too surprised to do more than nod as his low, sensual voice echoed her own chaotic thoughts, and tears clogged her throat.

A slow, suggestive smile curled up the corners of his mouth. He leaned forward and pressed a kiss on her forehead. "To be continued."

The peal of the telephone broke the spell. Seth rolled over and grabbed the cordless from the base. "Hamilton. Who's calling? Just a sec." He pressed the phone to his chest. "Do you want to talk to your sister?"

Jess closed her eyes. Next to her mother, Tina was the last person she wanted to talk to right now. But Tina being Tina, wouldn't be put off long. Resigned, she reached for the phone. "May as well get it over with."

Seth moved to the side of the bed. "I'll go make some coffee."

She put the phone to her ear. "Hi, Tina. For your information, he's my partner."

She tuned out Tina's rant and watched Seth stand beside the bed, back to her, and stretch. Breath caught in her throat at the sight of that tight ass and muscular body.

Boxers. I was right.

Spellbound, she watched as he bent over and plucked sweatpants from the settee and pulled them on. They rode low on his hips, and muscles rippled across his broad back as he rotated his shoulder. Her mind relived the velvety touch of his lips and the passion hidden below the surface.

How long would a fire that hot burn? Would it turn to ashes like it did for her parents?

He reached for his tee-shirt and caught her stare.

Invisible energy passed between them, connecting them. Her heart thudded once then fell into a steady rhythm.

He winked and walked away.

CHAPTER ELEVEN

SETH HUMMED TO HIMSELF AS HE EMPTIED THE COFFEE POT from last night and started a fresh one. He glanced at the wall clock and shook his head. Nine o'clock. They'd slept for ten hours. How long had it been since he enjoyed that luxury? *Having a beautiful woman tucked against your side doesn't hurt, either.*

Optimism surfaced for the first time in months, and with it, an appetite. He opened the fridge and found eggs, sausage, cheese, and butter, along with half a carton of milk and blackberry jam. "My favorites."

He placed the ingredients on the counter and put the sausage on to cook. A quick search of cabinets supplied a bowl, and he cracked one egg into it and reached for another when his cell phone rang. He rested the phone on his shoulder and broke the second egg. "Hamilton."

"We believe he's in Fort Worth."

Tom's straight-to-the-point statement stopped Seth cold. "Why?"

"PD found the Jeep in a strip mall parking lot last night. A dark

Taurus sedan was reported stolen from there, too, so we can assume they've changed vehicles."

Seth listened in silence as Phillips rattled off the car's license number, color, and make, committing the information to memory. Thoughts of the third man, still unidentified, prompted a question. "What about prints? Did they pull anything from the Jeep?"

"A couple of partials, but no ID yet. They did a half-ass job of wiping it down. Either they didn't care if we found something or were in a hurry." He paused. "Either way, I don't like it."

"I agree. We'll be vigilant." He added salt and pepper to the eggs. "Anything else?"

"No, that's it for now."

"Okay. Keep me posted."

Mind awash with possibilities, he finished the sausage and debated the eggs. Breakfast in bed might win him brownie points, or it may be a little too intimate right now. He moved the meat to a plate and filled two mugs with coffee. "I'll bring her in here for breakfast. This time."

♂⚲

"Did you hear me?" Tina's voice rang with suppressed anger. "Who the hell was that?"

Jess counted to ten, refused to let Tina's theatrics pull her in.

"It's not enough you nearly gave Mom a heart attack with your antics. Now you can't even call and tell her you're okay."

"I was—"

"She's so upset, I had to stay with her."

Upset is her specialty. And yours. Jess sighed. "I'll call her."

"Honestly, Jessica, do you ever think of anyone but yourself? You disappear for days and let everyone think some crazy killer kidnapped you." Tina's voice edged up more with each word. "And I have to drop everything to babysit Mom." She sucked in a breath. "And when you get home from your little escapade, you can't even find time to call." She paused for a breath. "But you find time to shack up with some guy."

She pushed her head deeper into the pillow and closed her eyes. Explanations were useless. If something didn't directly affect Tina, it wasn't important.

The product of Frank and Ivy's second marriage when Jess was twelve, Tina grew up the center of attention, leaving nothing for Jess and Frank's son Tony, who was three years older.

Had it not been for Tony, Jess would never have survived the emotional isolation and scorn she suffered at the hands of her so-called family.

He joined the Army the day after graduation, and she was left alone.

"Are you listening to me?"

Tina's shriek jerked Jess from the dark memories her call unearthed. "Yes."

"You have to come right now and take care of Mother. You know good and well I can't deal with her when she has one of her moods."

"I'm not able to—"

"Oh, so your boyfriend is more important to you than your own family?"

Jess sighed and tried to explain. "I'm hurt, Tina. I can't—"

"You're lying," she shouted, "You're mean and selfish and just don't want to help me."

It was no surprise when her sister hung up without a goodbye. For a twenty-one-year-old woman, Tina often acted like a spoiled teenager.

Jess closed her eyes and bit her lip until it throbbed in sync with her pulse. *I will not cry. I will not cry.*

Contact with her mother and sister was infrequent at best, for that was the only way to avoid the deep hole of self-pity in which they wallowed. Still, they were her family, and while she did love them, she didn't like them very much at times.

She jumped when Seth sat on the edge of the bed.

"Brought your coffee, and breakfast is almost ready."

Her throat ached with unshed tears, and she had to swallow hard to speak. "Oh, thanks. Just put it on the end table."

"What's wrong? Are you okay?"

She didn't trust herself to look at him. "I'm fine."

He placed both cups beside the lamp and tipped up her chin. "No, you're not. You've been through hell this week. I don't know what your sister told you just now, but I can see it upset you." His thumb traced her trembling lip. "I'm here, Jess. You're not alone."

The kindness in his voice broke through the wall and triggered the worst reaction imaginable.

A tear found its way out of one eye, followed by another. Then both eyes. Miserable and in pain, swamped with deep-seated fear, loneliness, and guilt, a sob escaped.

Tenderly, he pulled her into his arms. "Let it go, babe," he whispered, "just let it go."

She couldn't stop the flood of emotions that tore loud, choking sobs from the depths of her soul. Fear of being captured by Walls. Fear of losing Seth.

Fear. Of being alone. Forever.

"I'm here," he whispered as he rocked her back and forth. "I'm here."

CHAPTER TWELVE

Seth pressed his back against the headboard, and Jess nestled close to his side, her head on his chest. The heart-wrenching sobs dwindled to an occasional hiccup and shaky breath.

In his career, he'd seen a lot of women come apart at the seams when presented with shocking news or the prospect of going to jail. It was a simple enough task to separate himself from it and wait for the waterworks to cease, then continue with business as usual.

He couldn't do that with Jess. The sight of her shattered to the point of tears shredded his heart. He lightly rubbed one hand over her upper arm, mindful of her injured shoulder.

"I'm not a weak person," she sniffled.

"You're the strongest woman I know."

"Strong people don't cry."

"I cried when Bambi's mom got killed."

She rubbed her cheek on his chest and hiccupped. "How old were you? Six?"

"Thirty-seven."

"Bull. That was last year."

"Watched it with my niece and nephew. We all cried." When she remained silent, he added, "There are only a thousand words of dialog in that whole movie."

She stiffened against his chest. "Thank you...for not judging me."

He discovered early on how she hated to appear weak or dependent upon someone else. In her eyes, to break down in front of him would be nothing short of a catastrophe.

"Humans cry, Jess. No shame in that."

"Means you're weak."

"No. It means you're human." He patted her arm. "Time to eat." He eased her forward and made his way off the bed. "Breakfast is almost ready. Can you make it to the kitchen?"

"I'm gonna owe you big time, aren't I?" She sighed. "Cooking, babysitting."

He grinned. "I may have to start a list."

Jess glanced at the coffee cup on the bedside table. "I'll warm it up later. Right now, I need a hot shower."

"Okay. Need some help?" He didn't react when she looked everywhere but at him.

"The shower has a bench seat. Let me see if I can walk with the crutches."

A few minutes later, they stood in front of the vanity in the tiny bathroom. The exertion caused her to grimace, and sweat glistened on her upper lip, but she didn't complain. "I think I can make it from here if you take the bandage off my hand and forehead."

"Are you sure?"

"Doctor said I could take them off today and shower."

"All right." He helped her sit on the lowered commode lid, gently removed the bandages, and inspected her injuries. "Good. No signs of infection." He placed both hands on his hips, enjoying the play of emotions running across her face. "Sure you don't need help to undress?"

"Out."

"Okay, but leave the door open." He expected her objection and raised his hand, palm out. "I'll be in the kitchen or the porch. I have to hear if you need help." He used his index finger to make a cross over his heart. "I won't come in unless you call."

She took a breath and nodded.

Once in the kitchen, Seth stood at the back door with his coffee and surveyed the tidy yard enclosed by a new chain link fence.

Jess's home rested on top of a slight rise at the end of a cul-de-sac with no close neighbors. The western edge of Crawford Lake was visible from the small screened-in back porch, and a wooden gazebo in the center of the yard held a table and two chairs.

The cozy porch included two rockers and a glider swing, so he took his mug out there. He moved a rocker near the open door so he could hear if she called and sat down. The light breeze still had a bit of chill, but the bright blue sky promised a warm day. Two baskets with bright red blooms hanging from the eaves added a splash of color, and completed the homey feel. The softness of the place was at odds with the hard woman most people knew. And yet, it fit, for she was a woman of sharp contrasts, full of bright spots and dark shadows, and he couldn't wait to explore them all.

He blew out a slow breath and allowed the serenity of the scene to ease the tension in his soul. Leaning back, he set the rocker in slow, measured motion. The place spoke volumes about her. The need for tranquility and peace echoed in the pale-yellow paint in the kitchen to the soft colors of her bedroom and vibrant baskets of flowers on the porch.

This was her sanctuary.

No wonder she likes it here. Hell. I like it here.

He drained the last of his warm coffee and glimpsed at his watch. "Twenty minutes. Too long for a shower." Concern edged up, and he returned to the kitchen. He placed the cup on the counter and headed toward the bathroom as Jess hobbled down the hall.

Dressed in sweatpants and tee-shirt, hair still wet, she appeared exhausted. "I was headed to check on you." His gaze scanned her head to toe. "You're pale. Are you okay?"

"The process was harder than I envisioned, but I managed." She shook her head and sent water droplets flying. "Couldn't manage to towel my hair very well and didn't bother with the blow dryer."

She didn't protest as he helped her to the kitchen table.

"I brought your cup back in here. Want some fresh or just nuke it?"

"Nuke is fine."

He placed it in front of her.

"I could get used to being waited on."

The fact that she smiled when she spoke pleased him. "Every woman needs to be waited on now and then."

He went to the laundry room and pulled a towel from the shelf. "Let me see if I can dry your hair some more." He didn't give her a chance to object as he gently kneaded her hair. "That's better." He tossed it on top of the washer. "I'll finish—" The melodic chime of the doorbell interrupted him. "Would Bitsy come by this early?"

"No." Esther worked at a financial firm downtown and clocked a lot of hours. "She's at work."

Seth hummed to himself as he opened the door to a stranger dressed in an Army combat uniform with a Staff Sargent insignia.

"Who the hell are you?" the man snapped.

"Who wants to know?"

"Is Jessie home?" He craned his neck to look behind Seth. "Is she?"

A new boyfriend, maybe? In the time they'd worked together, there'd been only one man, and their relationship ended months ago. He took another look at the newcomer. Six feet tall, muscular, dark hair, brown eyes, unfamiliar features. Then he saw the name on his shirt. *Cantrell.* Her stepfather's name was Cantrell. But there were gaps in his information on her background, so he wasn't aware of a relative, but it was possible. "I repeat, Sargent," he demanded, "Who wants to know?"

The man took a step forward. "Where is she?" He peeked over Seth's shoulder toward the half-wall of the kitchen and suddenly rushed past.

Caught off guard, Seth stumbled against the door jam. Recovering quickly, he turned and followed the man into the kitchen and saw Jess slumped in her chair, cup cradled in her hands.

"Jessie!" The man rushed toward her.

Startled, she jumped and knocked over her mug.

"What the hell happened?" He cast a furious glance at Seth. "Did he do this to you?" He took a step toward Seth. "I'll kill him!"

Jess grabbed his hand and pulled herself up from the table. "Tony? Oh, God. Tony?"

The man hesitated, then pulled her against him in a rough embrace.

Jess moaned, and he took a step back. "Oh, Jess. I'm so sorry. Did I hurt you?"

Seth watched as the woman he loved tenderly touched the face of the man who held her in his arms and tried to ignore the crushing agony it caused. *She loves someone else.*

"I can't believe you're here," she whispered. "It's been two years."

Seth stood it as long as he could. "So, wanna introduce me to your friend, Jess?"

She swiped at her tear-stained face. "He's not a friend, Seth. He's my brother. Tony, this is my partner, Seth Hamilton. Seth, meet my brother Tony Cantrell."

Seth stepped forward and extended his hand, refusing to acknowledge the relief racing through him. "Sorry if I came across like a hard ass. I'm a little protective right now."

Tony shook his hand. "I should have told you who I was." He turned back to Jess. "I was in Iraq when I heard what happened.

Every newscast I listened to said something different." He examined her closely. "You look like hell. Are you sure you're okay?"

"I need to sit."

He helped her back to her chair while Seth cleaned up the spilled brew then filled two cups. "I'll finish breakfast while you guys catch up."

He turned back to the counter when the phone rang. He picked the cordless from the base. "Want me to run interference?"

Jess reached for the phone. "Probably Mary telling me my car warranty is expired."

ᛟᛏ

Jess took a sip of coffee and answered the phone. "Hello?"

"Good morning, Detective." Jack Walls' voice, low and sinister, vibrated with anger. "Hope you are feeling better today."

Heart lodged in her throat, she sputtered. "How did you get this number?"

"Nice place you have there. No close neighbors."

Unable to speak, she gripped the corner of the table. Walls knew where she lived.

"Tsk-tsk, Detective. No smart remarks, no sass. I'm disappointed."

"What do you want?" Even as she asked, she knew the answer.

"You'll find out soon enough. When I'm ready."

The line went dead.

Fear hit like icy water and chilled her to the bone.

"Jess?" Seth squatted down in front of her. "Answer me. Who was on the phone?"

It took several erratic breaths before she spoke. "Walls."

"The prisoner who escaped?"

Tony's question went unanswered as she stared at Seth.

He rested his hands on her thighs. "What did he want?"

"My recipe for margaritas." *Control. Get control.*

"Word for word," insisted Seth. "What did he say?"

His touch provided more comfort than she wanted to admit as she repeated the conversation with Walls.

"I'm calling Tom." Seth looked toward Tony. "How long can you stay?"

"Five days. I was lucky to get leave at all."

Seth stood and pulled his cell phone from his pocket. "I need to call this in."

Tony concentrated on Jess. "Tell me. All of it."

Jess relayed a condensed version of what happened while keeping one ear tuned to Seth's conversation.

"Now he's calling you." Tony slapped the table. "And he knows where you live."

Jess forced a calmness she didn't quite feel. "I'm a big girl now, Tony. I can take care of myself."

"I wasn't there when you needed me." He reached across the table and took her hand. "Let me help you now."

She glanced at Seth, then back to her brother. "I'll be fine, Tony. Really.

"I'll see if I can extend my leave. You don't need to be here alone."

"She won't be." Seth's comment brooked no opposition. He turned to Tony. "I need to get some stuff from my place. I assume you can stay until I get back?"

"Hello?" protested Jess. "I'm still here, and this concerns me, too." She hated being excluded from the conversation. "And I can take care of myself."

"You couldn't even get ready for bed last night without help," snapped Seth.

Heat scorched her cheeks at Tony's quickly shuttered expression. "Contrary to what you seem to think, Seth Hamilton, I am not a helpless bimbo."

That Cheshire cat smile did crazy things to her insides.

"You're the last person in the world *anyone* would ever call a bimbo, Tex." He took the phone from the table and placed it back in the base. "Tom's setting up regular patrols starting now. I'll be back in a couple of hours." He stopped beside her chair and tilted her chin up. "We're in this together, Jess. Don't ever doubt it." He turned to Tony. "There's sausage, eggs, and toast. Make sure she eats."

A horn sounded outside, and Seth stepped back. "My taxi's here. I'll be back in a couple of hours."

Tony silently watched Seth leave the room then turned to his sister. "I've worked with a lot of partners in my time," he declared, "but not one of them ever helped me get ready for bed."

CHAPTER THIRTEEN

"**G**ET HIM ON THE PHONE!" JACK SWEPT THE PIZZA BOX OFF the dirty mattress that served as their dining table. "Now!"

Koslow dodged the cardboard but not the half-eaten slice of pepperoni pizza that plastered to his chest. "I've called him twice, Jack. It went to voicemail both times."

If I didn't need you, asshole, you'd be dead now.

"I don't give a damn how many times you called him, Dipstick, you keep calling 'til he answers!"

Jack went to the window and parted the dusty, stained curtain. "He should have checked in by now."

The cell phone's musical tone made him turn toward Kos. "It's him."

"Of course it's him, you idiot. He's the only one with the number." Jack stomped over and grabbed the phone. "Why the hell didn't you answer my calls?"

"I have a job, Jack. I can't take calls at work."

"You think I give a damn about your job? You work for me, dammit! Me!"

"I did like Kos said. I drove the jeep." His high-pitched voice rose another notch. "I didn't know what he planned. I'm done. I won't help you again."

"You're done when I say you are," hissed Jack. "I want her place watched. I want to know everyone who goes in and comes out."

"I can't lose my job, Jack. Why can't you or Kos do it?"

"Because the whole damn state is looking for us!"

Jack ended the call before the loser could argue further. "I shouldn't have to put up with this crap," he muttered as he paced around the room. "It's all her fault, and she's gonna pay."

♂ ♀

"You were right about the tires," confirmed Phillips, "both had bullet holes."

"Did we get the slugs?" Phone pressed to his ear, Seth waited.

"No. One through and through and caught just enough tread to blow it. The other one hit the rim and blew out the whole back side. Could have used a rifle or handgun, but at that speed and the storm barreling down, it was just flat-out luck he hit anything."

"He'd have to be one hell of a shot," proclaimed Seth. "Did Kos have a military background?"

"I'm not sure, but we'll check it out next." He made a tsk-tsk sound. "I did ask the locals to scan the area and see what turns up. But with the storm that night, if something did hit the ground, no telling where it ended up."

Not the news Seth wanted to hear, but it didn't surprise him, either. "Okay. What about prints? Any luck on the Jeep?"

"Zip."

Seth swore under his breath. "I hoped we'd at least find out who the other man was."

"Yeah," said Tom, "me, too. The partials are small and smeared, but I'm sending them over to a fed I know. Maybe their high-tech equipment can come up with something."

"What about the stolen car?"

"Nothing new. Get this. That guy, Koslow? Well, he worked at the courthouse as a janitor until a couple of months ago."

That comment grabbed his attention. "That explains why Jess thought he looked familiar. She probably saw him around there."

"He worked there a little over a year. From all accounts, he was a model employee. Never late or missed a day and did his job. One day, out of the blue, he quit. Claimed he had family problems to deal with."

"Okay. I'm headed back to Jess's place now to drop off some stuff, and then I'll be in the office. I need to get our laptops."

"Not until medical releases you," insisted Tom.

"We need our laptops. I'll be in and out."

"No. I'll bring both of them by the house when I head home." Tom hung up without saying goodbye.

Seth climbed into the truck and buckled the seat belt. "Okay, Lucy, here's the deal." He cranked up and moved into traffic. "You have to be on your best behavior because I didn't tell her about you yet." He glanced at the towel-wrapped bundle on the front seat. "So, be nice, okay?"

Twenty minutes later, he pulled into Jess's driveway and parked beside Tony's rental. He grabbed the bundle from the front seat and headed for the door, which opened before he knocked.

"I saw you drive up." Tony moved aside for him to enter, then gaped at Seth's ride. "Is that a fifty-seven-step-side?"

Seth beamed. "Yeah. My grandfather used it at his hardware store. You can still see the logo on the door. Then my dad had it, and I got it from him."

"Sweet." Then he noticed the wiggling towel in Seth's hands. "And what is that?"

"This is Lucy."

"A cat. A black cat."

"She's a kitten. The vet thinks maybe seven or eight weeks old." He unwrapped her and placed her on the floor.

Lucy immediately clamped onto his pant leg and shimmied up to his chest. He plucked her off and put her on his shoulder. "She's a little skittish around strangers."

The kitten peered at Tony from behind Seth's neck and gave a soft '*meow*.'

Seth rubbed her nose. "It's okay, Lucy. He's a friend."

Tony shook his head. "You just destroyed your badass Marine image."

"Marine?"

He shrugged. "Met my share. Easy to spot."

Seth lifted one shoulder. "Long time ago."

Tony nodded toward the truck. "Need some help?"

"Sure. Thanks."

He put Lucy on the couch and pointed a finger at her. "Stay."

The kitten promptly hid behind one of the purple LSU pillows.

Fifteen minutes later, Seth stored the last of the groceries. "I'll take the couch tonight." He didn't bother to ask if Tony minded his presence. He wasn't about to leave. "You can have the guest room."

Tony stood in the middle of the kitchen, hands flexing at his sides. He inhaled, then blew it out through pursed lips.

"Something on your mind?" Seth leaned against the counter, arms crossed, and waited, even though he guessed what was coming.

"Yeah. My sister."

"What about her?"

One fist clenched, released. "She's special."

"Agreed."

"She's not as tough as she wants people to believe."

Seth uncrossed his arms and stuffed his hands in his front pockets. "I'm aware of that, too."

"She's dealt with a lot of shit."

"And?"

"Badass Marine or not, you hurt her, and I'll tear you apart."

"Understood."

"If you two Neanderthals are through chest-thumping," grumbled Jess from the other room, "Perhaps one of you can explain why a black ball of fur just ran under the couch."

♂♀

Even though Jess didn't hear the conversation between Seth and her brother, their body language explained everything. Both were in full-on-protect mode. Part of her did a happy dance that Seth was ready for battle, and another part dreaded being close to him for the foreseeable future.

He leaned over the half wall between the kitchen and the living room, pointed to the black nose peeking out from under the couch, and grinned. "That's Lucy."

Butterflies once again took flight in her stomach. *Holy mother of pearl. I'm worse than a dang love-struck teenager.*

"And Lucy is…"

When he came around the counter and dropped to the floor in front of the couch, Jess couldn't hide her shock. Big, bad Seth Hamilton was on his stomach, trying to coax a kitten out from under the sofa.

"She's a stray." He extended his hand toward the nose peeking out at him. "Here, baby, come on out. It's okay."

His falsetto sing-song voice was so out of character, Jess snickered.

He paused and looked up at Jess. "I found her two weeks ago." He wiggled his finger at the slowly approaching feline. "Neighbor's bulldog had her pinned against the fence." He shook his head. "That dog could swallow her with one bite, and there she was, full of piss and vinegar, hissing and slapping at him, daring him to try and get her." His grin widened. "Kinda like you."

She refused to show how much his comment pleased her.

Lucy suddenly darted out and jumped on Seth's shoulder, then buried her head against his neck, a pitiful mewling sound muffled by his collar.

He stood and walked toward Jess, caressing the distressed kitten. "Do you like cats?"

"Never had one."

"What about Cocoa?" asked Tony, then turned his gaze away when Jess scowled.

Frank forbid them to have pets of any kind. When Jess was thirteen, she found a stray cat in the shed behind the house. It took weeks for the brown and white feline to allow a touch and a little longer before Cocoa would let Jess hold her. When things got unpleasant at home, she would sneak off to the shed and spend time with Cocoa. Tony discovered her secret and helped her ensure the mouser always had food and water.

Until Frank found out.

"She uses a litterbox," continued Seth, "And I keep her indoors."

His comment pulled her from the dark memory of finding Cocoa's body.

"But, for now, I put her stuff on the back porch."

"No." She spoke a little too sharply, then softened her tone. "It's supposed to storm tonight."

"I can call my sister later and see if she can keep her for a bit. I just couldn't leave her alone again."

"She can stay."

His face impassive, Seth remained still for a heartbeat. "Are you sure?"

"I'm sure."

Lucy turned around and gawked at Jess. Her beautiful golden eyes opened wide as if to say, *Really? I can stay inside.*

She resisted the urge to stroke the ebony fur but couldn't keep from smiling at the tiny creature. "What did you find out from Tom?"

Seth tilted his head toward the kitchen. "Let's go sit."

The three of them sat down at the table.

She watched the cat, who switched shoulders and studied her with curious eyes. "She likes your shoulder."

"I put her there while I dealt with the dog." He reached up and stroked her head. "Guess it's her safe place now."

She eyed the kitten and huffed. "Just when I think I have you figured out, you go do something to surprise me."

He shrugged. "What can I say? I'm a pushover for a damsel in distress."

This tender Seth was new and unexpected. And sexy. Very sexy. She gave herself a mental shake and rolled her index finger in a get-on-with-the-story gesture.

Seth folded his hands on the table. "Right before we rolled, I thought I heard gunshots."

"Gunshots?" asked Tony, "Someone shot at you?"

Seth focused on Jess. "I wasn't sure because of the storm and asked Tom to check the back tires. Both had bullet holes."

"That explains why we rolled. I was doing over eighty when the first one blew. With the wind added in, the second took out all control."

"Someone wanted you dead." Tony sat up straight. "And they're still out there."

"They wanted Walls free," corrected Seth. "We were collateral damage."

Held captive by Seth's intense gaze, she didn't move.

"The call indicates Walls has another plan in mind," added Seth.

Heartrate accelerating, Jess took a breath. "He's taunting me. May even come after me." She paused. "And he wants to make sure I know."

Seth nodded. "I agree."

"Okay. What about the third guy? Any ID yet?"

He shook his head. "No. Tom did say Koslow worked mainte-nance at the courthouse."

"I must have seen him there. That's why he seemed familiar."

Tony glared at Seth. "What about him? Walls, I mean? What are you going to do?"

He pushed back from the table. "Find him and put him away."

When he placed Lucy on the floor, she scampered back under the sofa. "Tom said he'd bring our laptops by tonight, but I can't wait." He addressed Tony. "Can you stay here until I get back?"

"Of course."

"She's not to be left alone for any reason. I should be back in an hour or so."

"I want to go, too," snipped Jess. "I can get my laptop and check on a couple of things while I'm there."

"You need to rest."

Ready to tell Mr. Macho Man she didn't need him to take care of her business, she took a deep breath. But then Seth stood in front of her, his features all soft and sexy and full of concern, and for one moment, she thought—wished—he would kiss her and held her breath and waited.

He rubbed a knuckle on her cheek. "Tom will have a fit if we both show up." He hesitated. "I'll be back soon."

CHAPTER FOURTEEN

"So, tell me about your boyfriend." Tony rested his arms on the table.

Jess cursed the heat racing up her neck. "He's not my boyfriend."

"Phfft. Sell that to someone else," argued Tony. "I ain't buying it."

"It's …complicated."

"Relationships usually are."

"I don't…we're not…." She groaned and lowered her forehead to the table. "How did I let this happen?"

Tony chuckled. "That bad, huh?"

She tapped her head on the table twice. "I suck at relationships. Look who my role models were."

"You're not like either of them. And never will be."

"Only because I had you to keep me sane."

"Until I left when you needed me most."

She straightened and reached for his hand. "No. You made me believe I could do anything, be anything, despite them. If it hadn't been for you, for your letters, your support, I couldn't have pulled myself out of that mess."

"I remember the first time I saw you." His expression softened, and he covered her hand with his. "You were three years old, so small and skinny. All arms and legs." He paused. "Ivy brought you into the den and said, 'Jessica, this is your new big brother, Anthony.'"

Jess swallowed against the emotions clogging her throat. "I couldn't say Anthony. It came out Thoney and eventually Tony."

"I had no idea what a big brother was supposed to do, but I knew I had to protect you, take care of you."

"And then Tina came along, and you and I ceased to exist in that house."

"Except when they needed someone to blame for whatever went wrong. Or wanted something to eat or clean clothes to wear."

"Yeah. But we made it." She squeezed his hand. "Together."

Tony broke the extended silence. "I need to get gas for my rental. I should have done that sooner, but I was concerned about you."

"There's a convenience store less than a mile from here. You drive. I'll navigate."

He regarded the crutches. "Are you sure?"

"I need to get out of the house."

He laughed. "It's only been a day."

"Yeah, well, that's a day too long."

Seated in the front seat, she sent a quick text to Seth in case he came home before they returned.

Tony pulled up to the pump and grumbled. "Card reader is broken. I have to go inside to pay."

She got out, too, and hobbled to the gas tank. "You pay. I'll pump. And you can bring me back some—"

"I know," he droned, dragging out the last syllable. "Cupcakes and barbeque chips. Right?"

"Yep."

When he disappeared inside, another car pulled up on the opposite side of the pump, and a man wearing a local security company uniform exited.

Immediately, she thought of former Dallas Cowboy's Coach, Jason Garrett. Well, if Jason were six feet tall with wavy red hair. And a linebacker body squeezed into a skin-tight uniform.

He hooked his sunglasses on the neck of his shirt and nodded at the crutches. "Hope it's not as bad as it looks."

Add sky blue eyes to his list of appealing attributes.

Cop radar detected no cause for alarm, possibly because of the uniform. Still, she remained alert and cautious. "Better than it was." She nodded toward the pump. "Card reader is broken. You have to go inside to pay."

Tony waved from the door, and she inserted the nozzle and began filling the tank.

He leaned against the other pump, and an engaging smile revealed generous lips, even white teeth, and charming dimples in each cheek. "I was going to offer to help, but I think you got it."

She glanced up again, waited for cop radar to ping, and got nothing. *How about that? A good-looking man is hitting on me.* Go figure. "Yep, I do."

"An independent woman and pretty to boot. Killer combination."

His interest caught her off-guard a moment. "You always hit on women at the gas station?"

"Only the pretty ones." He scanned her left hand. "Married?"

The pump kicked off, and she replaced the nozzle. "No. You?" *Why did I ask that? He's cute, but I'm not interested.*

His interest, however, was apparent in the way he checked her out. "Nope." He straightened up. "Maybe we—"

"They didn't have cupcakes, so I..." Tony paused in mid-sentence. "Coach?" Tony stopped at the front of the car and stared at the man. "What the hell are you doing here?"

"You two know each other?" asked Jess.

Tony tossed the snacks on the dash and grabbed the stranger in a man-hug. "Are you lost?"

"I live here now. I thought you were still in Iraq," declared the man.

"On leave." Tony stepped back. "Sis, this is Luke Collins, better known as Coach. My sister, Jessie Foster."

The newcomer's eyes widened. "Your sister? You never told me you had a sister." He stepped forward and extended his hand. "And a beautiful one at that. Pleasure, ma'am."

His grip was firm, his hands calloused. "Nice to meet you."

Tony slapped his friend on the shoulder. "How are you, man?"

"I'm good." He stuffed his hands in his front pockets. "How about you?"

Tony leaned against the car beside his sister. "Great. On leave this week. What are you doing in Walker? Last I heard, you were in Dubai."

He hesitated, and Jess thought he suddenly appeared uneasy.

He shifted his stance, then spoke to Tony. "Remember Carter Reynolds?"

"Yeah, y'all got out about the same time and went to work doing private security."

"Yeah. Cushy gig. Decent pay. Nobody shooting at you." His eyes turned dark, and all humor left his face. "We came home on leave to celebrate his kid brother's twenty-first birthday." Sorrow cho-aked his voice. "Carter got caught in a damn drive-by of all things."

"I'm sorry, man."

"I was with him when it happened. Mason was the only fam-ily he had." He swallowed and looked up. "Anyway, I promised I'd look out for the kid." He spread his hands out, then shoved them in his front pockets. "You always talked about how great this place was, and Mason wanted out of Houston. So, here I am. Besides, I got tired of all that sand. Wanted something green for a change." The engaging smile returned when he gazed at Jess. "Had I known you had such a beautiful sister, I'd have moved sooner."

Jess opted not to respond to his flirtatious comment and focused on his uniform instead. "Good company. Several of our officers do part-time there."

"Jess is a cop," offered Tony, "Walker PD."

"I'm a detective," she corrected with a grin.

"Oh. Excuse me, *Detective* Foster," amended Tony before addressing Coach. "We should get together later, grab a beer and catch up."

"Got called back in tonight. We're short-handed." He glanced at Jess. "Maybe tomorrow?"

Tony pulled the receipt from his pocket and scribbled something on it. "Here's my cell number. Give me a call, and we'll set something up. I'm home till Friday."

Coach rattled off his number, and Tony added it to his phone. "Great to see you again."

"You too, Tiger."

"Miss Foster," he bowed toward Jess. "I look forward to seeing you again."

Jess watched him leave. "Tiger?"

He gave her a sheepish grin. "You know, like Tony the Tiger."

She buckled in and grabbed the snacks off the dash. "I'm guessing the nickname is because he looks like Jason Garrett."

He grinned. "Excellent work, Detective Foster. I'm impressed." He put the car in gear and exited the station. "They didn't have cupcakes, so I got you Ding Dongs instead."

"That'll work." She tore open the treats and took a healthy bite of the cake, followed by a handful of chips. "Yum. I've missed this."

"I never understood how you could eat that."

"There's just something about this flavor combination." She took another bite and closed her eyes. "Yummy in the tummy. Now, tell me about Coach."

"Not much to tell. We did a couple of tours together. He got a job offer with a high-stakes security company and opted out. Lost track of him a couple of years ago." He paused. "I like him and all," he stated cautiously, "but he's a player."

She opened her mouth to protest, but Tony interrupted. "I know, I know, you're a grown woman, and I have no say in who you see. Just not him." He kept his eyes forward. "Seth, now, there's a man for you."

She decided to drop it for the time being. But they were adults now, and she didn't need his approval of her dates—if she had any.

She bit back a grin. He would never stop being her big brother, and that made her happy.

A random thought flitted across her mind as Tony pulled into the drive.

Coach never pumped any gas. *Maybe he did just stop to hit on me.*

That irrational and improbable thought followed her in the house.

CHAPTER FIFTEEN

JESS ENDED THE CALL WITH HER MOTHER AND TOOK THREE deep breaths before opening her eyes.

Tony sat on the arm of the couch, expression conveying concern. "I can tell by the look on your face things didn't go well."

She rolled her lips and sighed. "Mom is…Mom." Jess noticed Lucy watched from the corner of the purple throw draped on the armchair to the right. Reluctant to spook the kitten, who inched closer and closer for the last half hour, Jess made no sudden moves. "She and Tina are two peas in a pod." She shook her head. "Know what she said?" Before he could respond, she continued, unable to conceal the hurt her mother's words triggered. "She asked if I made it all up just to get attention."

"She's not happy unless you're miserable, Brat." Tony slid down beside her. "Don't let her get to you."

She leaned her head on his shoulder. "You haven't called me Brat in a long time."

He hugged her against his side. "I try to remember you're a

grown woman and not that scrawny kid who used to follow me like a shadow."

"You were all I had, Weiner." She swallowed the urge to cry. "Still are."

He kissed the top of her head. "Yeah, well, I see a change coming now."

"What do you mean?"

"Beckett wants to…oh, sorry," apologized Seth. "Didn't mean to interrupt."

Tony stood. "We're done." He regarded at Jess with loving eyes. "You're stronger than her, Brat. Stronger, better, and smarter." He stretched his back. "And I'm beat. I think I'll take a nap. That flight was a killer."

"Thanks, Weiner." She watched him walk away and turned to Seth. "Beckett wants what?" Beckett was one of the detectives assigned to work her cases.

Two hours passed as Jess sat at the kitchen table with Seth catching up on emails and talking with detectives assigned to their caseload. It grated on her to have others do her work, but Tom gave no other options.

By four o'clock, her knee throbbed, and a headache made concentration difficult.

Added to that irritation was the constant memory of crawling over Seth this morning. And that kiss. He'd not mentioned it, which only made her discomfort more acute and made her wonder: *Does he want to pretend it didn't happen?*

"How bad is it?"

Seth's question caught her off-guard. "How bad is what?"

He stood and closed her laptop. "The pain."

"I'm fine. A little tired is all."

He bent down, his face inches from hers. A quick intake of breath brought with it the smell of coffee, Old Spice, and Seth.

And the kiss. *Dammit.*

"Liar. I can see it in your eyes." He stood. "Do you need a pain pill?"

She started to argue but changed her mind. He was too percep-tive. "I'll take some Tylenol." She met his gaze. "What about you?"

"I'm fine." He went to the cabinet and pulled out the medicine.

"Liar," she quipped, repeating his reprimand. "You've been rub-bing your temple and the back of your neck for the last half hour."

He placed the bottle of pills in front of her with a glass of water. "Beautiful *and* observant."

Her heart did a little stutter-step. That was the second time he called her beautiful. Only Tony ever told her that, but he was her brother, so it didn't count. "I'm a train wreck."

"Not to me." He took a step back. "Why don't you lie down on the couch, and I'll see about dinner."

She stared at him and frowned, tried to remember what she may have around to make a decent meal. Grocery shopping wasn't something she did often. "Dinner?"

"We have to eat, and I don't think you're up to cooking yet."

"I, um, well…."

He gathered up their laptops and paperwork and placed them out of the way. "I brought some stuff from the house. Your cupboard was rather bare."

"Not much point in cooking for one."

"Cooking is therapeutic."

She squinted and cocked her head to one side. "Who are you, and what have you done with my partner?"

He scooped the medicine off the table, returned it to the cup-board, and leaned against the counter. "I can't tell you how many silly tea parties I endured with my sisters when they were young. Later, Mom insisted we all learn to cook. It was fun. I enjoyed it. Still do."

She noticed he tried to hide the limp but frowned when he opened the cupboard to return the pills. He was exhausted and in pain, yet he took care of her first. The thought made her sag in the chair. "Seth…"

He turned, his face a cleverly vacant mask. "Yeah?"

"You don't have to take care of me. I can take care of myself." Even as the words left her lips, she wanted to take them back because she wanted someone to take care of *her* for a change.

"What if I wanted to take care of you?"

Swamped with a sudden chill, she pressed a hand to her throat and shivered. Had he guessed her secret desire?

More than anything, she longed for someone who *want*ed to take care of her for a change.

Tony once joked she was their family's personal Cinderella, and that fit the situation.

Frank and Ivy divorced when Jess was ten, and the loss of Tony broke her heart. He understood her. He praised her, made her feel she had value. And then he was gone.

Frequent bouts of depression and helplessness turned her mother into the child and Jess into the adult.

Two years later, Ivy and Frank remarried, and Tony returned. Life was better for a brief time, but then Tina came along, and things went downhill again. Jess ended up being the cook, maid, babysitter, and housekeeper. Frank was no help at all when he was around, often adding to the load she carried. Tony tried, but was older, involved in sports, and held a job. When he was home, he and Frank often clashed because his father was always broke and insisted Tony contribute most of his meager salary to room and board.

She was fifteen when Tony joined the Army.

And left her alone.

Each breath became a struggle. A tingling rush of adrenaline surged through her body. *How did he guess my secret?*

Seth took a step toward her. "Jess? What's wrong? What did I say?"

Tony's entrance saved her from a reply as she struggled for

control. His starched jeans and western shirt said he was going out. "Hot date already?" She hoped the quiver in her voice went unnoticed.

His gaze slid over to Seth. "Your bodyguard can manage things here. Thought I'd take a drive around town. See what's changed." He grinned and tweaked her nose. "If I run into any of the old crowd, I may be out a while."

"What about dinner?" she asked, trying to delay his departure, not ready to be alone with Seth and his all-too-perceptive eyes.

"I'll grab something while I'm out."

She stood on unsteady legs. "I think I'll take Seth's suggestion and lie down on the couch a bit."

Tony walked her to the sofa and propped her knee up with one of the large throw pillows sporting the LSU Tiger on one side, purple and gold stripes on the other. He placed two more under her head. "I won't be out long."

She heard the front door close and belatedly wished she'd asked for a throw or blanket. She kept the house cool and often had to wrap up to watch television or read.

Resigned, she closed her eyes, only to jerk them open when something touched her legs.

"Figured you might want this." Seth spread a soft purple throw over her.

Unaccustomed to having someone anticipate her needs and go out of the way to accommodate them was disconcerting. And wonderful. And scary. And not something she knew how to handle. "Thank you," she whispered and sagged further into the pillows, struggling to get a decent breath.

"My pleasure." He straightened and stared down at her. "I'm sorry for whatever I said earlier to upset you."

"You didn't—"

He squatted down beside the couch. "I meant what I said earlier." He placed one hand on her pillow, the other on her thigh.

"There's something between us, Jess. Something special. The kiss proved it. We owe it to ourselves to find out what that something is."

A tear found its way down her cheek, and he flicked it off with his thumb. "Dammit. I've upset you again. I'm so sorry."

It was too much. *He* was too much.

So many things to process. Walls, the wreck, her near kidnapping and narrow escape, the nightmares.

A flash flood of emotions surfaced all at once, making her body convulse and jerk. She couldn't get enough air, and her stomach pitched and rolled as the last ounce of defensive reserves melted away. "N-No. It's m-me. I'm a m-mess. I th-thought I had…I c-couldn't…." Humiliation overcame her. "Dammit. I h-hate a c-crybaby."

Head spinning, she squeezed her eyelids tight. She wanted to run, to hide, and avoid the pity she knew lodged in his eyes, afraid she would break down in front of him. Again.

"What is it, babe? Please…tell me."

His voice, so tender, so caring, was more than she could bear. *He called me Babe again.* She sucked in a ragged breath. "N-No one ever w-wanted to take c-care of m-me before. I d-don't know w-what to do."

There. The secret was out; her soul was bare. Resigned to the inevitable, she held her breath and waited for him to laugh at such a silly statement and leave.

Instead, he lightly stroked her cheek with his finger, wiping away the moisture lingering there. "Aw, Texas. I'm crazy about you." Then his lips covered hers.

Shocked by the gesture, she froze a moment, then melted into the kiss. Exhilaration surged through her, replacing the tension that tied her insides in knots.

Surprisingly gentle, his kiss was tender, and light as a summer breeze yet had the power to produce strong currents of desire.

He pulled back and gazed into her eyes. "I've waited a long time for you to need me."

She pulled her hand from the coverlet and gently touched his face. "I've known you for over a year," she whispered, "And I'm just now finding out who you are."

"And?"

"I might be crazy about you, too."

"Might be?" He leaned down and began a series of slow, shivery kisses, stopping once to repeat, "Might be?"

She trembled as his lips feather-touched hers with a tantalizing promise of more.

"How about now?" he whispered.

The heart-melting tenderness in his gaze released the last band from around her chest, and she took a full, deep breath. "I've never felt this way before, so I'm not sure what it is." She paused. "But I want to find out."

"That's a start." He brushed his lips across her forehead. "Now you're frowning again. Why?"

Out of her comfort zone, she swam through a maze of unfamiliar feelings and desires and said the first thing that came to mind. "I can't believe you went all day long and haven't uttered one word of trivia."

Whiskey-colored eyes sparkled with humor. "A snail can sleep for three years."

"The adder is the only venomous snake in Great Britain."

"A kangaroo can't fart."

"Pfftt. That can't be true."

"Rest." He stood and turned toward the kitchen. "I'll wake you when dinner's ready."

The pounding in her head increased with the rapid beat of her heart as she watched him walk away. The limp was still there but not as pronounced. Muscles rippled under the white shirt he wore, and his powerful, well-formed body moved with a natural grace, despite the limp. She licked her lips, reliving his velvety touch, and a delicious shudder coursed through her body.

Holy mother of pearl. I should have done this a long time ago.

She lowered her head against the pillows and saw Lucy staring at her from the arm of the couch. "What? I saw him first."

The kitten gave a soft *meow,* those golden-palomino eyes wide, as she glanced toward Seth, then back to Jess. *'Meow.'*

She patted a spot on her chest, delighted when Lucy inched toward it. "Amen, Sister. He *is* all that and a bag of chips."

♂♀

Thunder rumbled in the distance when Seth went to check on Jess. He smiled when he saw Lucy asleep on her chest. "Lucky cat," he mumbled.

The night before they left for Denver, he woke to find Lucy on the foot of his bed. Unaccustomed to anyone else in the house, he'd neglected to shut his door, and she made herself at home. When she gazed at him, he didn't have the heart to make her leave.

Now, apparently, she'd accepted Jess.

He turned back and checked the steaks he had marinating. Thanks to his mom, he not only enjoyed cooking, he was good at it, too. His friends gave him hell, but so what? He was a guy. He liked to cook. Besides, it helped him offset some of the madness he dealt with every day.

And he wanted to do something special for Jess tonight. A pan-seared filet in a red wine reduction, fresh salad, baked potato, and a chilled, creamy peach pie should do the trick.

Now that he knew her feelings for him went beyond partner and friend, he had the incentive to move forward. He hadn't planned to tell her how he felt just yet, but her distress shattered his plan. He just prayed it wouldn't backfire on him.

Nobody ever wanted to take care of me before.

Her statement broke his heart. He could only imagine what

life with Ivy and Tina encompassed since neither cared about any-one but themselves.

I'll make up for it, Jess, if you'll let me.

He double-checked to make sure he had the ingredients for the dessert he wanted to make and poured himself another cup of coffee when his phone beeped.

"Hamilton."

"Still no word from the feds on that partial print," complained Tom, as always, getting straight to the point. "Rangers are check-ing, too."

"What next?"

"I've got Driscoll and Harper going through everything on Koslow and Walls again. Maybe something will turn up." He took a breath. "Koslow was in the Army, honorable discharge. Marksmanship Badge. No arrests, not even a parking ticket." He gave a disgusted sigh. "How do you explain a model citizen who suddenly becomes an accomplice to attempted murder and helps a felon escape?"

Seth tapped the counter with his fingers. "I agree. It doesn't make sense. My gut says I'm missing something but can't figure out what it is."

"Well, considering that knot on your head, I'm not surprised. Headache any better?"

It wasn't, but he'd never tell his boss that. "All but gone."

"Bullshit. I've had two concussions myself. Hang on a sec."

He waited while Tom talked with someone who entered his office. The lack of any substantial leads was frustrating as hell.

When he came back on the line, his voice edged up with excite-ment. "Ranger Sampson just called. Some guy from a convenience store over on Parkdale called in. Koslow was there late yesterday. He's going to talk to him later. I'll let you know what they find out. Has Jess had any other contact from him?"

"No. Nothing. Not sure if that's good or bad."

"Yeah. Well, keep your eyes peeled. Get some rest." As usual, Tom hung up without fanfare.

Ten minutes later, the doorbell rang. Seth looked through the side window and saw a young man holding a vase with three yellow roses.

"Delivery for Detective Foster." The young man viewed the card in his hand. "Is this the right house?"

"Yes. I'll take them."

He glanced at the card envelope from a popular Dallas florist but didn't read the card. He placed the vase in the center of the table and went back to work on dinner.

At five-thirty, Jess walked into the kitchen, carefully avoiding eye contact.

"Hey, you're down to one crutch," gushed Seth. "That's great."

"Yeah. Trying it out." She sat down at the table and noticed the flowers.

"They came for you a while ago." He continued to toss the salad they would eat with supper.

She leaned forward and inhaled the delicate aroma that permeated the kitchen. "Who would send me flowers?"

"I didn't read the card." *Because I didn't want to know if they were from another man.*

"No one ever sent me flowers before." She reached for the card. "Well, Tony did a couple of times on my birthday, but that's all."

He made a mental note to send her flowers. Lots of flowers. Her sudden gasp had him swinging around to face her.

The color drained from her face, and the paper drifted to the floor.

Seth jerked it up and read.

I'll see you soon.

—Jack

CHAPTER SIXTEEN

"**D**ID YOU DO LIKE I SAID?" JACK'S SNARL BOUNCED OFF THE walls of the small motel room.

"Yes, Jack. I'm not an imbecile," snapped Kos, "I wore a disguise when I went to the flower shop. I asked the woman to write the message for me, then paid in cash and left."

"And you didn't stop anywhere or talk to anyone?"

"I stopped for gas because I was down to less than half a tank, and you told me it needed to be kept full at all times."

That stopped Jack in his tracks. "Where did you stop?"

"Some convenience store near the interstate four or five miles from here."

"Which one?" His fist clenched tightly with the need to punch the man.

Kos relayed the name of the station and the location.

It was far enough away it shouldn't be an issue, but still too close for comfort. *Dumbass is gonna get me caught again.* "Were you wearing the disguise? Who did you talk to? Was there anyone else inside?"

"Jeeze, Jack. What the hell? I wore glasses and a ball cap. The wig made my head itch. But I made sure no one was around except the guy inside. I paid for my gas and left."

Jack was not happy. Kos was an idiot, and his stupidity was going to cost him. Dearly. "You go back to that place now and make sure that bastard doesn't talk to anyone! You hear me!"

Kos's face turned bright red, the vein at his temple engorged and turned purple. "I'm not killing anyone, Jack. I'm done."

He turned for the door, and Jack grabbed his arm. His appreciation for Kos finally growing a pair was short-lived. "You think I give a shit about what you want?" Jack was close enough that spittle landed on Kos's cheek as he spoke. Unblinking eyes, cold as the arctic wind, locked on. "Do it, Kos, or die in his place. Your choice."

ơਠ

Phone cradled against his ear, Seth emptied water from the vase in the sink and tossed the roses in the trash.

"I've already called the shop," he told Tom, "And left a message on the answering machine for them to call."

"Pretty ballsy move on his part," asserted Tom. "I'll brief Sampson."

"Did he get anything from the convenience store guy?"

"He's tied up on something else. I'm going by there when I'm finished here."

"As soon as Tony gets back, I'll head over there. I don't want this to wait."

"I'm going, too." Jess's voice brooked no opposition.

Seth frowned and shook his head. Silence on the other end of the line said Tom sorted through the pros and cons of the idea. Deciding he needed a little extra push, Seth added, "Look, you're shorthanded as it is. I can handle talking to some jerk at a convenience store."

Another pause. "Okay. Fine. Get the tape if they have one. But that's all you do. And I want an immediate report."

"Roger that. Give me the info again." He jotted everything down.

"I'll drop by to get the card later. I doubt we'll get anything off it, but it's worth a try."

"I'll take it by the lab when I'm done at the store," offered Seth. "No point in adding to your day."

"All right. Keep me posted."

He ended the call and pulled a chair beside Jess. Taking her hands in his, he squeezed. "He's just trying to scare you."

"Yeah, well, it's working."

"Can I get Tony's number from you? I need him to come home so I can go check out the guy at the store."

She straightened. "No way. I'm going, too." She stood and reached for the crutch. "I went out with Tony earlier today and did just fine."

"No."

She nailed him with those coffee-colored eyes and damned if he didn't experience a flash of pure lust. The intensity was staggering.

"We're still partners. You go. I go. You stay. I stay. Choose."

He scowled. "I forgot how bossy you are."

"I'm not bossy. I just don't like being left out. Or ordered around."

"Are we having our first fight?"

She squinted at him. "We're not fighting. We're...discussing options."

He stepped forward. "Because if we are fighting," his voice dropped to a sensual whisper. "We can make up later."

Her slow smile was so damn sexy, his body throbbed in response.

"In that case, we're definitely fighting."

He brushed a quick kiss to her forehead. "Well, the steaks can sit a while longer. You ready to go?"

"Yeah."

"Let's roll, then."

It took less than ten minutes to grab their weapons and badges and head out the door.

Intermittent rain and evening traffic made getting to the location a chore and took thirty minutes. Once there, Seth opened his mouth to suggest Jess wait in the car but swallowed the objection. Crutch or not, she'd never let him go in alone.

Inside, the first thing he noticed was the absence of someone at the register. Hand hovering near his weapon, he checked out the old video surveillance camera on the wall. "Walker PD," he shouted. "Anyone here?"

The small, crowded interior smelled like day-old chili, cigarette smoke, and something else he preferred not to analyze. Six rows of merchandise stretched to his left, with just enough room at the end to walk around and access coolers along the wall. A crooked door, its top hinge broken, stood directly in front of him, and a short hallway led to the right. He eased toward the end of the checkout counter and looked behind it.

Nothing.

He inched toward the door with the broken hinge, looking right and left. Empty.

The hallway to the right led to a generic bathroom. Seth approached the open, graffiti-covered door with caution. "Walker PD," he repeated. "Anyone in there?"

Silence.

He glanced behind him at Jess, who stood beside the counter, weapon ready and pointed down.

He crept closer to the door, pushed it open with one hand, his gun at the ready. "Shit."

"What is it?" asked Jess.

"We got a body."

CHAPTER SEVENTEEN

A FTER SHE GAVE HER STATEMENT, JESS HOBBLED BACK TO THE car, scoping out the area along the way. A glance down the narrow alley revealed nothing except an overflowing dumpster.

The station sat on the corner of an alley and a narrow secondary street full of potholes in a rundown section of town. One dim streetlight highlighted the fact the place was in dire need of some TLC. Two dirty gas pumps sat under a blinking fluorescent light covered by a rusted canopy. Card readers covered, so cash only. She checked her watch—eight o'clock at night and not much traffic. The only businesses around were a tattoo shop, a small boarded-up salon next door, and a fast-food restaurant half a block over she wouldn't enter on a dare.

She shook her head. Poor techs would be there all night processing the place. If the dead guy was the caller, they were back to square one unless there was something useful on the surveillance tape, or better yet, they got a lead they could use.

It was doubtful the tape would provide anything useful. They already knew Walls and Kos were still in the area, though the 'why' of it was anyone's guess. Perhaps the third man was on there. It was worth a shot to find out.

A glance at the body showed a needle stuck in his arm, indicating a possible overdose. The only thing certain at this point was they were again one step behind Walls because every spidey-sense she owned screamed he was somehow involved.

The soft beep of her cell phone sent frayed nerves into overdrive until she checked caller ID. Tom. She leaned against the car and swiped to accept. "Foster."

"Y'all still at the crime scene?"

"Yes. Seth is talking with responding officers. Sampson's on his way. We should be able to leave soon."

"Okay. I'm still working on the other case with Driscoll. Damn fool Harper has food poisoning. Dumbass will eat anything."

Jess didn't reply, understanding the declaration was merely a reflection of the stress Tom faced.

"I did see a needle in his arm," she said. "But no signs of a struggle."

"What about an ID?"

"I don't know yet. Seth may have it." She took a breath. "We're taking the card by the lab on the way home."

He sighed. "Good. Maybe the techs can find something."

Seth walked up about then and mouthed the word "Tom?"

She nodded. "Hey, Tom…Seth just walked up. Hang on." She passed the phone to Seth, who leaned against the car beside her.

"The victim is our caller, Carter Dempsey. Priors go back eight years or so—petty theft, possession, DUI. Reynolds, the responding officer, knows him. Time of death was between six and seven. Will have to wait on the autopsy for official COD, but overdose is likely since he still had a needle in his arm. I'll drop the card by the lab on the way home. Anything else?…Roger that."

Seth handed the phone to Jess and opened the car door for her. "No signs of foul play." He got behind the wheel, then maneuvered around the small lot packed with police vehicles. "Damn place still uses the old VCR tapes for security, and the machine was empty."

"Think someone pulled the tape?"

He shrugged one shoulder. "Not sure. The owner is on his way now, and Reynolds will find out when he gets here. They're also going to key on the hotels and motels in the area. Maybe we'll get lucky."

"Now what?"

He paused at the edge of the parking lot. "You up to taking the long way home?"

"Sure. What do you have in mind?"

"There are some older motels around here. I thought we'd drive by and look around. If something worth checking out pops up, we'll call in back up."

"Works for me."

A quick stop at the lab to leave the card, and they headed for the first of the motels Seth wanted to check out.

An hour later, they sat in the parking lot of the last one on Seth's mental list.

"Well, that was a waste of time," she grumbled.

He stared at the almost empty lot. "They're around here somewhere. I know it. Probably out to eat."

"I agree. Hopefully, the locals will find something later." She paused, then looked at Seth. "Speaking of eating…"

He grinned, put the car in gear, and turned around.

Once home, getting out of the car proved to be more of a challenge than she cared to admit as her banged-up body protested the activity.

If Seth noticed her discomfort, he didn't mention it, though he stood close enough to help if needed.

She made it to the kitchen and dropped into the nearest chair.

"You want coffee?" he asked. "Or would you rather have

something else?" He opened the door to the fridge. "What's this pink stuff in the orange juice container?"

She snorted. "That's an Esther special. I'll pass for now. I haven't had a pain pill, so wine is fine."

He squinted at the repurposed jug. "What is it?"

Heat crept up her neck, and she avoided his inquiring eyes. "If you must know, it's a concoction she and some of her cronies came up with in college." She hesitated. "They call it Pink Panty Pulldown."

His throaty laugh gave her gooseflesh. "I'm afraid to ask what's in it."

"Tequila, Crystal Light pink lemonade, and water."

"That's all?" He pulled out the open bottle of white wine and poured two glasses, passing one to her.

"Trust me. That's enough." She tried to relax in the chair, but every muscle in her body hurt to some degree. "She had some left from a party and brought it by before we left for Denver. That stuff will make you pay bills you don't owe."

He pinned her with a look that sent her blood pressure up a notch.

"No, I never did," she added.

"Did what?"

"Drink too much. Someone had to be the adult." She took a sip of her wine, admitting to herself alone she was at the end of her endurance rope.

Silent, Seth went back to work.

Her stomach growled when the first steak hit the pan, and the aroma filled the room.

She watched him move about her kitchen, perfectly at home as he finished their meal. The man was a study in contrasts. One minute the bad-ass cop, the next a man who cooked, rescued kittens, and watched kiddie movies with his niece and nephew. *I thought I knew all about him, but I'm just now seeing the real Seth. The more I see, the more I like.*

Uncomfortable with her train of thought, she focused on work. "Do you think he OD'd?"

"Probably. Officer Reynolds knew the guy. Longtime user."

"A little too coincidental for my taste."

"Yep." He placed the steaks on a platter. "They need to rest a few minutes." He brought out two salad plates, followed by baked potatoes and all the trimmings. "We can start with the salad and add fixings to the potatoes."

"I feel bad that you're doing all this, and I'm just sitting here," muttered Jess. "You're kinda like company."

"Mother insists every woman needs to be waited on some time." He sat down across from her, and his voice softened. "She'd be upset with me if I didn't wait on you now."

"I think I'd like her."

His steady, unblinking gaze fixed on her. "She'd like you, too."

The words, soft as a caress, went straight to her hammering heart and rendered her speechless.

Seth recovered first. "Eat. We don't want the steaks to get cold."

They ate in companionable silence, neither wanting to destroy the mood by talking shop. When the last bite of steak was gone, Jess drained her wine glass and sighed. "That was, without a doubt, the best steak I have ever had. And you cooked it on the stove, not the grill."

He stood and picked up the empty dishes, placing them in the sink. "Secret is the cut of meat, seasoning, and the marinade. Ready for dessert?"

The chime of her cell phone interrupted her reply. Anticipating Tom's call, she didn't check caller-ID. "Foster."

"Enjoy your little drive tonight?" snarled Walls.

Jess sat up straight and hit the speakerphone icon.

"How did you know I took a drive?"

"You have caused me a great deal of trouble, Detective. And for that, you will pay," Walls sputtered on the other end.

Seth pulled out his cell phone and began a rapid-fire text, pausing long enough to give her the keep-him-talking signal.

She swallowed hard, dug deep for the courage to taunt the devil as the delicious meal now rested like a rock in her stomach. "You're a murderer. I'm a cop. It's my job to cause you trouble."

Walls sucked in a breath. "You got a smart mouth on you. It's time you learned a woman's place. And it will be a pleasure to teach you where it is."

Jess chuckled. "You think a stupid little weasel like you can teach me anything?"

"Don't call me stupid," snapped Walls.

She ignored the fierce look on Seth's face. He wasn't happy about her tactic. Too bad. They needed Walls to make a mistake. Ticked off people made mistakes.

"You're a stupid, pretentious little moron," she declared with false bravado.

"You'll pay for calling me stupid," Walls growled.

"You practically signed your own death sentence with all the evidence you left around Lottie." She paused. "And you better believe I'll be drinking champagne when they stick that needle in your arm." Voice steady, one hand gripping the edge of the table, she ignored Seth's head shake and goaded him again. "You're a stupid little man who gets off on hurting women, especially those who can't fight back."

Immediately, his voice changed. "Oh, but you're wrong," he cooed. "I like for them to fight back. I want them to." He made a tsk-tsk sound. "Alas, few do." He took a noisy breath. "But you... you, I think, will fight extremely hard. In fact, I'm praying you will."

The line went dead.

"Dammit!" Seth jumped up from the table and raced to the front door.

Shaken by the encounter, Jess was slow to rise and follow.

Cell phone pressed to his ear; Seth stared out the front door.

"No. There's no one out here. I saw taillights down the street. Are you sure? Where? Okay. Keep me posted." He ended the call and stuffed the phone in his pocket.

"The expression on your face says bad news or worse news," announced Jess.

"He was down the block." Seth's voice radiated controlled anger. "The sonofabitch called from down the block."

CHAPTER EIGHTEEN

"KOS TOLD ME YOU WERE A CRAZY BASTARD, AND THIS PROVES it."

The irritated voice on the other end of the line made Jack clench his fist.

"Or maybe you think you're too smart to get caught?"

Jack took a breath to control the anger rising like hot lava from the depths of his soul. No one questioned Jack Walls' decisions. Ever. "I don't owe you any explanations," he snapped. "You work for me."

"I told you. I'm done. It's gettin' out of hand. If I had known what Kos was up to when he asked for my help, I would never have agreed to do it. Now I'm done."

Jack's body went rigid as steel. Molten fury raced through him, followed by a deadly calm. "Let's see…aiding and abetting an escape, accessory to attempted murder. And of a cop no less," he continued with exaggerated restraint. "What's the going rate for that, I wonder? Ten years? Twenty? The death penalty?"

He waited, not surprised his statement met with stony

silence. "You're done when I say you are. I want it taken care of on schedule."

Jack ended the call and tried to relax. *He isn't nearly as controllable as Kos led me to believe. Now I must deal with him, too.* "It's all her fault," he mumbled, "If she'd stayed out of my business, none of this would have happened."

A garbled snore from Kos, where he slept on the other bed, drew his gaze, and anger again threatened to overcome him. *The dope he gave the kid took care of the problem, but then that smart-mouth detective and her partner showed up and nearly caught him. But at least there wasn't a tape. Though I don't suppose it really matters now.*

The muted television in the corner was tuned to a local news station. Jack glanced up in time to see their pictures flash across the screen. *By the time they get things figured out, I'll be on my way to Mexico with that detective along for company. And entertainment.*

He turned to Kos, who slept soundly, unaware of the danger he brought on himself. *Thanks to Kos, they'll be checking motels around here, so now I have to look for a new place to hole up.*

He moved to the foot of the bed. "So, you think I'm crazy, do you?" He whispered to the sleeping man. "You ain't seen nothing yet." Jack scrubbed his face with both hands and paced around the room. Time to put his plan into action.

But first, he had a problem to solve.

⚭

"They didn't find anything." Seth dropped down on the couch beside Jess, his heart rate still in the stratosphere. "Crazy bastard called from a block away."

She rubbed her arms as though to ward off a chill. "I'm not a spooky person, but he scares me."

On impulse, he moved closer and placed an arm around her, pleased when she leaned into him instead of pulling away. "We'll have to settle for drive-by patrols tonight. Tom will try to have a car out front starting tomorrow, but he's pretty short-handed, so that may not fly."

Lucy perched on the arm of the couch beside Seth, and her golden eyes flicked back and forth between them.

Seth couldn't hold his tongue any longer. "You pushed Walls pretty hard." He tried to keep his voice steady but watching her taunt a ruthless killer scared the hell out of him.

She sat forward, and those hazelnut eyes shot daggers at him. "You would have done the same thing."

Before he could muster a decent counter, she continued. "And if you value your life, you will not speak whatever male chauvinist comment you're thinking about."

He paused at the realization she read him so well and spoke the truth. "I care about you, Jess." His voice softened. "I care."

The ready-for-battle glint in her eyes vanished, and she leaned back against him. "I care about you, too."

"He's unstable and unpredictable, and that makes the situation even more perilous."

She nestled in the crook of his shoulder as though it were the most natural thing in the world. "And he's escalating, which is why I pushed. He might make a mistake."

"Or maybe you'll push him into doing something not only stupid but dangerous."

Before she could reply, Lucy hopped from the arm of the couch to Seth's leg, then moved to Jess's lap and climbed up to rest on her shoulder, a low mewling sound in her throat.

Jess rubbed the nose pressed against her cheek with one finger. "It's okay, Lucy," she cooed, then grinned up at Seth. "We aren't really fighting."

"Humph. And just like that, she's your cat?"

Lucy crawled over to Seth's shoulder as if to say, *'I'm not playing favorites.'* She turned and stretched out, half of her body on his shoulder, the rest on Jess's head.

Jess grinned. "Just make yourself comfortable, Lucy."

When the kitten settled in, her gentle purr a buzz in his ear, Seth continued. "Okay. Let's walk through this. It's clear he's fixated on you, but why?"

"Well, I started the Potter case right before you came on board, but we both worked it," she mused, "and I was the lead investigator in Lottie's case."

"I think there's more to it." He got distracted when Lucy's purr grew a little louder. He loved that sound and took a moment to enjoy it. "I've been thinking about the stuff he said in the car."

Jess squinted and shook her head. "It's obvious he has women issues and thought I talked down to you."

"I don't think it's all women." He absently rubbed his hand over her upper arm. "Tough women set him off, and you're one of the strongest women I know."

"Aww, you're being all nice again."

His shoulder lifted, then dropped. "It's the truth. You're strong, intelligent, independent, and beautiful to boot."

She tilted her head, hampered by her new cat-hat. "That's the third time you called me beautiful." She peered at her cut and bruised hand resting on his thigh. "Even though I don't feel that way at the moment, I thank you just the same."

"You're welcome."

Seth savored the moment and let her nearness soothe his troubled soul. *Everything I ever wanted is here right now. I'm home.*

Lucy's gentle purr mixed with the fading adrenaline rush worked like a sleeping potion, and his eyelids drifted shut.

"He's coming after me, isn't he?" Jess's whisper broke the contented quiet.

The denial died on his lips. She deserved the truth. "Yes. He is." He edged the cat over and kissed the top of her head. "I won't let him get to you."

She snuggled closer to his side. "I'll hold you to that."

Suddenly, Lucy jerked her head up and focused on the front door.

Seth rose from the couch and pulled his weapon. "Stay here."

CHAPTER NINETEEN

ETH'S SHARP ORDER BROOKED NO OPPOSITION, AND FOR ONCE, Jess didn't argue.

He walked to the front and eased the curtain back from the narrow side window, then relaxed. "It's Bitsy," he called over his shoulder and opened the door.

"What took you so long, Studly?" All five-foot-nothing Esther Scott stomped past him. "Where is she?"

"Hello to you, too, Bitsy." He shut the door and followed her into the living room.

Her best friend since college, Esther was petite, sported a Barbie-doll body, platinum spiked hair, and a near-genius IQ. A computer whiz, she worked at a downtown investment banking firm. She and Seth delighted in baiting each other.

"I'm gonna hit the shower," announced Seth and strode off down the hall. "Let you two catch up."

Esther watched him leave, one arched brow raised as she sighed. "An ass made for grabbing." She sat down beside Jess, one eye on Lucy, who still rested on Jess's shoulder.

"Yes, I know it's after ten o'clock at night, but…start to finish. All of it."

The next few minutes passed in a blur of questions until her friend was satisfied.

"I'm sorry I couldn't get here sooner. Mom…" Esther's voice dropped off, and then she brightened, both brows wiggling up and down. "But I doubt you missed me."

Jess cursed the heat crawling up her neck. "We're partners. That's all."

"Right. And I'm the Tooth Fairy."

Jess huffed and leaned against the back of the couch, careful not to disturb Lucy. "It's such a bad idea on so many levels."

"But right on the most important ones."

"You're not helping me make the right decision."

"Please. Like there's even a question."

Their conversation halted when Seth walked past them, arms full of clothes. "Hamper's full." He headed toward the small laundry room off the kitchen.

The women tracked his movements in silence.

"A body built for sin," whispered Esther and grabbed Jess's arm. "And he does laundry."

"He rescues kittens," added Jess on a quick intake of breath. "And cooks."

Esther cast a flushed glance toward the kitchen, then back to her friend. "Da-yum, girl. If I thought I had a snowball's chance in hell of stealing him away from you, I'd have him roped and tied by sunrise."

"He's not—"

Esther's palm in her face silenced a reply.

Just as well since it was a lie anyway.

"He definitely is," snipped Ester. "You just aren't ready to admit it." She squared around and faced Jess. "Now, what's the plan to catch this psycho?"

"Not sure at the moment."

Esther pinned her with a hard stare. "What does that mean?"

"It's…complicated."

Seth entered about then, and Esther turned on him. "What the hell, Studly?"

Seth blinked twice; his face clouded with confusion. "What'd I do?"

Bitsy jumped from the couch, hands fisted on perfect hips, and marched to within two feet of him. The fact the top of her head didn't even reach his chin was irrelevant. She was in full-on Ninja mode. "Why aren't you out there looking for this guy?"

He side-stepped Esther's ire and sat on the arm of the couch. "The whole department is. Rangers, too." Lucy hopped on his thigh, and he rubbed her back. "Me and Lucy here are bodyguards."

"That's just great." Esther waved both hands in the air. "A kitten and a beat-up cop. She's in great hands."

"She is," barked Seth firmly. "And you know it."

Esther stood there a moment longer, then relaxed her combative stance. "Fine. She's safe." She sat back down beside Jess and reached for her hand. "What can I do to help?"

Happy with the change in the atmosphere, Jess relaxed. "Thanks, Ess. We'll have a patrol car out front some and regular patrols through the night."

"Your cupboard is almost always empty," admonished Esther. "So, what do you need?"

"I got it covered, Bitsy," announced Seth. "But thanks for the offer."

Jess blushed under her friend's intense stare.

"He cooks. He does laundry, *and* he shops for groceries." Esther winked and got up from the couch. "It's obvious I'm a third wheel here, so I'll go."

Seth stood and placed Lucy on his shoulder.

"Oh," Jess kept her voice casual. "Tony arrived today and will be staying here a few days."

Esther's expression became guarded. "Oh? That's nice. How long will he be in town?"

Her indifferent appearance didn't fool Jess. She'd had a thing for Tony for years, but neither of them appeared ready to act on it. "Not long. Friday, I think. He left earlier to check out some of the old haunts and see if he ran into anyone."

Esther nibbled her lower lip, then turned for the door. "Well, tell him I said hello."

Jess didn't want to embarrass her friend by saying more in front of Seth, but now Esther knew. The rest was up to her. "Thanks so much for coming by. I've missed you."

Esther glanced at Seth, then back to Jess, and winked. "Of course, you miss me, sweetie." Then she stepped in front of Seth and jabbed a finger in his chest. "You better watch out for my friend, Studly, or I'll be on your ass like morning glory on a fence post. Got it?"

Jess couldn't help but smile at her friend's attempt at intimidation. She might tip the scales at a buck-twenty tops, but she was also a fifth-degree black belt in Aikido and could easily back up her threat with action.

"I got it," answered Seth. "How's your mom?"

Her rigid stance softened, and she shrugged. "Not sure how much longer she's gonna last."

"I'm sorry. That's gotta be tough on you."

"Yeah, well, it is what it is." She turned for the door, then stopped and looked back. "Thanks for asking, Studly. Take care of my friend."

☋

Jess settled against Seth when he joined her on the couch. The warmth and strength he emanated soothed her frayed nerves. "Now what, *Kemosabe*?" she asked at last.

"It's eleven-fifteen. We go to bed."

135

She froze. Uh-oh...

His light chuckle vibrated against her cheek where it rested on his chest. "Like I said this morning...neither of us is at our best right now." He pulled back and tipped her chin up to face him. "But never doubt this."

The underlying sensuality in his voice captivated her, and the low, husky timbre sent currents of latent desire surging through her body.

"I want you so bad it hurts."

She swallowed hard, his words igniting a fire hidden just beneath the surface. "...You do?"

"And when the time is right...."

The smoldering promise in his eyes took her breath away.

"I intend to make love to you the way I've dreamed of for months." He brushed his lips against her forehead. "After that..." He kissed the tip of her nose. "You will never..." His lips feather-touched each cheek. "...ever...want another man." He lightly kissed her lips. "I promise."

Oh. My. Goodness. If she had any saliva left in her mouth, she would have drooled as the images his statement generated filled her head.

One finger caressed her lips. "If you have any objections to my intentions, tell me now, and I'll never bring it up again."

Duh. Do I look stupid? Unable to speak, she slowly shook her head.

He pulled her back against him. "Good. I'll put Lucy in the laundry room in a bit. That's where I put her stuff, though she probably won't like being cooped up there." He hissed out a long breath. "Tell me when you're ready, and I'll help you to bed."

Memories of the nightmare surfaced without warning. A cold chill washed over her, and gooseflesh peppered her arms. Walls' ominous voice rang through her brain, and she shivered. "Um...could you do like before?" Her voice quivered. "I mean…just be beside me." She took a shaky breath. "I don't want to be alone."

He hesitated, then pulled her tighter against him. "I'll be here," he whispered. His warm breath tickled her cheek. "I'll always be here."

CHAPTER TWENTY

JACK HAD TO FIND ANOTHER RIDE, AND THAT INFURIATED HIM.
Traffic was light in this part of town at one o'clock in the
morning, and options were almost non-existent. "It's Kos's fault
I have to change plans again," he muttered. "Dumb shit." Thoughts
of his cousin elicited a moment of regret because Jack needed help.
"Too late now," he muttered. "He served his purpose."

The guy Kos brought in refused to cooperate. Out of options,
Jack had no choice but to increase the pressure. "He'll do it or else."

A glance in his side mirror showed a police car pulling up to
a stop sign from a side street on the left. "Shit." Jack made a quick
right down a narrow alley and parked behind a dumpster. Pistol in
his hand, he waited until the unit rolled past. Another ten minutes
elapsed before he ventured out.

Anger rolled off him in waves. "Jack Walls doesn't hide out like a
common criminal." He hit the steering wheel with his fist. "This is all
her fault. If she'd stayed out of my business, none of this would have
happened." He flexed his fingers and took a breath. "She's gonna pay."

Once back on the main road, Jack debated where to go next.

He had another motel in mind, but it was on the other side of town. The coffee he drank an hour ago now made a pit stop necessary, too. "I should have pissed in the alley," he mumbled, then turned toward an older section of town where a couple of rundown bars and a convenience store offered opportunities for a new ride.

He pulled into the first bar parking lot he came to, but a group of rowdy cowboy-types hovered near a beat-up truck. Cautious, he left and headed for the convenience store a block away. As he circled the building, he saw two kids at the register. He parked on the side and waited until they walked out and headed off in the opposite direction. He got out and peeked around the corner. Restrooms were at the back. He scanned the area again to ensure the coast was clear.

Before he stepped around the building, a new, dark green Mustang pulled up to the front. A shapely blond wearing a next-to-nothing tank top stepped out and swayed a moment before she reached across the seat for her purse. She tugged on the hem of her skimpy red skirt, took a deep breath which caused it to inch back up, then staggered toward the door.

"What a waste," he muttered, then moved to the corner where he watched her stumble toward the restrooms. After a quick look to make sure no one else lurked in the parking lot, he shuffled over and tried the handle. Unlocked. And the keys hung from the ignition. *My lucky night after all.* In less than a minute, he raced across town to another shabby motel that didn't ask questions.

He resisted the urge to make another pass by the detective's house. He'd seen cops in the neighborhood last time, so best not to take any chances. He grabbed a burger at a fast-food joint and headed for the motel.

He stepped into the musty room, dropped his bag and the food on the bed, and then rushed to the bathroom.

A few minutes later, he sat on the edge of the bed and briefly wished he'd brought the tipsy blond along for fun. She was either drunk or high, but he knew pain was the ultimate sobering solution.

"It won't be long now, Detective." Even as he made the declaration, doubts crowded the corner of his mind, but he pushed them aside. His plan *would* work.

He lay on the smelly mattress and pictured just how he would teach the uppity bitch what happens when you mess with Jack Walls.

♂♀

"You're mine, now," he taunted. "You won't get away this time."

Hampered by total darkness, Jess inched forward. Where was Seth?

Fear, a foreign emotion, crawled over her skin like ants at a picnic, freezing her steps. Leg muscles tightened, her fight or flight reflex intensified.

"It's just you and me, Detective," he hissed. "Your partner is dead."

What? Dead? No! She inhaled, then exhaled slowly, and tried to calm her racing heart. Where am I? Where's my gun?

Walls spoke again, closer now. "But he died much too fast." He paused. "You, however, won't be so lucky." The sinister promise in his words chilled her to the bone.

She took another step, found the corner of a wall. Oh, God. Where is he? A whisper of warm air caressed her cheek a split second before he spoke.

"I've got you."

Strong arms wrapped around her, cutting off any hope of escape. Ignoring the pain in her body, she twisted and kicked, tried to break his hold. "No! No. Let me go."

"Jess? Wake up. It's Seth. I've got you. I've got you. You're safe."

Jess whimpered and tried to hold back the shriek lodged in her throat.

Seth's arms held her tight to his chest, his voice calm and soothing. "It's okay, babe. Just a bad dream. It's over now."

Tremors racked her body, and her heart pounded so hard her chest hurt. Each breath whooshed in and out as she struggled for calm. "Oh, God," she whispered. "It was so real."

Seth reached over and turned on the bedside lamp, then pulled her back against him, rubbing his hand up and down her arm. "But it was just a dream, Jess," he repeated. "And it's over now."

Suddenly, the bedroom door swung open, and Tony rushed in. "Take your damn hands off her!"

Brain still foggy from the nightmare, Jess barely recognized his intent. "No, Tony. It's okay," she stuttered. "It's okay."

"I heard you scream *no* and come in to find this prick holding you down."

Seth's arms never lessened their hold. "She had a nightmare, Tony."

Jess tried to sit up, then leaned back against Seth, needing his strength more than she cared to admit. "He's right, Weiner," she babbled. "An awful nightmare."

Tony stopped beside the bed and touched her cheek. "Are you sure, Sis? Cause if this jerk is pushing himself on you, I'll take care of his ass right now."

She covered his hand with hers and tried to smile. "I know you would. It's one of the things I love about my big brother."

He glanced between her and Seth. "Are you sure you're okay?"

She took a breath. "I am now. God. This has been the week from hell. I guess things just caught up with me."

He paused and glared at Seth. "Hurt my sister, jerk, you'll answer to me."

"I'd expect no less."

Tony hesitated, then nodded and walked out, easing the door closed behind him.

Jess went limp against Seth's chest. "It...was so real."

"I know." He shifted them on the bed until she nestled against his side, her head on his shoulder.

"He said...he told me you were dead...I heard him, but I couldn't see him."

"Just a dream, Jess. It's over now."

"It doesn't feel over, Seth." Heart still racing, she huddled closer. "It feels like it's just beginning."

"We'll get him. I promise."

She shook her head. "Don't make promises you can't keep."

He tipped her chin up until she met his gaze. "You do understand I'd die before I let him hurt you, right?"

She reached up and caressed his cheek. "I do, but—"

"No buts, Tex. I won't let him get to you."

Safe in his arms and spent from the fading adrenaline surge, she snuggled closer. Out of nowhere, a question popped in her head and out her mouth. "I've always wondered about something."

"What?"

"Why do you call me Tex or Texas?"

He hesitated. "Because there is nothing sexier than a beautiful woman with a kick-ass attitude and a hot Texas drawl."

She heard the contentment in his voice.

"And you, Texas, are all that and then some."

She lapped up the compliment like a double scoop of rocky road ice cream. "Okay then. I won't complain about it anymore."

His silence didn't last long. "Prairie dogs say hello with kisses."

"I like prairie dogs." She yawned and splayed her hand over his chest. "I'm glad you're here, Seth."

He kissed the top of her head. "So am I, Texas. So am I."

CHAPTER TWENTY-ONE

SETH WAITED UNTIL JESS FELL ASLEEP BEFORE HE EASED OUT of bed. A night light by the door illuminated the room enough for him to pull on his sweats and leave. He walked to Tony's room, not surprised to find the door open. He sat in a chair by the window, his face clouded with concern.

Seth stood in the entrance and cocked his head so he could hear if Jess called out. "I care about her," he declared without preamble. "We care about each other. More than partners."

"Since when?"

He shrugged. "Been building for a while, but all this kinda brought things to a head."

"Explain what 'all this' means."

Seth paused to listen, then turned and gave Tony the condensed version of things up to now.

All color drained from his face, and Tony sat up straighter. "You really think he'll come after her?"

"I do. For whatever reason, she ticks off some buttons for him." He crossed his arms and leaned against the door jam. "There's no question she's a tough lady, Tony, but the last few days have taken a toll on her."

"The nightmare?"

"It's not the first one."

Posture rigid, Tony's dark eyes drilled holes in Seth, but he didn't look away.

"Do you love her?"

"For some time now." He paused. "But she's not ready to hear it yet."

Tony's stiff posture relaxed, and he bent forward, elbows on his knees. "Okay. What can I do to help?"

"Be here when I can't."

"Okay."

"She'll pitch a fit at being coddled, but there's no other way. Walls has at least one, maybe two others with him. I won't take chances with her life, whether she likes it or not."

Tony sat up, eyes wide, and grinned. "I don't envy you, man. Telling Brat she can't take care of herself will cause you a world of hurt."

"Yeah, well, I'd rather she be mad than dead."

"Copy that."

Seth turned to go, then stopped and looked back. "By the way… Esther came by earlier. Said to tell you hello."

Tony's eyes widened, and his expression softened. "Uh, okay. Thanks."

"Jess told her you'd be here a few days."

He changed the subject. "I have to report back on Friday, so I need to leave late Thursday. You gonna have him locked up by then?"

"That's the plan." Seth paused, then turned to go.

"Seth?"

"Yeah?"

"She deserves some happiness from life."

"I'll do my best to provide it."

Jaw set, Tony walked toward him and stopped a foot away. "I hope so." He paused. "Because if you hurt her, they'll never find your body." He calmly shut the door in his face.

Seth knew that wasn't a threat to an officer of the law; it was a promise from a protective brother.

Back in their room, he kicked off the sweats and slid under the covers. Jess sighed and offered no resistance when he pulled her to his side.

Exhaustion plagued him, but he pushed it away, cherishing the intimacy of their bodies side by side. It felt...right. He wanted a lifetime of these moments and planned to do whatever it took to make it happen.

Jess grunted and eased her bad knee over his thigh, then trailed her fingers across his chest.

He trapped the wandering appendage under his hand and re-minded himself they were both banged up and needed rest more than, well, anything his wayward brain tempted his body with now.

"Tony okay?" Her smoky voice took him by surprise.

"Yeah."

She rubbed her leg over his. "Sorry if he gave you any grief."

"Nothing I wouldn't do for my sisters. It's in the big brother creed."

She yawned against his chest. "You're really a nice guy, aren't you?"

He lifted one shoulder in a slight shrug. "I try to be. Unless you're a bad guy, then all bets are off."

She stretched out beside him, sleek and sexy as hell, her head on his shoulder.

"Don't wait too long."

"For what?"

Her warm breath drifted across his upper body. "To make me forget other men."

He smiled and caressed the arm draped over his chest. "Sure you don't wanna see who can hold out the longest?"

A soft snore answered him.

♂♀

Jess woke to the steady thump of Seth's heart in her ear, her body meshed against him, her sore knee balanced on his thigh. The soft glow of the night light cast the room in blue-black shadows.

After the nightmare, she expected sleep to elude her, but it didn't. Now, awake and teased by the warmth of his body, she was acutely aware of every spot they touched.

I intend to make love to you the way I've dreamed of for months.

Just the memory of his voice fueled the flame of desire never far from the surface. She eased up on her elbow and glanced at the bedside clock—five a.m. On a typical day, she would rise and go for a five-mile run or head for the gym near the station.

But today wasn't normal. A killer stalked her.

She repressed the thought, refused to let Walls steal this moment, and focused on Seth. Sometime in the night, he'd taken off his tee-shirt, and his bare chest revealed hidden scars. One on his left shoulder resembled a bullet wound, two more on his side, possibly knife or shrapnel wounds. Though long healed, their evidence remained.

Her heart jumped at the realization any one of them could have proved fatal in the right circumstances. She drew a shallow breath and closely examined him in slumber. One arm lay across his waist, and the other rested on her hip. Her gaze roamed over his upper body to his face, then fixed on his lips. She took a breath and traced the line on his side with one finger, then leaned down and kissed the marred flesh. Her mind replayed the warmth of his kisses, and a delicious shudder heated her body.

What have you done to me?

The sense of connection she'd discovered in Seth amounted

to finding a piece of herself she didn't realize she missed—the one that made her whole. *Did he feel it, too?*

Without a doubt, they shared an intense physical awareness, but was there more to it?

Could it be love? A part of her said absolutely, but another doubted she even knew *how* to love. She certainly had no role models by which to evaluate the sentiment. Tony was the only loving, stable factor in her life and the one she could always depend on to be there for her.

Until Seth.

But questions plagued her. What if he decided she carried too much emotional baggage? What if he got what he wanted and tossed her aside? Half of her bewildered brain argued he wouldn't. The other side chided *he might*.

Even though doubt clouded her vision, one thing remained clear; her feelings for Seth went beyond friendship or partners, even sexual attraction. Exhilarating and intense, they were like nothing she'd ever experienced before and may never experience again. *I may as well enjoy it while I can.*

And pray he didn't break her heart.

She sifted her fingers through the dense curls on his torso and delighted in the slow spread of heat in her body. *Will he make good on his promise?*

She couldn't ignore the spark of excitement elicited by the thought. She leaned closer and inhaled his masculine scent as her pulse skittered in anticipation.

Immediately, she felt the change in his body and glanced up. Cognac-colored eyes watched in soundless anticipation.

The point of no return approached.

His nostrils flared, and his rib cage barely moved when he breathed.

She moved forward, dark hair creating a veil that brushed his face, and teased his lips with hers before she traced the seam with her tongue. "You win," she whispered.

The solid thump of his heartbeat under her palm increased in strength and speed. "Win?"

"Uh-huh." She met his gaze. "You win."

Narrowed eyes studied her. He drew in a long, shaky breath. "What did I win?"

Her mind grappled for a decent reply. Now would be a great time to be flirty or coy, but to her dismay, she never quite got a handle on using feminine wiles, so she opted for her strong suit and got straight to the point.

"We may not be a hundred percent," she murmured, one finger tracing swirls on his breastbone. "But unless you got plans to do this upright, we can probably work around the sore spots."

One brow kicked up, and his mouth curled into that sexy smile that always turned her insides to mush.

"The vertical part can wait." Seth eased her down beside him and rested on his elbow, his large hand splayed over her stomach. "I meant what I said before." His husky voice faltered. "There's something between us, Jess. Something special." His hand drifted lower, then stopped. "I'm crazy about you. This isn't a fling for me."

She took an erratic breath and swallowed. "Ditto." Her bewildered mind chastised her for such a lame reply, but it was all she could muster.

His fevered gaze traveled the length of her body before coming to rest on her face. "You are so beautiful." He brushed a tender kiss to the cut on her forehead, another to her bruised lip while his hand traveled down her hip, across her thigh. "And your sexy, sassy mouth drives me crazy," he whispered. His words were smothered in a hungry kiss that went on forever yet not near long enough. His lips skimmed over her cheek, her earlobe, down her throat. Hypersensitive skin tingled in his wake.

She winced when she lifted her sore arm, and Seth stopped.

"What did I hurt?"

She caressed his cheek with her uninjured hand. "Nothing." She took a breath. "But stop now, and I will hurt *you*."

He grinned and swept his lips against hers, once, twice, then covered her mouth in a slow, tender kiss that sent shivers of want through her. She gasped when he moved to the pulsing hollow at the base of her throat, skimmed across her collarbone, then back up to her lips for a mind-numbing kiss. He slipped his hand under the edge of her sleep shirt, and calloused fingers, rough but gentle, explored the soft lines of her waist, her hips.

She returned his kiss with all the unsated desire she denied the existence of for months. The pain in her shoulder forgotten, she wrapped her arms around him, fingers digging into the corded muscles of his back.

Raising his mouth from hers, he gazed into her eyes and reached for the edge of her shirt. "It may hurt to take this off."

She pushed herself up. "I don't care."

He lifted the edges and eased one arm out, then the other. He noted the sport bra and black lace panties. "Nice combination." The bra soon lay on the floor with her shirt, followed by his boxers, and he stood naked before her.

Her mouth went dry. "Oh my," she whispered as her gaze scanned his body. Another scar drew her attention. About six inches long and half an inch wide, it crossed his left thigh. Silent, she inspected it, then met his gaze.

He shrugged in typical Seth fashion. "Shrapnel."

Her heart squeezed again. *He could have been killed.*

She pushed the thought aside and feasted her eyes on Seth. Despite the wounds, his body was solid and well-proportioned, with broad shoulders, trim waist. Her gaze dipped lower, and a soft moan of pure desire escaped.

Oh yes, he can make good on his promise.

"Hold that thought." He lifted his pants from the back of the settee and removed a foil pack from his wallet. He paused, then reached for another before he rejoined her on the bed, tossing the condoms on the lamp table.

"Now. Where were we?"

The heat of his gaze on her breasts turned the peaks pebble hard, and breath shot from her lungs. She reached for the waistband of her panties.

He pushed her hands away. "Uh-uh. I'm taking those off." His fever-bright eyes darkened to deep chocolate brown. "It's part of my dream."

He eased her back on the bed. Straddling her hips, he knelt over her. He blew out a long, slow breath and skimmed his hands down her body, then back up and cupped her breasts, his thumbs rolling across the rigid nipples. He lowered his head and teased the buds with his tongue, then nipped them with his teeth before taking each in turn into his mouth.

Jess squirmed beneath his touch and arched upward. She stroked the strong tendons in the back of his neck, anchoring him to her chest.

"So beautiful," he murmured as his hands and mouth intimately examined her body, discovering hidden pleasure points along the way.

He paid particular attention to every cut and bruise marring her creamy flesh. With each tender kiss and whispered word, all doubts and fears drained away.

Coherent thought fragmented under his hungry exploration; his lips seared a path down her ribs, across her abdomen. She inhaled sharply when his warm breath blew over her core. "Seth..." Her fingers fisted in the sheets, and her hips bucked upwards. "Seth..."

He tugged on the scrap of black lace. "I almost hate to get rid of this," he murmured and pulled. His lips followed the track of the fabric as it slid down her body.

She shivered when his tongue licked the tender skin below

her navel, then slithered over the apex as he drew the panties down her legs, then tossed the wisp of material aside. Desire-glazed eyes locked with hers.

Anticipation sucked all the air from her lungs.

Then he retraced the panties' route with his mouth, beginning on the inside of each thigh.

Her body shuddered, and she gasped for air when his warm lips hovered over her cleft. Impatience grew to explosive levels, and she grabbed for him. "Now, Seth…"

He pushed her hands aside. "I promised to make you forget…"

One nip almost sent her over the edge.

"I always keep my promises."

His expert touch pushed her to a higher level of arousal, holding back just enough to keep her from going over.

He moved up her body, nibbled each breast, then captured her lips in a passion-fueled kiss while his fingers teased her core.

Desire erupted like molten lava, robbing her of all thought but him. She closed her eyes and surrendered to his expert seduction.

"Seth…please," she panted. "Now."

He sheathed himself, then lowered his body over hers.

She moaned as delicious heat coursed her entire length, filled her, consumed her. The slide of his sweat-coated body over her highly sensitized nerve endings added another layer of sensory perception that fast approached critical overload. Explosive pleasure engulfed her, and she bit her lip to suppress a cry.

"Open your eyes," he groaned through clenched teeth. "Open your eyes."

She obeyed his command and discovered a whole new level of intimacy, a connection she never knew existed. The sense of completeness astounded her. Two became one. They held nothing back, savoring the moment that bound them body and soul. Gazes locked, they moved in perfect harmony. Fast. Slow. Gentle. Hard.

Waves of ecstasy crashed through her, screaming for release.

She clawed his back, unable to stop the cry pulled from the depths of her soul.

He brought them to the brink, only to hold back again and again until they crested the wave together, exploding in a downpour of blistering sensations.

She sucked in deep soul-drenching gulps of air that carried with it the scent of him, of them, that imprinted her soul.

She was whole at last.

Arms trembling, he held the bulk of his weight off her and touched his forehead to hers, their ragged breathing the only sound in the room.

At length, some semblance of normal returned, and he rolled to the side. "I'll be right back."

He returned a moment later, and she burrowed against him, her back to his chest, their legs intertwined. Peace and contentment filled her.

"Are you all right?" he asked. "Did I hurt you?"

She refused to tell him how much she ached right now. Besides, the result was more than worth it. "Who knew sex was a pain killer?"

"Do you need your pills?"

Okay, so he guessed she wasn't totally honest. "Not yet." She paused a moment. "I like a man who keeps his promises."

He nuzzled her neck. "That was just a practice run," he whispered. "Wait till you see the real thing."

Oh boy.

Her imagination soared on his hushed promise.

CHAPTER TWENTY-TWO

SETH WOKE TO THE WARMTH OF JESS'S BODY PRESSED AGAINST his, sunlight leaking around the blinds. Making love to her exceeded his every dream. And now he knew she cared about him, too, even without saying *I love you*, which told him they had a chance.

He glanced at his watch—eight-thirty. More than anything, he wanted this to be the start of the rest of their lives together.

The subtle tension in her body told him when she woke. He could almost hear the wheels turning in her razor-sharp mind and waited for her reaction.

"So, I'm guessing this is where the awkward morning-after stuff comes in." Her smokey voice held more than a hint of uncertainty.

"I wouldn't know. There's nothing awkward about it for me." He kissed the top of her head. "How about you?"

She turned to face him, her head on his shoulder, ebony curls fanned out on his arm. She chewed her lower lip, then shook her head. "Me neither." She paused. "It's just…"

The worry in her eyes made him cringe inside. "Just what?"

Avoiding his gaze, she traced the scar on his shoulder with her finger. "I've never...been in this position before."

"You mean totally and completely satisfied?"

She snorted. "Well, that, too."

"What else?" His chest tightened. *Please don't let her say she regrets what happened.*

Her warm breath tickled the hairs on his chest. "I never...woke up like this."

It took a moment for her words to penetrate his brain still preoccupied with their night of lovemaking. "You mean you, or he, never stayed all night before?"

Silent, she nodded.

Happiness surged through him. "So, I'm your first sleepover?"

Before she could reply, another thought struck him. "Although, technically speaking, I did wake up in your bed yesterday, so that qualifies as a sleepover, too." He pulled her closer, and his arousal pressed against her hip. "But this is much better."

When she didn't reply, a twinge of unease crept up his back. He braced himself for an answer he didn't want to hear. "Do you regret this, Jess?" he asked softly. "Do you regret us?"

She pushed up on her elbow and faced him, cheeks stained a lovely shade of pink. "No, Seth. Never."

"I hear a 'but' coming."

She looked away, then back to him. "I suck at relationships," she murmured. "And I don't want to mess this up. But at the same time, I don't want to lose what we had, either." She hesitated. "I don't want to lose my partner."

Swamped with relief, he released a breath. "The department doesn't have a specific policy against partner's being involved. They just don't encourage it."

When she didn't say anything, he spoke again. "I asked Mildred in HR about it a couple of weeks ago."

Her mouth moved, but no words came out.

Alarm bells rang. *Did I go too far?* She didn't resist when he maneuvered her onto her back and positioned himself alongside her.

"I've known for some time my feelings for you went beyond partners or friendship."

"For real?"

"Yes. And I wondered—well, hoped that you felt the same. So, I sort of asked her one day in the breakroom if a policy existed."

She groaned. "That explains all the I've-got-a-secret looks I've been getting from her."

He let the comment pass. "I promised myself I'd use the trip to Denver to find out where we stood with each other." In the space of a heartbeat, he knew the time was right. "When I thought I'd lost you…that Walls had you—I was out of my mind. I couldn't bear it if something happened to you." He brushed a wayward curl away from her cheek and trailed his fingers down her jaw. "I realize you don't place much stock in love, Jess, but I do." He paused. "And with God as my witness, I love you."

☌

Jess blinked several times in rapid succession. *He loves me.* Try as she might, words refused to come. The quiet became uncomfortable for her, but Seth didn't appear affected.

She tried again to speak, but he silenced her with a finger to her lips.

"I can see this is a lot for you to take in. But it's important to me that you understand exactly how I feel. Here. Now." He cupped her cheek with one hand. "You're it for me, Jess," he whispered. "And you care for me, too. That's enough for now."

"Seth—"

A sharp tap on the bedroom door interrupted them.

"Y'all awake?" Tony's muffled voice penetrated the door.

"Yeah," she stammered, putting distance between them. "What's up?"

He cracked the door open but didn't enter. "There's a Texas Ranger here to see you. He's in the kitchen."

The door clicked shut, and silence filled the room.

Suddenly self-conscious, she debated a good exit move as she sat up, the sheet clutched to her chest.

Seth showed no signs of discomfort when he threw back the covers and stood. "Must be Sampson." He grabbed his clothes from the floor. "I'll give you time to—" He glanced up and froze, his expression shooting from casual to hot in the blink of an eye. A shuddering breath wracked his body. "Do you have any idea how sexy you are at this moment?" His whispered voice came out gruff and scratchy.

Breath stuck in her throat at the heat in his gaze. She couldn't look away even if she wanted to.

He didn't move, just stared. "Your hair's all over the place; that sheet barely covers you. That I've-been-loved-but-good expression on your face." He hissed in a breath. "I remember how you got that way." He moved to the side of the bed and pressed a quick kiss to her lips. "And I can't wait for it to happen again."

Before she could answer, providing, of course, her mouth and brain connected on some level—any level, he stepped back and threw on his clothes.

Dressed, he stood there with his arms folded. "Well?"

The smirk on his face dared her to get up as he watched.

She never could resist a dare.

She let the sheet inch down and swung her legs over the far side of the bed and stood.

"You'd be closer to your clothes if you got up on the other side," he grumbled.

Air whistled through his teeth as she slowly limped toward him.

"How much fun would that be?" Shocked by her brazen behavior, she nonetheless found it exhilarating. Never in a million years did she think she could be like this or that this would happen.

He loved her.

And she loved him.

She stopped a foot away.

Tawny eyes blazed with heat raked down her body. Air swished in and out of his mouth. "You're gonna pay for this, woman."

She slid her hands up his arms. "Is that a threat, Mr. Hamilton?" She inched closer. "I am a cop, you know. I could arrest you."

His expression was all male, and her insides hummed with excitement.

"I'll furnish the cuffs." He kissed the tip of her nose and strutted out.

CHAPTER TWENTY-THREE

SETH HEADED DOWN THE HALL, UNABLE TO KEEP THE GRIN OFF his face. Jess was everything he ever wanted in a partner, friend, and lover.

Now he wanted her as his wife. The realization shocked and excited him at the same time. The sheer possibility of that dream materializing put a bounce in his step. Even the appearance of the Ranger couldn't dampen his good mood as he entered the kitchen.

He found Tony leaning against the counter, a cup in his hand, and Ranger Drake Sampson stood next to the table.

"Catching up on your beauty sleep, Hammer?" Drake walked toward him, a wry grin on his face.

Seth gripped his outstretched hand and grinned. "What can I say? It takes more than it used to." Seth tilted his head toward Tony. "I guess you already met Jess's brother."

"I did."

"I'll take my coffee to the porch." Tony moved toward the back door. "Nice to meet you."

"Same here." Drake waited for the door to shut behind him.

"Well, at least you're getting around better than when I saw you in Amarillo. How's Jess?"

Seth liked Drake and was happy to have him on this case, but the shrewd look on his face right now caused unfamiliar warmth to creep up his cheeks. "Better. She'll be here in a minute." He gestured toward the table. "Have a seat. Coffee?"

"Sure."

He filled two cups and passed one to his friend.

"We found Koslow," said Drake without preamble.

"What? Where?" Coffee sloshed out when Seth's cup clunked down.

"Earlier this morning. Some fleabag motel out by the interstate." Drake shook his head. "Door was partially open. Another customer walked by and saw Koslow on the floor covered in blood. Locals called me as soon as they ID'd him."

"Dead?"

He cupped his mug in both hands. "No. Bad shape though. Two stab wounds. One to the chest, one to the stomach."

"Damn."

"Yeah." He blew on his coffee before taking a cautious sip. "He's still in surgery. We won't know the full extent of his injuries until he gets out. I've got locals standing by to talk to him when, or if, he comes around. Techs are still processing the scene." He shook his head. "Popular place with the by-the-hour crowd. Gonna take a while."

"Any idea what happened?" Seth's mind reeled with questions.

"Not yet. The rooms on either side were occupied at different times last night by Joe Smith." Disdain filled his voice. "Who knew there were so many Joe Smith's in Walker?" Drake set his cup down and folded his hands in front of him. "Signs of a struggle, though." He heaved a disgruntled sigh. "Short of dusting for prints and hoping they're in the system, it's doubtful we can track who rented those rooms." He shook his head. "All paid in cash, and the info used is likely bogus." He snorted. "Koslow rented the room under Jack Frost."

"So, no witnesses?" asked Seth

"No witnesses to what?" Jess limped into the room wearing grey sweatpants, an LSU tee shirt, and fluffy purple house slippers. She'd twisted her hair up into a messy-looking glob on top of her head, but a few tendrils escaped and framed her face.

She looked adorable.

The thought made him bite back a grin. *She'd kick my ass if I called her adorable.*

Both men stood as she approached the table, and Drake extended his hand. "Nice to see you again, Jess. You look a lot better than the last time we met."

"Feel better, too." Cheeks flushed a pretty shade of pink, she eased down into a chair without looking at Seth.

Drake sat across from her. "How's the knee? I see you still have the crutch."

"No permanent damage. I should be on desk duty in another week. Good as new in a month."

Seth placed a steaming mug in front of her.

She took the cup but didn't glance up, and the stain on her cheeks deepened.

Seth peeked at Drake. He was too good a cop not to notice the subtle change in their relationship. While it bothered him that she may be embarrassed, he didn't care who knew.

Expression neutral, Jess faced the Ranger. "Who did you find? Walls?"

Jess and Seth were already interviewed separately about the accident and Walls' escape and cleared of any wrongdoing, so there was no need for separate conversations now.

"We should be so lucky," grumbled Drake. "It was Koslow." He sat down and repeated what he'd told Seth.

Jess straightened and peered from one to the other. "Had to be Walls, but why try to kill Koslow?"

"Who knows why he does what he does?" groused Seth. "The man is certifiable."

Drake pulled a notebook from his pocket. "I spoke to the clerk at the motel. He wasn't keen on cooperating but finally identified Koslow as the person who rented the room a couple of days ago. Paid in cash for a week." He scanned his notes. "Bed covers were tangled, obvious signs of a struggle." He flipped a page. "Defensive wounds to both hands, blood under two nails so may get some DNA, and he had some bruising on his cheek." He closed the book. "He didn't give up without a fight."

"It doesn't make sense." Jess's fingers drummed on the table. "Walls used him to escape and for some of his leg work, so why kill him?" Before they answered, she continued. "And a knife is personal."

"A knife is his preferred method," offered Seth. "And Walls is quick-tempered." He rotated the cup around on the table. "It's logical to assume they had an argument and Jack lost it."

Expression thoughtful, Jess added, "Lottie told me the first beating happened because she questioned something he said."

Drake's piercing gaze settled on Jess. "Which brings me to another point. Why is he after you?"

She shrugged and shook her head. "Maybe Angie Potter. He did it, Drake." She tapped her knuckles on the table. "I'm sure of it. I just can't prove it. Yet." Gaze focused on the back wall, she paused in thought. "I urged Lottie to leave him, or at least press charges more than once, but she refused. Even after two trips to the ER." Head lowered, she sighed. "And he killed her."

"You're not to blame for that, Jess," declared Seth firmly, placing his hand over hers, unconcerned about what Drake might infer from the action. "She had a choice. She made the wrong one."

"I realize that, but..."

"No buts. You did all you could." He squeezed her hand. "We both did. He's to blame for her death. No one else."

Drake tapped his pen against the notebook. "Okay. Let's go over everything again, starting with how Koslow knew about Walls' arrest and transfer."

Seth held her hand a moment longer, then released it and stood because movement helped him think. "Timeline shows Koslow arrived in Denver a couple of months ago, shortly after he quit his job here. He rented an apartment over on the west side a week later under his own name. Landlord confirms Walls was there but wasn't sure at what point he arrived." He stopped pacing and turned to Drake. "Talk about coincidences. Three weeks ago, he started work as a janitor at the jail where they held Walls. It would have been easy for him to find out the details." Seth reached for his cup and drained it. "Walls' only call was to Koslow the day after he was arrested." He sat back down. "Still have no idea who the third man is unless you or the feds have something."

"Nothing yet," grumbled Drake. "But we're still checking."

An hour later, Drake closed his notebook and observed them in turn. "Well, that's where things stand right now. We've added Walls as a person of interest in Koslow's attack. The possibility he may have stabbed Koslow, a relative, someone he depended on, is further evidence he's out of control." He turned to Jess. "And for whatever reason, he's targeted you."

She shivered, and Seth covered her hand again. "We'll get him, Tex. We will."

Her hesitant smile never reached her eyes. "I know."

Drake stood and stretched. "Well, I'm off to the hospital to check on Koslow." He paused. "Glad to see you two are doing so well. I'll be in touch."

"I'll walk you out." Seth gave Jess's hand a quick squeeze and followed the Ranger.

Once at the door, Drake faced him. "I talked with Tom earlier, and it doesn't look like they can park anyone out front right now. Too short-handed. But they will make regular patrols through here."

"I figured as much when I talked with him yesterday." Seth shook hands with him. "Thanks for the updates."

Drake headed for the door, then turned. "There's no telling what Walls will do next."

"Agreed."

He held Seth's gaze. "Just to be clear... Jess needs someone watching her back every minute until we get him."

"Roger that."

"He's a cagey bastard."

"He won't get near her."

Seth watched his friend walk down the sidewalk to his truck and prayed he could back up that statement.

CHAPTER TWENTY-FOUR

JESS PINCHED THE BRIDGE OF HER NOSE AND TOOK A BREATH. "Mom…I already told you I can't come today. I can barely walk, and I'm not released to drive yet." She didn't bother mentioning the reasons behind her inability to jump at her mother's call. It would make no difference. Ivy Cantrell only thought about Ivy.

Her mother lived in a small apartment complex geared for senior adults. Not one of those assisted living facilities but one with folks around to help the tenants with whatever they needed. Ivy, however, insisted it was Jess's responsibility, not theirs, to take care of her.

"What am I supposed to do?" whined Ivy. "I'm out of everything. I need to go to the store, and I can't drive myself."

Of course you can't.

She struggled to keep her voice calm. "The store is three blocks away. You can drive that far. Or call Tina. She's out of school and can take you."

"She can't."

Jess clamped her teeth together when Ivy amped up the poor-pitiful-me tone.

"I need *you* to come, Jessica."

"What about the transportation service provided by the complex? That's what it's for."

Ivy's voice firmed up a notch, and Jess braced for a meltdown.

"It is not their responsibility to take care of *your* mother, Jessica," huffed Ivy. "Besides, all this drama with you and that man has wrecked my nerves, so I can't drive. You'd know that if you bothered to come by and check on me."

Jess stiffened her back. *Oh no you don't.* "What about me, Mom? When was the last time you called to check on me?" She'd spent most of her life taking care of things, walking on eggshells around her mother, afraid she might say or do something to upset her. Not anymore.

"I was in a car wreck on Friday. A bad one. And nearly kidnapped by a deranged killer. I survived because I was swept away by a dust storm and spent the night in a flooded ditch clinging to a root to keep from being washed away." She kept her voice calm despite the urge to shout in hurt and frustration. "I was unconscious for hours in the hospital. I've been home two days. Not once have you called to check on me. So, forgive me if your inability to function as an adult isn't on the top of my priority list today."

Ivy's silence spurred Jess to continue, "Since you won't call Tina and won't use the transportation provided by the complex, you'll have to wait until I can get by there."

"Well," blustered Ivy. "I guess I know where I stand."

Before Jess could say anything, even if she wanted to, the line went dead.

She placed the phone on the table and rubbed her temples. Tears of guilt and frustration clogged her throat. Why couldn't she have a normal mother? A normal family? And why the hell did she feel so guilty for standing up to Ivy?

Hands gently kneaded her shoulders, and she stiffened.

"You okay?"

Seth's quiet question wrenched her from the chasm of self-pity she inched toward. "Yeah."

"I take it your mother needs something?"

It didn't surprise her that Seth guessed the caller was Ivy. "Has to go to the store." She leaned her head against his arm. "Wasn't happy when I told her I couldn't go today."

"Frankly," declared Tony from the kitchen. "I'm glad you stood up to her. Surprised, but glad." He placed his cup on the counter and walked toward her. "About time, too."

She gave him a trembling smile. "It's…complicated."

"Family usually is." He nodded to Seth, who kept his hands on her shoulders. "I'll check on Ivy this afternoon. She won't push me around like she does you."

Jaw tense, Tony crouched down in front of her, one hand resting on her uninjured knee. "I'm worried about you."

She sighed. "I know you are, but really, I'm fine."

"No, you're not. As if Ivy wasn't enough, you've been through hell the last few days, and a madman with a grudge against you is still out there."

"I can—"

"Seth claims Walls is one mean SOB." He took a breath. "You're a kickass cop, Jess. I understand that. But, promise me, promise me you won't take any chances."

Her heart swelled with love. Her big brother never changed. "I've missed you, Weiner."

"Don't change the subject," he snipped. "You'd go bear hunting with a switch if you thought you needed to."

She leaned toward him. "I won't take any unnecessary chances. I promise."

"Don't think I didn't notice the word *unnecessary*," scoffed Tony.

Seth gave her shoulders a light squeeze then walked to the

fridge. "Had breakfast yet, Tony?" He pulled out bacon and eggs. "We're starved."

"I ate earlier." Tony rose and winked at Jess. "Unlike some folks, I didn't sleep in all nice and cozy."

Jess cursed the heat rushing to her cheeks. "Don't knock it if you ain't tried it."

His warm chuckle followed him down the hall toward his room.

"I need to make a grocery run this morning." Seth placed breakfast items on the counter. "He gonna be around?"

"Uh-huh. I mean, he's going to check on Mom at some point, but I could—"

"No, you couldn't," he interrupted, then squatted down in front of her. "You're a strong, independent woman, Tex. It's one of the many things I love about you." He lightly caressed her calves. "And I understand you hate feeling helpless, but…." He paused and leaned forward. "Let me take care of you a while longer." His voice dropped to a whisper. "Please."

The plea in his voice undid her. How could she say no to someone granting her fondest wish? She blinked to conquer the rush of tears burning the backs of her eyelids. "Okay," she stammered. "Just this once."

Animated dark eyes crinkled at the corners as he stood. "I promise to let you wait on me next time."

They enjoyed a cheerful breakfast infused with small talk like a long-standing couple. A sense of rightness, of home, surrounded them, and she basked in the change.

Tony returned and grabbed a water bottle from the fridge. Twisting off the top, he joined them at the table. "I wanted to talk to you about something, Sis. If you have time."

"Of course." She pushed her plate aside and folded her hands on the table. "Shoot."

Seth got up and reached for the empty dishes. "I'll leave you two alone."

"Actually," countered Tony, "I'd rather you stayed. If you don't mind."

"Let me clear this out of the way." He placed the dishes in the sink and sat back down.

Tony spun the water bottle on the table and took a deep breath. "I'm getting out of the Army."

Jess stared at her brother while the words filtered through her brain. "That's great!" Then noticing his wrinkled brow, she paused. "Isn't it?"

"I think so." He leaned back in his chair. "I went to see Mr. McKay yesterday."

"I thought he closed the shop." She glanced at Seth. "Tony worked at Mr. McKay's garage when he was in high school."

"He works a couple of days a week. Fussy about what he takes on because of his age." Tony shifted in his chair. "I came home last year, and we talked a long time." He took a drink of water. "He offered to sell me the place and help me get up to speed on things."

"You came home? And didn't stop by?" Jess couldn't keep the hurt from her voice.

"I did come by, Brat, twice, but you weren't home." He reached for her hand. "I called the station, and they told me you were on vacation. I only had three days' leave left, so I couldn't wait. I tried to leave you a voice mail, but your box was full."

Her anger dissipated. "You might know. My first and only vacation, and I missed you." Composure restored; she studied her brother. "Are you sure that's what you want?" Caution edged into her tone. "You've been in since you graduated."

"I've always loved tinkering with motors. That's what I do in the Army. But I want more." He looked between them. "I want what you have."

Before she could respond, he directed his attention to Seth. "How long were you in? Was it hard to adjust when you got out?"

He bobbed his head. "Eight years. Mainly in combat situations, so, yeah, it was a little difficult at first. But I had my family to support me." He focused on Jess. "Having people around who love you, who understand and want you to succeed is the key." He turned back to Tony. "I wanted to be in law enforcement, so as soon as I got out, I concentrated on that, and they backed me all the way."

"You're my big brother, Tony. I want whatever is going to make you happy. I'd love nothing more than to have you around again. And if leaving the Army and buying McKay's is what you want, then go for it." She smiled at Seth. "We'll be here for you. And I'm pretty sure there's someone else who will be happy, too."

His cheeks turned pink, and he sighed. "I hope so."

"I know so." The thought of her brother and best friend getting together made her heart sing.

Tony stood. "Got a couple of calls to make. I started the ball rolling last year before I was a hundred percent sure it's what I wanted, but after talking with Mr. McKay yesterday and you today, I'm certain the time is right."

"Can you hang around long enough for me to make a grocery run?" asked Seth, "or do I need to go later?"

"No, now is fine. Most of what I need to do can be accomplished over the phone. I'll wait until you get back to check on Ivy."

Seth pulled a notepad from his pocket. "Need anything?"

Tony handed Seth some bills.

"I got this," argued Seth. "You're company."

"I insist." Tony yawned and dropped the bills on the table. "Guess I'm still a bit jet-lagged." He turned, then stopped. "Oh, Coach may stop by later this evening to catch up if you don't mind."

Jess watched her brother. "Of course. It's fine."

"Who's Coach?" asked Seth.

"Old Army buddy of mine. He lives here now."

"We saw him at the gas station yesterday." Jess shifted in the chair. "I swear, he could pass for Jason Garretts older, better-looking brother."

"Should I be jealous?" teased Seth.

"Not a bit."

"I'll be in my room." Tony started down the hall. "Holler when you leave."

"Will do." Seth laid pen and pad on the table. "You're looking pale again."

She rose and reached for the crutch, unable to stop the upturn of her mouth. "Didn't get much sleep last night."

He rose and pulled her into his arms. "I love you." He kissed the top of her forehead. "You know I'll do anything I can to help, right?"

"Yes. I do." Her heart skipped a beat. She loved him more with each second that ticked away.

"It's going to be okay. You and me. We got this."

She sighed. "Yeah. We got this."

CHAPTER TWENTY-FIVE

JACK GLANCED AT THE BEDSIDE CLOCK AS HE DIALED THE NUMber; six p.m. "He'll answer this time." The call went to voicemail—again, and he threw the phone on the bed. "Jerk." He raked stubby fingers through greasy hair and paced around the small space. "He'll regret not taking my calls." His voice bounced off the paper-thin walls as he grabbed the back of a chair in a white-knuckled grip. "Nothing is going like it should." He pushed away and stomped toward the grime-coated window. "Her fault," he muttered as he yanked the curtain aside. "It's all her fault."

He took a deep breath and surveyed the parking lot. The muted light of sundown showed the motel for what it was—a shabby, run-down eyesore that reeked of failure and disappointment. "I shouldn't have to live like this," he muttered. "She's gonna pay for that, too."

Movement caught his eye, and he watched an older model crew-cab pickup pull into a parking space near the end. A moment later, a cowboy exited and staggered toward the last room, stumbling against a metal support post for the upper level. He regained his balance and pounded on the door. "Open up. It's me."

Jack lost sight of him when the door opened. He closed the curtains and wandered around the dingy room. "I need a new ride, Kos," he mumbled. "The Mustang stands out too much." He turned, expecting to see his cousin, belatedly realizing he was alone. He scanned the empty room then scrubbed his face with both hands. "I told him not to question me." He shook his head. "Too late now."

A grumble from his stomach said it was time to eat. Last night's pizza sat on the dinky table by the window. He curled his nose, then walked to the dresser and grabbed his wallet along with a 9mm Beretta he found in the Mustang's glove box. Only one clip, but it will have to do for now. He turned and plucked the phone off the bed, then opened the door and stopped. "The cops are sure to be on the lookout for the Mustang now," he muttered to himself. "I shoulda kept the van."

He hesitated a moment, then ambled over to the pickup. Sure enough, it wasn't locked. Five tense minutes later, he had it hotwired and drove toward a nearby fast-food restaurant. Food in hand, he headed for the abandoned warehouse on the outskirts of town he'd used in the past. Homeless people had recently taken up residence, but Kos convinced them they needed to move on. "I just hope he got things in place."

A fleeting moment of regret surfaced, then vanished. Kos had no one to blame but himself for what happened. He knew better than to question Jack's orders.

The phone rang as he pulled around toward the back. "About damn time," he mumbled. "Why the hell haven't you answered my calls?"

"Did you try to kill Koslow?" the panicked voice snapped without preamble. "Did you?"

Walls froze. *Kos isn't dead?* "What are you talking about?"

"It's all over the news," barked the caller. "They found him in some motel room. Somebody stabbed him, and they think you did it." His brittle voice cracked. "Did you try to kill him?"

"He isn't dead?" Hope and fear warred for Jack's attention. *Kos is alive.*

"Haven't you been listening?" he shrieked. "He's alive, no thanks to you." He drew in a raspy breath. "Things are out of hand. This grudge of yours has gotta stop." He paused. "You're in way over your head."

Anger flared, and Jack gripped the phone tighter. "Don't tell me what to do." A deadly calm filled his voice. "Don't ever tell me what to do."

"Every cop in the state is looking for you, man," he reasoned, "you'll never get away with it."

"Let 'em look," he snarled. "They're not smart enough to catch me."

"So how did you end up in jail in Colorado?"

The man's sarcasm sent Jack's temper back up a notch. "That was Koslow's fault," he snapped. "And he paid for his mistake. Just like you will if you don't do what I say."

"You'll never get near her, Jack. She has a bodyguard now, and her brother's there, too. Both ex-military."

"Who gives a shit? They bleed like everyone else."

"Think about it, man. Cops are all over the place."

"I don't care," he snarled. "She owes me. I want her. And you damn well better help me get her, or you'll be the next one to pay."

Silence and heavy breathing lasted a long moment. "I don't get it. Why her?"

"She ruined my life," Jack shouted. "I'm living like a criminal because of her."

"She's a cop, dumbass."

A scornful laugh sealed his fate.

Nobody laughed at Jack Walls. Nobody.

"And you killed your girlfriend, Jack." He gave a quick disgusted snort. "And tried to kill her. Now Kos. Lord only knows who else. Why wouldn't she come after you?"

A deadly calm settled over Jack. *When this is over, you're a dead man.* "Lottie questioned me. So did Kos. People who question me don't live long."

"Yeah, well, Kos is still alive," he taunted. "He'll tell them everything."

Jack paused. He had a point. But, really, what difference did it make? That bitch already had him pegged for Lottie's death without even knowing how she forced his hand. And Kos, well, he got what he deserved, too. "Follow the plan," he ordered. "No changes."

The man gave a weary sigh. "I won't kill anybody, Jack. I mean it. And I'm done after this." He quickly ended the call.

"Yes," Jack whispered. "You are."

☍

Jess sat on the couch and continually pressed the channel selector button on the remote. Lucy dozed on her shoulder. "A gazillion channels to choose from," she muttered, "and nothing to watch." She finally clicked it off and tossed the device onto the end table. "I'm going stir crazy, Seth. I need something to do."

"It's only been a few days," Seth voiced from the kitchen. "Give it time."

Careful of the kitten, she rose and limped toward him as he put away the groceries. "You were hurt, too, and look at you." She waved in his direction. "You're sashaying around almost like new."

He put away the last of the provisions he'd bought and faced her. "Men don't sashay. And your injuries were more serious than mine."

"I'm so bored," she moaned. "I can't stand it."

He gently rubbed up and down her arms. "Patience, Texas. Patience."

Lucy tugged at Jess's hair, and he grinned. "Enjoy the downtime, babe. Read a book." His brow furrowed. "Do you have a hobby?"

"My work *is* my hobby." She burrowed into his embrace, enjoying their closeness. "There has to be something I can do."

"You can help me make dinner."

"Oh, that." She leaned back and faced him. "I forgot to tell you. Coach—Tony's friend is coming over and bringing goodies from the Chinese place downtown."

He followed her to the table. "What's his real name?"

"Luke Collins." Jess sat and placed Lucy on the floor. The kitten scurried over and inched up Seth's leg. "His nickname is Coach because he looks like a bigger, more handsome version of Jason Garret." She watched Seth's expression go from casual to focused in the blink of an eye. "They did a couple of tours together before he opted out. Now he lives here."

Seth glanced down at Lucy, who now hung onto his belt. "I'll talk to Tony."

"You're going to check him out?"

He gave her his best you've-got-to-be-kidding-me look.

"He works for Exide Security. He's been fully vetted."

He bent down and kissed the top of her head. "Not by me."

He hustled off down the hall. She assumed to find Tony, with Lucy dangling from his waistband like an accessory. Not long ago, his taking control would have raised her hackles big time, but now, she simply smiled. *He loves me.*

Spirits higher than before, she looked around the kitchen. "At least I can get dishes down." Before she could stand, her phone rang, and she answered without checking caller-ID. "Foster."

"It won't be long now, Detective."

CHAPTER TWENTY-SIX

WALLS' RASPY VOICE SKATED OVER HER SKIN LIKE SPIDERS. Instinct took over, and she quickly set her phone to record the call and put it on speakerphone. "Before what?" She steeled herself for the answer.

His breath wheezed when he inhaled. "You're going to die. And it won't be an easy death."

She needed an edge and forced a taunting laugh. "That a fact? Well, I hope you do a better job than you did on Koslow because, really, Jack. That was sloppy as hell."

His ragged breathing got louder. "He had it coming. Just like you."

She ignored the implied threat. "You screwed up, Jack. Again. You can't do anything right."

For a moment, the only sound on the line was rapid, harsh breathing. "You won't be so sassy when I'm finished with you."

She heard Seth enter the kitchen but kept her focus on the call. He sat across from her and launched rapid-fire texts.

"He's gonna make it, you know," goaded Jess. "He'll live to

testify against you. DA's gonna have a field day racking up charges." She kept a cheerful tone. "The death penalty is a slam dunk. And I can't wait."

A heavy silence followed. Her body trembled as images of Lottie's crime scene flashed through her mind. *He won't win. I won't let him win.*

"Whatever," hissed Jack at last. "You won't be around to gloat."

His guttural snarl made her skin crawl, but she switched gears and prodded again. "We know about the third man, Jack. And we know he's still around because you can't do anything on your own. It's just a matter of time before we get him, too. And then what, Jack? Who's gonna do your dirty work?"

Jack's silence said she struck a nerve, so she pressed the advantage. "You know, for someone who claims to be so fricking smart, Jack, you do some really stupid shit."

"Don't call me stupid," he sputtered.

She could almost see the spittle flying from his mouth, and it took monumental control to keep the fear freezing her body from showing in her voice. "Then stop doing stupid things. It's time to end this. Turn yourself in."

Labored breathing was the only sound on the line for several heartbeats.

"That's a wonderful idea, Detective," he whispered at last. "Why don't we end this?"

The line went dead.

Body trembling, she drew a ragged breath. Shoulders so tight, they hurt, she forced herself to relax.

Seth tugged the phone from her cramped fingers. "Are you all right?"

Silent, she licked parched lips and dipped her head.

"What the hell?"

Tony's sharp question made her jump. "You startled me."

"That was him, wasn't it? The killer you're after."

"Yeah." Seth kept his eyes on Jess. "It was him."

Tony joined them at the table. "Do you have to deal with this kind of crap a lot?"

She lifted one shoulder in a slight shrug. "Comes with the badge."

"Yeah, well, that sucks."

"Does for a fact."

When his phone rang, Tony stepped out to take the call.

"The trace?" asked Jess.

"No." Seth's frustration leached into his voice.

"I didn't think so." She heaved a sigh. "I did hope we'd get lucky, though."

"Tom can't put someone outside 24/7 right now. The best he can do is a couple of hours at a time." He covered her hands with his and squeezed. "Drake's gonna see if he can wrangle some help, too."

"I hate that I'm causing Tom more problems," she griped. "He's short-handed as it is."

"You'd be the first in line to cover if it were anyone else. And, besides, you're worth it." He changed the subject. "I talked to Tony about Coach. He likes him well enough and admires what he's doing for his friend's brother." His jaw tightened. "He also said the guy was hitting on you at the gas station."

"Yeah," she cooed. "It was kinda nice." She leaned forward and kissed him. "But I'm a one-man woman."

"Good." He cupped her face with both hands. "Because I'm a one-woman man."

The warmth of his lips took the ice from her body, and she leaned into the kiss.

"Sheesh, you two," complained Tony when he returned. "Get a room."

Seth grinned and sat back.

Tony grabbed a glass from the cabinet and filled it with water. "Coach is gonna be a little late. His relief is on baby watch, so he has to wait for a replacement." He sat down across from Jess. "Should be here around seven-thirty." He drank half the water before setting the glass down. "I told him we'd just gnaw on a bone till he got here."

"Are you all right, Weiner?" asked Jess. "You still look tired."

He drank the rest of his water. "I'm good. Jet lag hits me hard. Takes longer to go away than before."

She studied her brother a moment and changed the subject. "Well, we won't have to wait long. It's already a little after seven, so the time is fine." She got up and moved toward the cabinets. "I can set the table."

Seth stood, his face broadcasting the argument in his mind.

"Don't even," she snipped.

He sat down. "Yes, ma'am."

Tony yawned and spoke to Seth. "Sorry. I hope Chinese was okay with you."

"It's fine. I'm not picky."

Jess smiled to herself. He was more a steak and potatoes kind of guy, but he never complained if she had a taste for something different. Even if the place didn't serve beef, he'd still go along. In hindsight, she recognized many of his "giving-in" actions for what they were—acts of love. For her. *How could I have been so blind?*

She stacked everything on the table and returned to wash her hands. The window over the sink provided a glimpse into the restful backyard. A lot of time, energy, and hard work transformed the small space into her personal oasis of peace and tranquility. The fact she did it herself was an immense source of pride. Same with the interior.

She turned around and was pleased to see her brother and her lover chat like old friends. She could easily picture sharing meals with Seth at the table, making love in the bedroom, planning a future together.

And having Tony home again was icing on the cake of her life. For the first time ever, the future she craved was within her grasp.

She retrieved a pitcher of tea from the fridge and placed it on the table.

Seth stood and grabbed the glasses, then filled them with ice. He grinned at her when she scowled. "I have to feel useful."

Jess sat down, and Tony watched her. "Tell me about this man, Walls. What's his deal?"

She hesitated, not wanting to say anything that might cause him extra worry. "Just another creep who killed his girlfriend in a fit of rage."

Though his eyes clouded with concern, his gaze didn't waver. "And he has it in for you because…."

"Because she's a damn good cop," interjected Seth as he resumed his seat. "She knew he did it and won't rest until he's behind bars waiting for the needle."

"Aww," she murmured with a smile. "You say the sweetest things."

Tony snorted. "You two are made for each other."

"That we are." Seth tapped his glass against Jess's in a mock toast. "That we are."

When the doorbell rang a few minutes later, Tony stood. "I got it. Probably Coach."

She caught Seth's gaze. "Have I told you lately how much I love you?"

His smile made her happy heart sing.

"Not often enough."

She leaned toward him. "How shall I ever apologize for that?"

"I have some ideas."

Tony walked in, followed by Coach, carry-out sacks in both hands, two uniformed officers behind them. "They want to make sure you're okay with this." Tony grinned at Seth.

"We were making rounds," offered the first cop. "Saw him pull in the drive. Just making sure it's all right."

Jess spoke to the officers. "Evening, Parker. Johnson. Can I get y'all something? Water? Coffee?"

"We're good, Jess," replied Johnson. "Thanks, though."

She took a breath. "Thanks for being here."

"You'd do the same for us."

Coach's fair complexion turned bright pink as he surveyed the group and settled on the first officer. "What gives, Parker?"

"Just doing my job, Luke." The officer turned to Seth. "You okay with everything?"

"Yeah."

Parker nodded. "We can't stay long. We'll radio for another car when we leave, but it might not be right away. We're spread pretty thin."

Jess felt terrible. The team was already overworked. "I'm so sorry I'm adding to the problem, Parker."

"You'd do the same for us."

Seth moved toward the living room. "I'll walk you out."

Coach placed the bags on the table and looked at Jess. "Does this have something to do with your accident?" Before she could reply, he continued. "I saw what happened on the news."

"Just work stuff." Seth's tone ended the conversation.

After a moment, Coach began pulling items from the bags. "Tony said you liked it all, so I brought some of my favorites." He flashed a thousand-watt smile. "Hot and sour soup, spring rolls, fried rice, Kung Pao chicken, and Beef Stir Fry." Lastly, he drew out a smaller sack. "And, of course, fortune cookies."

Jess inhaled the aromas. "It smells wonderful."

Everyone sat, and containers were passed around the table. Jess grinned when Seth handed his cup of soup to her. The first time she coerced him into trying it, he barely swallowed one bite. He took small portions of the rice, chicken, and beef but passed on the chopsticks.

"Thanks again for doing this." Jess tasted the soup. "I love this stuff."

"Me, too." Coach picked up his container. "And you're more than welcome." He slurped the lukewarm contents, then used chopsticks to grab a bite of chicken. "Mason started working there a couple of months ago. Makes deliveries, helps out in the kitchen." He frowned around a mouthful of chicken. "He kinda hopped around from job to job for a while but really likes Chen, the owner. And he's teaching Mason to cook."

"What's his story?" asked Tony. "If you don't mind me asking."

Eyes focused on his food, he shrugged. "Smart kid but no direction. He job hopped a couple of years after high school, then finally enrolled in the local junior college, trying to decide what he wanted from life." He moved a slice of beef around on his plate. "Carter was all the family he had left. They were tight, so his death hit pretty hard." He shook his head. "I hoped the change in scenery would help...."

"How old is he?" asked Jess.

"Just turned twenty-three," answered Coach. "Though some days he acts like a teenager to me. And hates it when I call him a kid." He sat up a little straighter and watched her. "I see you still have the crutch. Any better?"

As one who didn't share much, she understood his reluctance to say more. But then, he and Tony were friends. She waved around her chopsticks. "Better every day."

He met her steady gaze, his dimpled expression no doubt perfected to entice interest. But today, she felt nothing. Seth ruined her for any other man.

Just like he promised.

"Maybe when you're well, we could grab dinner sometime? Or a movie?"

Seth's back stiffened, and she hastened to reply. "Sorry, but I'm seeing someone."

"Ahh. The beautiful ones usually are." Crystal blue eyes narrowed, but his smile never wavered. "Can't blame a guy for trying."

"I understand you and Tony served together." Seth's question came a little too fast, and his voice lacked any degree of warmth.

Jess chanced a quick side-eye. *Is he jealous or simply distrustful?*

"Two tours. Got out about three years ago."

"Why private security?"

"Good money," he replied around a mouthful of food. "And no sand."

Jess appeared to be the only one concerned with the grilling as Tony watched in silence, and Coach ate his food.

"Why Walker?"

This time, Coach stopped eating and met Seth's intense stare. "I made Carter a promise to look after his kid brother. Tiger talked about this place all the time, so we ended up here about a year ago. I wanted Mason out of Houston, and this seemed like a good place to start over." He took a breath. "I went to work for Exide two months after we arrived. Mason's still adjusting." He paused and glanced at Jess, then back to Seth. "And I'm smart enough to recognize a no-trespassing sign when I see it." He picked up his chopsticks. "Any more questions?"

Before Seth answered, his phone rang. "Hamilton." He listened a moment, expression unreadable. "Thanks, Baker. No, that's all. I appreciate the quick response." He ended the call and forked a slice of beef off Jess's plate.

"Can I assume I passed scrutiny?"

"For now."

Unfazed, Coach directed the conversation to Tony. "So, Tiger, how long you home?"

Somewhat strained at first, they soon relaxed in semi-friendly conversation as the newcomer entertained them with stories of his life in private security and tales of exploits shared with Tony.

Seth wore his detective-assessing-the-situation look the whole time. His only interaction was to pick something off her plate to nibble on, thereby painting the no-trespassing sign bright red.

And she loved it.

"My favorite time, though," laughed Coach as he pointed his chopsticks toward Tony, "was in Du Bai on our first tour." He chuckled. "Remember that?"

"What happened in Du Bai?" asked Jess when her brother didn't respond.

Face flushed; Tony scowled at his friend. "Nothing I want my little sister to hear about."

"Now I really wanna know," quipped Jess.

"And we need to talk about something else," objected Tony. He focused on Jess and took a deep breath. "I was gonna tell you later, but, well, I got the call earlier. It's official. I'm out in three months, two weeks, and four days."

She clapped her hands together. "I'm so happy for you, Tony."

Coach's eyes widened in surprise. "You're getting out?"

"Yeah. I've been thinking about it for a while. Time's right."

Seth reached across the table and shook Tony's hand. "Congratulations. Tell me if I can do anything to help."

"Thanks. I will."

Coach sat back in his chair. "Wow. That's great. What will you do? We can sure use help at Exide. I'd be glad to put in a word for you."

"Thanks, but I've already got something lined up." He fiddled with the spoon resting beside his half-eaten cup of soup. "I'm buying a garage here in town."

His friend beamed. "That's right up your alley, Tiger. I'm happy for you. We get to hang out again." He yawned and covered his mouth. "Excuse me."

A different ring tone had Seth glancing at his phone. "I have to take this." He got up and walked toward the living room.

"I can't believe you finally did it," uttered Coach. "I pegged you for a lifer."

"Yeah, well, things change."

"They do for a fact."

Seth returned and stopped beside her chair, his gaze flicking from Tony to their guest before landing on her. "He's awake." His voice radiated suppressed excitement. "I need to go."

Koslow.

She jumped from the chair and swayed when she stood too fast. "I'm going with you."

He caught her shoulders. "You had a concussion, and you're not ready yet," he stated firmly. "Please. Stay here with Tony." He nodded toward the front. "Parker and Johnson will be here a while yet."

She wanted to argue but suddenly felt more light-headed and sat back down. "I just got up too fast. I'm fine."

He squatted down in front of her. "I'll call you if I learn anything." His gaze skimmed between the two men.

"I got this, Seth." Tony tapped his chopstick on the table. "Don't worry."

Coach sighed and stood, bumping the table leg when he turned. He steadied it with one hand. "It's obvious your boyfriend isn't comfortable with me here without him, so I'll go." He turned to Jess. "It was nice seeing you again, Miss Foster." His smile lost some of its brilliance. "Guess I won't have to fake needing gas next time."

His comment surprised her, but she quickly recovered. "Please. Stay. He's a little overprotective, is all." She bent forward and placed a quick kiss on Seth's cheek. "And I love that about you, but really, he's Tony's friend."

Jaw tight, Coach shook his head. "It's okay, ma'am. Another time might be better." He yawned again and covered his mouth. "Sorry. Been pulling extra shifts lately, and I guess it's catching up with me." He reached for a fortune cookie. "Can't leave without this."

Tony stood and shook hands with him. "Thanks for coming by and for supper. Hopefully, we can meet up again before I head back."

"Sounds like a plan." He nodded toward Seth, and Tony followed him out.

Once out of earshot, Seth quipped. "I don't trust him."

"Do I detect a note of jealousy, Detective Hamilton?"

"Maybe." He brushed a quick kiss over her lips and stood. "I'm not sure how long it'll take, but you know the drill…Glock and phone with you at all times."

She got woozy when she rolled her eyes. "I'm not a rookie, Hammer, or helpless."

"No, but you are injured." His voice softened, and he caressed her cheek with his thumb. "And I care about you."

Her heart melted. "I know."

Tony returned and dropped into his chair.

"You okay, man?" asked Seth. "Your face is a little flushed."

"I'm fine."

Jess snickered. "Thinking about Du Bai?"

Silent, Tony waved his hand in dismissal.

Seth hesitated. "Sure you're okay?"

"Yeah, I'm fine." He straightened in his chair. "Jet lag. Go. I got things here."

"All right." He glanced down at Jess. "Back soon."

She watched him walk out and wondered why he moved so slow. She squinted because the thought made no sense. Did she take too many pain meds today? No, she only took one this morning. Or did she? She blinked and shook her head slightly. *That concussion is playing tricks on my mind.*

Head foggy, she focused on the cookies, bewildered when she had to reach twice before making contact, then awkwardly slid one toward Tony. She opened her mouth to speak but her tongue felt thick, and she had difficulty forming words. "'member for-ton lash time?" Even to her muddled brain, the words sounded slurred.

He swayed in his seat. "Yeah. 'Don' know fu-ture, here's cookie.'"

His voice sounded peculiar, like he spoke from a deep well. She wanted to ask what was wrong, but her mouth wouldn't cooperate. A new wave of dizziness made her stomach roll, and panic followed. "Sah-thin's 'rong."

"Wh-tha…"

Tony's body slid to one side, righted, then slid again. His features blurred, and she barely registered the crash of dishes on the floor as Tony vanished from view.

A strange noise from the back door pierced the fuzzy veil seconds before blackness swallowed her.

CHAPTER TWENTY-SEVEN

SETH HURRIED DOWN THE HALL TOWARD KOSLOW'S ROOM. Two uniformed police officers stood outside the door along with Drake.

"Did something happen?"

Drake shook his head. "The doctor's checking him over."

The door opened, and a tired-looking older gentleman in a white coat stepped out.

"How is he, Dr. Warren?" asked Drake.

"Critical but stable. He lost a lot of blood, and frankly, he's lucky to be alive."

"Can we talk to him?"

His gaze drifted from Drake to Seth. "Five minutes. No more."

"We just need a couple of questions answered." Seth barely contained his apprehension.

Dr. Warren shook his head. "I doubt you'll glean anything substantial out of him. He's heavily medicated." He gestured toward the woman behind him. "Nurse Austin will observe. If the patient shows any signs of distress, you are to leave at once. Understood?"

The men nodded in unison, and the doctor walked away.

Nurse Austin spoke to Drake as they entered the room. "I wondered if it was your case."

"Lucky me."

"It's good to see you again."

Seth watched the exchange with interest. There was a story there.

Turning his attention to the task at hand, Seth scanned the room. The rhythmic beep from a machine on the left side of the bed coincided with peaks and valleys on the small monitor while an IV bag fed liquid into his arm.

Seth tried without success to match the ashen-faced man in the bed to the photo of Koslow in the file.

The two men stepped closer to the bed, and Drake leaned down.

"Koslow? Can you hear me?"

The man's eyes shifted underneath closed lids, and his mouth opened slightly.

"Nod if you hear me," urged Drake.

A long moment passed before Koslow's head inched up and down.

Drake shook his head. "Doc's right. I don't think we'll get anything useful tonight."

"Try."

Drake bent lower. "Who did this, Koslow?"

The man's lips moved, but no sound came out.

"Was it Jack? Did he do it?"

Beeps from the machine increased in speed, and his chin raised. The nurse kept a watchful eye on both the device and her patient.

"The other man, Drake," urged Seth. "Who was the other man?"

Koslow's eyelids fluttered open then closed again as the beeps got faster. His mouth opened on a whisper.

"His name, Koslow?" Drake leaned closer, his voice vibrating with urgency.

The injured man moved his head slightly, exhaled a gentle breath, and lay still. The beeps from the machine slowed to a steady rhythm.

Nurse Austin stepped forward and checked the patient. "He's out. I'm surprised he lasted that long."

"How soon before we can talk to him again?" asked Seth, unable to keep the irritation from his voice.

Accustomed to such situations, she didn't react. "Tomorrow. Right now, he's dealing with the after-effects of the anesthesia plus the pain meds."

Drake smiled at her. "Thanks, Julie. Any chance he might wake up later tonight?"

"It's possible, but I doubt it." She gazed at Drake. "I'm on till seven in the morning. I could give you a call if he does."

His fingers tapped against the bed railing. "I'd appreciate that."

She glanced at Seth, and he dipped his head. "I'll wait outside."

While he waited for Drake, he confirmed with the officers that only hospital staff, he, and Drake were to enter.

When Drake came out a moment later, Seth raised a brow at him.

"A friend." He walked toward the elevators.

"We need to find out who the other man is," muttered Seth as he matched Drake's stride. "And if he's still around."

"I'm betting he's still here." Drake punched the down arrow.

"Why do you say that?"

The doors opened, and they stepped inside.

"Just a hunch. Koslow dropped everything and headed to Denver when Walls called. He's the one who rented the apartment there. After Walls' arrest, Koslow was his one phone call, and he rented the hotel room. We also believe Koslow is the one who sent the flowers to Jess. Which tells me Walls needs a minion."

"I see your point, but if that's the case, why try to kill him now? He still hasn't gotten to Jess."

The doors opened to the ground floor. They walked in silence through the busy lobby to the parking lot.

Drake picked up the conversation. "Based on Walls' background, I believe he got mad about something and just reacted."

Seth recalled Lottie's crime scene photos and shook his head. "He's unstable, and it doesn't take much to set him off, so I can see that being the case."

Drake stopped and faced him. "Tom doesn't have the manpower to put a full-time car on Jess's place."

"Yeah. I talked to him on the way over here. He had a car there when I left. They were to stay until I returned, or they got a call. I hated to leave but wanted to hear firsthand what Koslow had to say about where Jack might be hiding. Besides, I'm confident Tony can handle things. Especially if a unit is out front." His phone rang, and he glanced at caller-ID. "It's Tom." He swiped the screen to answer. "Hamilton."

Breath froze in his lungs, and his heartrate skyrocketed. "What? I'm on my way." He struggled to stay calm as he faced Drake. "Tony's hurt, and Jess is gone. I bet he has her."

♂♀

Fifteen minutes later, Seth arrived home with Drake right behind him. Official vehicles littered the area. Flashing red and blue lights created a kaleidoscope against the house. The absence of a coroner's van gave him hope.

Yellow crime scene tape circled the yard, and techs busied themselves dusting for fingerprints and looking for evidence. His white-knuckle grip on the steering wheel tightened even more. Air burst in and out of his lungs, and sweat peppered his brow. Adrenaline rushed through his veins like a tsunami making his head swim. "Please, God, let me find her in time."

He jumped from the car and rushed forward, Drake on his heels. They signed in with the officer overseeing the log and found Tom waiting by the porch.

"How bad is it? What did they find?"

Tom's stricken face told him more than words ever could.

Seth closed his eyes and inhaled deeply, forcing everything from his mind except doing whatever it took to get Jess back.

"What happened?" asked Drake. "Are we sure he has her?"

"We're still piecing things together." Tom's voice radiated weariness. "Johnson and Baker were first on the scene. Johnson found the man unconscious on the floor and called it in. ID said Tony Cantrell." He looked at Seth. "Ring any bells?"

"He's Jess's older brother. On leave from the Army."

"Is that his Honda over there?"

"No. Belongs to Jess's friend, Esther Scott."

"Short woman? Blonde?" asked Tom. "The one who's a computer whiz and does all that Ninja crap?"

"Yeah." He swallowed hard. "Is she okay?"

Tom sighed. "No sign of her yet."

"Okay if I check things out?" asked Drake.

"Go ahead," instructed Tom. "I need to talk to Seth."

His voice flat and monotone, Tom confirmed Seth's greatest fear.

"Signs of a struggle in the kitchen. Found some blood smeared on the door facing and more signs of a struggle outside."

A plaintive mewling sound came from behind a potted plant on the porch. Seth followed the noise and spied Lucy peeping around the pot, her anxious meow's loud and clear. "I need to get the kitten." He walked up the steps and scooped up the frightened feline. "Hey, girl," he cooed. "What are you doing out here?"

Lucy clung to his shoulder, nose pressed against his neck, her yowl noisy and insistent.

"Yeah, outside is a scary place, isn't it?" He walked back to Tom. "How's Tony? You said he was unconscious."

"In and out. Already on his way to Memorial." His boss rested both hands on his hips. "How well do you know him?"

"I just met him. Why?"

"He a user?"

"I don't think so." Seth thought back over the last few days. "No red flags. Why do you ask?"

"The cut on his cheek was minor." Tom gave his brow a tired swipe. "Probably from a piece of broken glass. No other visible injuries." He met Seth's gaze. "But he was out cold. Walk me through what happened before you left."

Seth took a steadying breath. "We were sitting around the table, talking, eating. Tony's friend, Luke Collins, was there. He picked up food from the Chinese place downtown."

"Who is Collins?"

"Army buddy of Tony's. I had Baker run a check earlier. He's clean. Works security for Exide. He left about the time I did." *Maybe I should have swallowed my pride and left him there with Jess, too. She'd be safe instead of missing.*

"I need to talk with him next. I'll have Parker get his info from Exide. Any other contact from Walls? Or anything unusual happen?"

"No other calls. Unless something happened after I left." A sudden thought made him look toward the house, then return his gaze to Tom. "You said Tony was out cold."

"That's right. We barely got a mumble out of him. They've already taken him to the hospital. What's on your mind?"

"After Tony walked Luke to the door, I noticed his face was flushed and asked if he was okay. Claimed it was jet lag." Another thought had him standing up straight. "Right before that, Jess stood up and got dizzy. I thought it was from the concussion." Heart hammering, he stared at Tom. "Check Tony for drugs. And the food. Check all the food for drugs."

Tom grabbed his phone. "Done."

Seth's mind raced, and he forced himself to think like a cop and not a man in love. Jess was gone, and there was no doubt in his mind Walls had her. But how did he manage it? He addressed the two officers who were first on the scene.

"I understand you've already spoken to Tom, but I need to hear it myself. Please. Walk me through what happened."

"Parker radioed when he and his partner left and asked for a unit to take their place." The first patrolman, Jed Baker, a ten-year veteran, answered. "They had a domestic call and had to leave. We were the closest unit."

"How long was she unprotected?"

Fear and guilt made his voice harsher than necessary, and the man flinched, but Seth didn't care. Nothing mattered except getting Jess back unharmed.

Seeming to understand the anger, he calmly continued his report. "We were about twenty minutes out when Parker called."

The second officer, Riley Johnson, a rookie from Austin, resumed the story. "Baker thought we should tell them we were outside, so I went up and rang the bell. When I got no reply, I knocked and called out." His face clouded with concern. "I noticed a light on near the back of the house and thought maybe they were outside. I told my partner I was going to check around back. When I rounded the corner, I saw the open door. I approached with caution and found a man lying on the floor. An overturned table and a couple of chairs were near the door, and some broken dishes scattered around." He swallowed hard. "My partner came up about then and immediately radioed it in."

Drake walked up, stripping latex gloves from his hands. "The back door was forced open. Signs of a struggle in the kitchen and around the back porch." He focused on Seth. "There was blood on the door facing, more on the porch railing." He inhaled then blew it out slowly as though to calm himself. "A section of fence on the north side appears to have been cut. Looks like he may have carried her out that way."

"What about Bitsy?" He shook his head. "Esther Scott, Jess's friend. That's her Honda out front."

"Nothing yet."

Rage and fear warred for Seth's attention, and he forced himself to remain calm. "Okay. He had to be watching the house and saw me and the patrol car leave." He took a deep breath and focused on the task at hand. "Parker's unit was only here a few minutes after I left. And there's roughly a twenty-minute gap before the next car got here." Heart sinking, he paused. "That's more than enough time."

"But what happened?" asked Riley, his face stricken. "The guy was out. She was hurt, so who did he fight with?"

"Could be Jess's friend, Esther," asserted Seth. "She's a fifth-degree blackbelt. If she happened in at the wrong time, she'd definitely try to kick ass." He turned to Drake. "I think they were drugged."

Drake pinned his stony gaze on Seth. "How?"

"The only thing that makes sense is the food."

"Did you all eat the same thing?"

He shook his head. "I'm not a fan of the meal choice. I nibbled on some stuff, then you called, and I left." He turned grief-stricken eyes on Drake. "I left her alone. And now he has her."

"What about the others?" asked Drake. "If it was the food, then it had to be something they all ate."

He struggled to remember. "I think they all had the soup. I don't care for it. I put mine in the fridge so Jess could have it later."

"Okay, we'll find it. In the meantime, I've got guys looking for a trail out back."

Seth pounded his fist against the hood of a nearby patrol car. "We don't know shit. Was it Walls or the unknown man? What he was driving or where the hell he might take her."

Drake's radio crackled, and everyone listened. "We found a female, hurt but alive."

Seth's heart jumped, and they all hurried for the location he gave.

"It's not Detective Foster, though," the voice continued.

"This property backs up to a new subdivision under construction," Drake stated as they ran. "Maybe a hundred yards or so from the fence."

They found a medic assessing an unconscious Esther. "How bad is it?" Seth asked.

"Hard to tell right now," the man replied. "Blow to the head probably knocked her out. Numerous bruises, cuts, and abrasions. Defensive wounds on her hands and arms. We need to get her to the hospital as soon as possible." He pushed Seth back, and they loaded Esther onto a gurney.

He watched in silence as they raced toward the waiting ambulance.

"We'll find her, Seth," declared Drake. "We will."

Seth's phone chimed with an incoming text. When he checked the message, his knees threatened to fold, and breath lodged in his throat.

She's mine now.

CHAPTER TWENTY-EIGHT

JACK GLARED AT THE UNCONSCIOUS WOMAN ON THE FLOOR, then back to the man. "What did you do?"

The man paced around in circles, light from the small battery-operated lantern resting on the single rickety table casting shadows on the walls. He stopped and faced Jack, rubbing the back of his neck with one hand. "You told me to get her, so I did." He paused, then resumed pacing. "I never should have gotten involved. I wish I'd never met Kos. Nothing has happened like he said it would. I should never have done any of this."

Jack barely contained his rage. He had no patience for whiners. "Stop bellyaching." He took a deep breath. "And you didn't follow the plan." It took massive control not to use the knife at his waist. "It wasn't supposed to happen until I was ready." He clenched his fist, anger more intense than anything he'd ever felt before, consumed him. "And I wanted her awake when she got here."

The harried man stopped pacing and rubbed his hands up and down his thighs, never making eye contact. "Yeah, well, your plan sucked." His voice cracked, and he glanced up. "I saw an opportunity and took it."

Jack suddenly noticed the cuts and scratches on his face. "She do that to you?" He salivated as he pictured her fighting back.

"No. Her damn cat. And then some chick showed up right before I hauled her out the back door. Pulled some Ninja shit on me. I almost didn't get away." The man stood a little straighter. "She can identify me, man. I'm done. I want my money so that I can get out of town."

Jack ignored the demand. "What did you give her?"

He hesitated. "Ketamine. Not a lot. It'll wear off in a couple of hours."

"And what do I do in the meantime?" An intelligent man would be afraid of the lethal tone in Jack's voice, but this guy didn't have a clue.

"That's your problem, man. She's here. I want my money."

Jack shoved him so hard he stumbled back against the wall, then grabbed him by the front of his shirt with both hands and lifted him off the floor. "Don't ever back-talk me. Ever."

"I was just supposed to drive the Jeep, man." His shaky voice rose an octave. "Kos promised me five grand to drive," he stammered. "I didn't want any part of the rest of this, and now I'm screwed. I want my money, and I'm out of here."

Jack snorted. Leave it to Kos to mess things up. Even if he had that kind of money, he wouldn't waste it on this useless excuse for a man.

No reason to tell him that just yet since Jack may need his help later. "You get paid when we're done."

The man twisted out of Jack's hold. "I told you. I'm done. That's it."

"You're done when I say you are," he snapped. "And not before." He nudged Jess with his foot. "Tie her hands and feet and secure her to that post." He passed him a length of rope and two long zip ties and chuckled. "Wouldn't want her to wake up and run off before the party starts."

The man didn't move, and Jack placed his hand near the knife at his belt. "You deaf?"

He mumbled under his breath and followed instructions.

ơひ

Angry voices leaked through the foggy veil of her mind, but Jess couldn't unravel the words. She urged her body to move but couldn't even open her eyes. Her mouth felt like she'd eaten cotton balls, and a headache pounded in her temples. Darkness snaked around the corners of her awareness as she struggled to make sense of what happened. Visions, scrambled and unclear, flashed in and out too fast to untangle, adding to the panic and causing her breath to hitch and her heart rate to soar. *Drugged. I've been drugged.*

Moments of clarity mingled with confusion. *Musty smell. Dark room. No. Eyes are closed.* Something crawled over her hand, but she couldn't brush it off. *Please don't be a rat.* She concentrated on opening her eyes but only managed a small slit. *Large room. Lantern on a table. Two men.* Mind racing, her eyes slid shut. *Oh God. What happened? Where am I?*

Someone, a man, judging by the whiff of *Old Spice* she smelled, lifted her shoulders and pulled her along a rough concrete floor. He propped her against a metal post of some kind and bound her hands and feet.

A voice, soft and gentle, whispered, "I'm so sorry, ma'am. I'm so sorry."

A rope circled her upper body and secured her against the post.

A moment before the darkness returned, the strange voice whispered, "There's a knife in your back pocket."

ơひ

Seth paced outside the exam room where the ER doctors examined both Tony and Bitsy.

"Only a few more minutes," reassured Drake. "And we can go in."

"I should have been there. I could have stopped it."

"Maybe, maybe not," countered Drake. "We still don't know what happened."

Before Seth could reply, a patrol officer stepped out of a room down the hall and walked toward him.

"Heard you were down here." The man extended his hand to Seth. "Eric Conner. I got your person of interest, Luke Collins, back in six."

Seth shook his hand and nodded toward the room he indicated. "What happened?"

"Blew through a stop sign and hit a parked car an hour ago. Said he's been working double shifts all week and must have fallen asleep. Luckily, he wasn't going fast, but airbags deployed on impact. Gave him a bloody nose, some bruises. Nothing serious."

Drake tensed. "Have they run a tox screen yet?"

He nodded. "Positive for Ketamine. Just enough to make him groggy." Conner paused. "But swears he didn't take anything." He shook his head. "I do part-time with Excide and have worked with him several times. Not sure what's going on, but he just doesn't strike me as a user at all."

"We'll be in to talk with him as soon as we're finished here," said Seth. "Thanks for letting me know."

"No problem." Conner turned and walked away.

Drake shook his head. "Has to—" His phone rang, and he glanced at the screen. "It's Perkins from the lab. Drake here. Are you sure? Okay. Keep checking the rest. Thanks." He ended the call and spoke to Seth. "Ketamine in the soup."

Seth checked his watch. "They'll be closing soon."

"I'll get someone over there to talk to them."

Seth waited until he finished phoning instructions to one of his men. "There were four containers."

"He checked all the soup cups first since it was a liquid and easier to mix in. He's going to check the rest but thinks that's where it came from."

"I passed on the soup," confirmed Seth. "But I ate some of the beef and chicken and suffered no symptoms. Granted, I didn't eat much, but if it contained anything, I would have likely felt something."

They both turned when the doctor pushed back the cloth curtain and stepped out.

"How are they?" asked Drake. "Can we talk to them now?"

"Ms. Scott is alert and oriented. Mr. Cantrell is awake but groggy." He scanned the charts in his hand. "Mr. Cantrell had a minor cut on his cheek and tested positive for Ketamine. Enough to put him to sleep but not enough to cause significant side effects. No other injuries. Ms. Scott's tox screen was clean. She suffered two bruised ribs, multiple cuts and scrapes on her torso, and considerable bruising consistent with a physical altercation. A hard blow to the head caused a slight concussion and knocked her out for a brief time." He closed the chart. "Mr. Cantrell will be dismissed tonight. We'll keep Ms. Scott overnight for observation, but I don't foresee any issues other than being extremely sore tomorrow."

"Thank you," said Seth.

He and Drake hurried into the room and stopped between the two beds.

Seth flinched when he saw the battered woman under the sheet, her petite form making her appear more child-like. A bruise discolored her left cheek, and two small white strips marked a cut over her left eye. The visible part of both arms sported dark blue splotches, and cuts and scrapes covered both hands.

Tony struggled to get off the bed. "Jess?"

Seth placed a hand on his arm and eased him back down. "Easy, big guy, easy."

"Jess. Did he get her?"

Seth swallowed hard. "Looks that way."

Tony sat up again, and Seth pressed him back down. "We need to know what happened."

Tony gently rolled his head side-to-side. "Don't know. After Coach left, I went back to the kitchen. Remember thinking jet lag was never this bad. I sat down and lights out." He took a deep breath. "Bits and pieces of things until I woke up here." His gaze swung from Seth to Drake. "Doc said I was drugged."

"Ketamine," offered Seth. "In the soup. You were already suffering from jet lag, so the drug may have hit you quicker."

His eyes closed then snapped open. "What about Coach? He had the soup, too."

Seth and Drake exchanged looks.

"He was in an accident about an hour ago," said Seth. "He's here. Not sure of his exact status, but he wasn't too severely injured. We're going to talk to him next."

He studied Seth. "You don't think he had something to do with this, do you?" Tony's face pulled into a deep scowl. "He wouldn't."

"It's too early in the investigation to make any assumptions," said Drake. "We don't have all the facts yet."

Seth glanced at Esther, who blinked multiple times as though trying to focus on him. "Hey, Bitsy. How are you doing?"

"I tried to stop him."

Her voice broke, and Seth moved to her side and gently placed a hand over hers. "Can you tell us what happened?"

"I really tried to stop him," she whimpered.

"Take your time." Seth gently squeezed her hand. "Stop who? What happened."

She closed her eyes and swallowed hard. "I called her cell, but she didn't answer. I was worried, so I drove over." She licked her lip, a tentative smile edging up one corner of her mouth. "Hoped I'd be interrupting something interesting." A quick intake of air produced a gasp of pain. "I knocked and rang the bell, but no one answered." Anguish filled each stumbling word. "The kitchen light was on, so I went around to the back." When she opened her eyes and gazed at Tony, tears trickled down her cheeks. "I thought you were dead."

"I'm okay, Ess," Tony whispered. "I'm okay.

"What happened next?" urged Drake. "What did you see?"

She swallowed again; tormented eyes still fixed on Tony. "You were on the floor, and Jess was slumped over the table. A guy was standing behind her, and it looked like he was trying to lift her." She moistened her lips again. "Your cat jumped on his head and clawed his face before he flung her across the room. Is she okay?"

"She's fine. Go on," pressed Seth.

"Things happened so fast." Her face scrunched up in a frown. "I yelled, and he kinda froze a moment. Then he came at me." She hissed when she took a breath.

"Take it slow, Bitsy." Seth tamped down the urge to rush her. "Then what?"

"Traded some punches. Nearly had him down, but he landed a blow on my head and rolled away." She paused, and more tears trickled down her cheeks. "He caught me in the side with a chair, and I went down. Couldn't breathe. He slung Jess over his shoulder and headed for the door."

"Did you recognize him?" asked Drake.

She shook her head. "No. Never saw him before."

Drake stepped around Seth and spoke to Esther. "Ms. Scott? Can you look at this picture, please?" He pulled Walls' photo up on his phone. "Is this the man who took her?"

She examined the image. "No. He was younger. Tall. Slender build, with longish, dark hair."

"What happened after he grabbed Jess?" urged Seth.

"I had trouble getting my breath. Used a chair to help me stand, then followed."

"You have a couple of bruised ribs." Drake's voice softened. "I'm surprised you could move at all."

Lips compressed, she winced and tried to take another breath. "Hurts like hell," she muttered. "I tripped or stumbled, not sure which, and fell down the back steps. I had trouble getting back up, but I couldn't let him get away." Her voice broke again. "Caught up to them on the other side of the fence. I yelled, and he dropped her. We traded more licks, though I wasn't at my best. I don't know what he hit me with. Maybe his fist, but it did the job. I was out." Tears flowed freely now. "I couldn't save her, Tony. I'm so sorry I couldn't save my best friend."

Seth didn't stop Tony as he stumbled from his bed to Esther's. He sat on the side and gently folded her in his arms. "It's okay, Ess. It's okay." He glared at Seth and Drake. "They'll find her and make that bastard pay."

CHAPTER TWENTY-NINE

SETH APPROACHED THE HOSPITAL BED WITH ANGRY STRIDES.
"What the hell?" muttered Coach as he waved a hand toward the door. "They just told me I tested positive for Special K." He took a deep breath. "I don't do drugs, man. Ever." He leaned back in the bed, face haggard. "Thank God no one was hurt." He shook his head. "A DUI will ruin me."

Seth didn't have time for his woes and got to the point. "You told Tony you'd be late getting off work. What time did you leave, and where did you go?"

Coach tensed, and his face pulled into a fierce scowl. Then he sighed and met Seth's glare. "My relief was late. I left the site at seven-twenty. Picked up the food and got escorted inside your place about seven-forty." He blew out a long breath. "You can verify all of that at the site and through the GPS on my car or my phone." He paused. "It's in my pants pocket." He scanned the small room. "Not sure where my belongings are but feel free to check." He relayed his passcode and sank back against the pillow.

Seth turned a page in his notebook. "Was the food ready when you arrived or did you have to wait?"

"It was ready."

Even though Coach was the most likely suspect right now, Seth doubted he deliberately drugged himself, then got behind the wheel. He may not like the man hitting on Jess, but his gut said Coach was a victim, too, not a perpetrator.

So, who the hell is responsible?

Baffled, he went back to his notes. "Do you eat there often?"

He shrugged. "Couple of times a week."

"Anyone have an issue with you?"

"Not that I know of. Why?"

"Are you familiar with any of the staff?"

"Couple of the wait staff and Chen, the owner, who handles the register. Mason works there, but I already told you that."

Drake stepped forward. "Who's Mason?"

"Mason Reynolds," said Coach. "He lives with me."

Drake's brow inched up.

"Not like that," snipped Coach. "His brother was a friend, and when he died, he asked me to look out for the kid."

A nurse walked in, and the conversation stopped. She placed a plastic bag on the side of Coach's bed near his hand. "Here are your clothes and personal belongings, Mr. Collins. Can you check to make sure nothing is missing?"

Coach shuffled the contents of the bag, then handed his phone to Seth. "Knock yourself out." While Seth opened the phone, Coach glared at Drake. "Will I be booked for DUI?"

"As soon as they are done with you here, you'll be taken into custody."

"I'm ruined."

Seth scrolled through the phone and stopped. His heart rate jumped, and excitement filtered through his voice when he held the phone toward Drake. "Take a look."

"What?" asked Coach. "What is it?"

Silent, Seth held the phone out for Coach to read the text on the screen.

Don't eat the soup.

ᘙᘖ

The sudden blast of a freight train horn as the line sped past jolted Jess from a dream-filled stupor. Her body protested movement as she straightened from a slumped position against the post. A low groan inched up her throat. Her shoulder throbbed, and a headache slammed against her temples. She forced herself to remain upright, then paused and cautiously opened her eyes. There were several windows on the right, all but one covered with graffiti-covered plywood. Feeble light from a streetlamp trickled past the broken covering of one window halfway up the wall, casting the area in muted grey shadows. A glance to the left revealed only darkness.

She was alone. For now.

After a gulp of musty air, she willed the cobwebs in her mind to disappear. The headache intensified to the point of nausea, and she swallowed hard to quell the urge. She leaned her head against the metal beam and closed her eyes. *Think, Jessica. Think.* Without question, she knew who was responsible. Jack. Which meant she must escape before he returned. "And how do you plan to do that?" she scolded. "You're tied to a post. You have no phone, no weapon...." *A knife in your pocket.* She froze as the thought flashed through her mind. *A knife? I don't carry a knife.* A memory? A drug-induced dream?

"No. I heard him." A quick test of the zip tie around her ankles and wrists revealed little wiggle room. She leaned forward and pulled at the rope around her chest, gritting her teeth against the pain in her injured shoulder. *Did it loosen?* She leaned back, then pushed forward again. *Yes! It moved.* Two more attempts to further relax the bonds failed, and she sat back, head pounding, energy depleted.

She cursed under her breath. "I won't give up." She braced against the post, then pressed her heels into the rough floor and pushed. Inch by agonizing inch, she worked her way up the bar until she stood on shaky legs. Shoulder throbbing, her knees threatened to fold, and she braced against the pole. She firmed her jaw and concentrated on her next move. "Okay, you're up. Now what, genius?" She took a breath. "I get free, that's what."

Fortified with new resolve, she ignored the pain in her shoulder and pulled against the rope. Time and again she tugged until, at last, it shifted to her waist. A few more yanks, a little shimmy, and it hit the floor. Unable to believe her semi-good fortune, she stared at the coiled length at her feet. Then she stepped away and took a moment to get her breath, leaning against the post to steady herself.

Thoughts of the knife filtered through her mind again. *Was it a dream or not?* She shifted until she touched her left pocket. Empty. She barely stifled a cry as the pain in her shoulder intensified when she reached for the right one. *Work through the pain, Jess. Get free, or Jack wins, and you die.*

She touched the right pocket. Yes! Something's there.

Once again, she tested the bonds around her wrists, wincing when the hard plastic cut into her skin. Not much play, but enough to maneuver, and since her palms faced outward, she managed to grip the knife.

Lack of circulation made her clumsy, and she feared dropping the only weapon she possessed. Forcing herself to move at a snail's pace, she finally gripped it securely. Weak with relief, she sagged against the post to regain her composure.

"You can do this, Jess. You can do this." Encouraged, she fingered the smooth, metal body and decided it was a switchblade about four inches long. Rather than risk dropping it, she left the blade in her pocket while she searched for the button to open. Once open, the knife wedged in her pocket. "Dammit," she muttered and gently worked to free the blade.

Cutting the plastic tie proved a challenge and took several long minutes and two nicks to her skin to accomplish. Shivers racked her body as the restraint fell away, and she quickly cut the one around her ankles.

Loud voices and the creak of a metal door opening sent a torrent of fear racing through her veins.

Oh, God. He's back.

She scanned the area and found no suitable hiding place on either side. Behind her, only darkness loomed. Gripping the knife tightly in one hand, she eased away from the post on shaky legs. Careful not to make any noise, she moved to the wall and slid deeper into the inky space. Gasps coming in rapid succession, she fought a wave of dizziness.

Slow, deep breaths, girl. Come on. You know what to do.

Step by step, she crept along the wall until an object stopped her progress. She halted to listen, then touched the surface. A desk? A table? *No, it's metal and cylinder-shaped.* She felt her way around the piece and found three more stacked side-by-side. Moving around them to the wall, she inched further into the void, stopping when another cylinder, this one lying on its side, blocked her way.

An angry shout punctured the darkness. "You imbecile. You let her escape."

Without hesitation, she dropped down and slithered inside the pipe.

CHAPTER THIRTY

JACK'S WHOLE BODY SHOOK WITH OUTRAGE. HOW COULD SHE be gone? His plans were ruined. He dropped the flashlight, bathing the darkened room in spots of light as it rolled across the floor. A guttural roar escaped as he grabbed the unsuspecting man by the shirt and slammed him against the nearest wall, his feet dangling inches off the floor, and used his body to hold him in place. "You had one job," he hissed. "One. Job." Jaw clenched so tight it hurt; he got in the man's face. "Tie the bitch up."

"I-I did," he stammered and pushed at the hands gripping his shirt. "Y-you saw me."

The terror in the man's eyes gave Jack a little thrill, and he pushed harder on his chest. "Then how did she get free?"

"I-I d-don't know." His feet flailed back and forth just inches off the floor. "I d-don't know."

Muscles quivering, Jack held him steady. He hated incompetence. With hindsight being twenty-twenty, it was a mistake to keep him around and think he could be manipulated like Kos. *I can't do anything about that now.* He glared at the man. "You don't know."

He loosened his grip until the man's feet touched the floor. "It's your job to know."

The man squirmed free, and Jack let him think he did so on his own. Like a cat playing with a mouse, it was his favorite part of the game.

"I don't have a fricking job," he shouted. "I never wanted to be a part of your stupid idea." He poked a finger in Jack's chest.

Rage-fueled adrenaline coursed through Jack's veins, and a red haze clouded his vision. His nostrils flared as he drew in rancid air. *He's gonna pay for that.*

"Kos was right. You're crazy." He poked Jack again. "You're bat shit crazy. Forget the money. I'm outta here."

A quick jab to the stomach bent the man over, and a second one dropped him to the floor in a wheezing heap. "Nobody," hissed Jack through clenched teeth as he booted him in the side. "Nobody pokes Jack Walls."

He curled into a ball as though that would help, but it only fueled the rage. Jack kicked and stomped him repeatedly until he tired. Panting from the effort, he put his hands on his knees and glared at the semi-conscious man. "I ought to kill you here and now." He pulled the gun from his belt, aimed, then paused. Only eight shots remained, and he might need them later. He stuffed the gun back in his belt and pulled his knife.

A scurrying noise made him grab the flashlight off the floor and scan the room. Two enormous rats darted out of the beam toward the back. He fingered the gun again. "Damn rats. I told Kos to get rid of them."

He turned back to the man who managed to snake toward the door. Annoyed, he grunted and kicked him again. "That's for messing up my plans."

He dismissed him from his mind and focused on the woman. She was here, and he'd find her.

ᓂ

"I'm waiting," snapped Seth.

"It has to be a joke," insisted Coach as he sat up straighter. "He likes to cook, and Chen lets him work in the kitchen. Today, he got to make the soup again." He rubbed his temples and blew out a long breath. "That's why I made sure I ordered it." He gave a lopsided grin. "The last time he made the stuff, he didn't do it right, and they had to toss it and start over, so I thought he was making a joke."

"A joke?" Anger and frustration leached into Seth's voice. Jess's life was on the line, and every second mattered.

"It has to be. I called him after I saw the text." Exhausted, Coach leaned back and sighed. "It went straight to voicemail." He looked at Seth, eyes glazed with worry. "Masons had a tough time since Carter's death. This job is the only one he's hung on to for more than a few weeks. When Chen said he could work in the kitchen, he was on cloud nine. Getting to make the soup again was important to him." He took a weary breath. "He was just making light of it."

"Have you spoken to him tonight?"

"No. But I need to call and let him know what happened. He should be getting home soon and will worry."

"What's his number?" asked Seth. "I'll call him."

He paused, then rattled off the number, and Seth made the call using Coach's phone. When it went to voicemail again, he passed the device to Coach. "Tell him to call A-SAP."

Collins left a terse message and ended the call. "What's going on, Hamilton? Is Mason in trouble?"

"How well do you two get along?" asked Drake.

"Fine. Why?"

"Have any arguments or disagreements lately?"

"No. What the hell is going on?" His angry voice edged up a notch.

"He have any reason to want to harm you?"

"What? No. Of course not." He sat up in the bed. "What's this all about?"

"Any idea where he might be right now?"

"No. He rarely goes out and has few friends." He switched his glare to Seth. "I may not be much, Hamilton, but I'm all he's got. What the hell's going on?"

Seth hesitated. "If there's something you're not telling me, Collins, now's the time." When Coach said nothing, he continued. "The soup contained Ketamine. If you didn't put it there, then Mason is the next likely choice."

"That's ridiculous." His face turned an angry shade of red. "Mason's an upright kid, and he would never do anything like that."

"You delivered the food, and Mason prepared it." He paused to let that sink in. "You, Tony, and Jess all ate the soup, and you and Tony ended up here." He waited for a beat. "And someone kidnapped Jess."

All color drained from Collins' face. His gaze flicked between the two men. "No. He couldn't. He wouldn't."

"Someone drugged the soup, and Mason warned you not to eat it. Now Jess is gone, kidnapped by a slender man with dark hair." By the time he reached the end of his speech, Seth leaned on the bed, and his hands fisted the top sheet. "And if either of you had anything to do with it, you will never see the light of day again."

Drake laid a firm hand on Seth's shoulder. "Easy."

Seth took a step back, but his gaze remained fixed on Collins.

He slowly shook his head. "I don't know what happened, Detective." His voice rippled with sorrow. "But I know Mason, and he would never be involved in something like this."

"He's involved," snapped Seth. "You know it, and I know it. The question is, how deep."

His jaw clenched and released twice before Coach spoke again. "I failed him. I promised Carter I'd look after his brother, and I failed him."

"What does he drive?" asked Drake. "I'll issue a BOLO."

Coach supplied the information, and Drake phoned it in.

"Where would he go?" Seth tapped his pen against the notebook. "Is there anyone he'd reach out to?"

Collins rubbed his forehead and squinted. "Not really. There was an older guy who used to come in and talk to him. They shared a similar family history and kind of bonded over that. I'm a bit fuzzy on stuff right now. He was gone for a while and recently came back. He asked Mason to ride with him to Colorado last week to deliver something or pick something up. I'm not sure. He was only gone overnight." He paused. "Now that I think about it, he's been nervous since he got back. Hasn't had much to say."

Seth glanced at Drake, cop radar pinging off the charts. "Who was he? Do you have a name?"

His face scrunched up, then relaxed. "I don't remember. It was unusual, though. Reminded me of a grocery store chain, but he called him something else."

"Grocery chain?" prompted Seth. "You mean like Walmart?"

"Not that one." He squinted at the ceiling and huffed out a frustrated breath. "Something like…shit. What was his name?"

Despite the overwhelming desire to shake the answer free, Seth didn't push.

Coach rubbed his temples, and his face wrinkled into a deep frown. "What the hell was his name?" Suddenly, his eyes widened, and he snapped his fingers three times in quick succession. "It was… it was… like, like Costco, you know, the chain store. But he called him something else. Cos, maybe?"

Adrenaline hit so fast, it made Seth dizzy. *Koslow. How did he get mixed up with him?* "Are you sure about that?" Seth managed to keep the rush of excitement from his voice. *The third man is Coach's ward?*

"Yeah. He said something about how Cos understood his loss." Despair filled his voice. "Like I didn't."

"Any idea where this Cos fellow lived?" Drake all but bounced from foot to foot. "Or who he worked for?"

He shook his head. "No. My mind is still a little fuzzy. I wanna say he was a janitor or something, but I wouldn't swear to it."

Finally. At last. A lead they could use. But Koslow was still out and of no use to them until tomorrow at the earliest.

Impatient, Seth glanced at his watch. "Harper's gonna be back soon to take you in for booking." For reasons he couldn't explain, he suddenly felt the need to comfort the man. "I'll do my best to bring him in unharmed."

Collins slowly nodded. "He's solid, Seth." His rough voice shook with emotion. "I don't know what's going on, but he's a good kid."

Before Seth could respond, Coach's phone rang.

He peeked at the screen. "It's Mason."

"Put it on speaker," ordered Seth.

"Keep him talking," added Drake as he pulled out his phone and punched in a number.

"Mason, where—."

A muffled sob escaped as Mason stammered, "So sorry…all my fault."

"What's your fault?"

"Didn't know…what he planned."

"Who, Mason? Who?"

Ragged breathing was the only sound coming through the phone.

"Mason? Can you hear me?"

"…yes."

Coach glanced at Seth then placed the phone face-down on the bed. "Something's wrong. He's hurt." He spoke into the phone again. "Mason? Are you all right? Where are you?"

"…mad…didn't…do like…he said."

Coach buried a fist in the covers. "Where are you?"

"Doonn…know."

"Shit," muttered Coach. "Are you hurt?"

"…yes…sorry, Coach. So stupid."

"Mason," Perspiration popped out on his brow, but Coach's voice remained calm. "Listen to me. Whatever happened, we'll work it out, all right? I'll help you. But you have to tell me where you are."

"…can't."

"Can't? You don't know where you are?"

"…s-sorry." A garbled breath hissed over the line.

Coach pounded his fist on the bed and pleaded. "Mason, please. Tell me where you are."

"…try to kill me."

"I won't let him hurt you again. Whatever's wrong, we'll work it out together."

"…too late." A muffled noise came across the line, then silence.

"Mason? Mason!" He jerked his gaze to Drake even as he redialed Mason's number. "Please tell me you got a trace."

"We got it. Northwest of the interstate, about six miles from here. Have a car en route." He paused, then added, "And an ambulance."

"Seth?" Coach's voice stopped them at the door. "You'll let me know as soon as you find him, right?"

"I will."

Officer Conner met them at the door. "Doc said another hour, and we should be able to take him downtown for booking."

Seth locked eyes with the officer. "He seems pretty groggy yet and might need to chill out here a bit longer."

Conner hesitated, then nodded. "Yeah, I can see he's still not himself, but I can't babysit him."

"I'll be responsible," said Seth. "He won't go anywhere. Will you?"

"No."

Conner nodded and walked off.

Once outside the room, Seth stopped. "He's had her over two hours, Drake." He slapped his notebook against his thigh. "And I made it possible."

"Blaming yourself won't help matters any."

"I feel so helpless." He punched his fist into his other hand. "I don't even know where to look." He stopped and glared at Drake. "We're running out of time. All these bits and pieces add up to squat. And now this kid. How the hell did he get involved?"

Drake's phone rang before he could reply.

Seth stopped pacing to listen.

"Drake. What? How bad? No. Let 'em transport A-SAP. We'll talk to him here." He ended the call and faced Seth. "Kid was unconscious. Took a beating. I'm surprised he managed to drive. Found him parked under that old railroad trestle near the golf course. Motor was still running."

Encouraged, Seth stood straighter. "Okay. Assuming Walls is responsible, he has to be in that area, right?"

Drake nodded. "Yeah. An abandoned industrial complex is out that way, along with several older empty buildings. I'll have teams start checking, but it will take some time to work through them." Hands fisted on his hips; he blew out a long breath. "We need to narrow down the prospects."

"Think it's worth a shot to talk to Koslow again?"

"No. Julie said earlier he'd be out till tomorrow."

"So, Mason's our only hope."

"Looks that way."

Heart filled with dread; Seth headed for the emergency entrance to wait.

Hang on, Tex. I'm coming.

CHAPTER THIRTY-ONE

JESS HELD HER BREATH AND LISTENED TO SOUNDS OF A SCUF-
fle bounce off the metal walls. Whoever Jack fought didn't appear to fight back.

The silence that followed was deafening. Total darkness at
this end of the building was disorienting, and Jess struggled not
to panic. *Just like in my dream.*

She clutched the knife tighter. *I should have grabbed the lantern.* She stopped when the sound of something, a chair perhaps,
being dragged across the floor filtered down. The beam of a flashlight danced across the area, and the small lantern flared to life.

"I know you're still here, Detective," Jack sneered. "There's
only one way out, and it's through this door. Just in case you
wondered."

He sighed, the sound sending chills up and down her spine.

"You have much to answer for, you know." He made a tsk-tsk
sound. "Your constant interference in my life was very annoying.
But, staying one step ahead of you was an enjoyable challenge.

You're a worthy adversary." He paused. "I rather hate for that part to end."

A rat crawled up her leg and across her butt. She clenched her jaw and didn't move. When it reached her arm, she flicked it through the opening. The creature scratched across the floor, the sound resonating in the room.

"How do you feel about rats, Detective? I don't care for them myself, but some people like them. Even have them as pets. I've seen some doozies in here." He gave a low whistle. "I saw one the other day the size of a small cat. And the buggers will eat anything. Dead or alive."

His evil snicker made her skin crawl.

"But I won't let them get to you. At least, not until I'm through."

The chair scraped again, and Jess flinched. *Is he coming this way?* She edged toward the opening and saw the flashlight's beam dancing like a strobe light around the room, revealing metal beams down the middle of the hollow space and bounced off an assortment of boxes, debris, and other objects scattered around.

"Come, come, Detective," coaxed Jack as he walked forward. "You're just delaying the inevitable. We could be having so much fun right now."

She moved backward through the end of the pipe, hoping his voice would cover any sound she made.

"I'm losing my patience," he hissed. "And you do not want that to happen."

She slithered through the pipe, belatedly wondering if she'd be able to get out. Relief flooded her as she inched through the opening and worked her way toward the wall as fast as she dared, feeling for anything that might provide cover or a weapon. A large cardboard box, the kind homeless people often used for shelter, blocked her way. She inched around and found the wall made a ninety-degree turn. Her heart sank. *Was it the back of the building? An internal office? Another room?*

The light skipped around the middle of the space as Jack ambled toward her. "It's only a matter of time," he snapped, then stopped when something rolled over the floor on the other side of the building. He swung the light toward the sound and changed direction. "Ahh…is that where you're hiding?"

She hurried along the wall, happy to discover a small boxed-in room, and reached the other side before Jack resumed his search.

"Damn rats," he mumbled and started forward again.

Jess crouched down and felt around on the floor. Pieces of metal mixed with assorted trash littered the floor, but nothing that would suffice as a weapon. Though she still had the knife, she'd have to be up close and personal to use it and preferred a little more distance from the man.

"Ah-ha," he cooed when his light found the office. "Maybe you're hiding from me in here."

He rushed forward, and Jess slinked along the wall. She heard him mutter but couldn't make out the words. He kicked something, a piece of wood maybe, and cursed again.

"You won't get away from me this time."

She heard him kick and throw things as he continued his fruitless search. No light came from the room, so there were no windows. She shimmied down the wall, kicking an unseen can that rolled across the floor. *Dammit!*

In his haste to investigate, Jack must have fallen because she heard him grunt, followed by a string of profanity before the light once again bounced around the open room.

She ducked behind another cardboard box as he approached. He was close enough she heard his heavy breathing and smelled the rank body odor emanating from him.

He swung the light over the area, stopping when it hit the box.

Her heart sank. It was over. There was no escape. She'd never again know the warmth of Seth's embrace or the thrill of his kisses. Her happily ever after dream died today. With her.

She stood and gripped the knife tighter as the box flew away and the light fixed on her. She blinked rapidly and looked to the side, away from the blinding light.

The gun in his hand didn't waver. "You didn't really think I let you get away, did you?"

I love you, Seth.

CHAPTER THIRTY-TWO

"**D**AMMIT ALL," THUNDERED SETH. "I NEED TO TALK TO HIM now."

Drake tugged him away from the exam room where hospital staff tended to Mason Reynolds. "Let them finish."

"We're wasting time, Drake. He knows where she is. I know he does."

"I've got teams combing the area now. If Jess is there, we'll find her."

"But we're walking blind. She could be miles away." Seth raked shaky fingers through his hair. "It's all my fault. I should never have left her alone."

Drake opened his mouth, and Seth held up his hand. "Don't. I promised to protect her, and I didn't."

Just then, the same doctor who treated Tony and Bitsy stepped into the hallway.

"How is he?" Seth's voice radiated urgency. "Can I talk to him?"

"He's barely conscious and in a lot of pain," said the doctor. "He has three broken ribs, multiple facial contusions, possible fractured wrist, and we've yet to rule out internal injuries." His weary gaze traveled between the two men. "But he's refusing treatment until he speaks to the police."

Seth moved toward the door, and the doctor grabbed his arm. "He needs further medical treatment, and surgery can't be ruled out. At the very least, he needs pain medication. He's injured and in great pain, so make it quick."

Seth nodded and rushed into the room. Mason's pain was the least of his concerns.

The pungent odor of antiseptic, blood, and urine hit him as he approached the bed where Mason lay. Two nurses stood on either side near his head. One monitored his vital signs, and the other watched him and Drake. Their mask-covered faces failed to conceal their scowl of disapproval.

"Make it quick," ordered the nurse who watched them. "He's hurt and needs attention."

"So does the woman he helped kidnap," barked Seth. "And handed over to a psychopath."

Her eyes widened, but she didn't reply.

He leaned closer. "Mason? Can you hear me?"

He turned his head toward Seth. One eye was swollen shut, and the other barely opened. "Pah-leesh?" Swollen lips corrupted his words.

"I'm Detective Hamilton, and this is Texas Ranger Sampson." That exceeded the limit of his patience. "Where is she, Mason? Where did you take her?"

"So sorry," he whimpered. "Din'nt want to."

Seth punched the bed. "Dammit! Where is she?"

The nurse stepped forward, and Drake grabbed his arm. "I'll handle this."

Seth started to object, then stepped back, hands fisted at his sides as he struggled to breathe. Seconds counted. Jess needed him. Now. He paced in circles, a helpless rage building inside.

"Mason? I'm Ranger Sampson. Can you hear me?"

"Yes."

"Did you take Miss Foster? Did you take her to Jack?"

He whimpered again. "Yes. Din'nt wan to. Made me."

"I get that, Mason. I do. You didn't want any part of it."

"Gave her knife."

"You gave Miss Foster a knife?"

His undamaged eye closed, and he nodded.

"That's good, Mason," encouraged Drake. "I'm glad you did that."

Seth stepped closer to the bed. This was taking too long. He needed answers now. "Listen, asshole—"

Drake pushed him back, the fierce glare on his face a warning not to be ignored before he turned back to Mason, his voice firm. "Where is she, Mason? Where did you take her?"

Mason struggled to get a breath, and the nurse stepped forward.

"Not yet," snapped Drake.

"He can barely breathe," she argued.

Seth scrubbed his face with both hands. "If he doesn't tell us what we need to know," his voice rose higher with each word. "The woman I love is going to die tonight."

"Mason?" prodded Drake. "You asked for the police, and we're here. I know you're in pain and need help, but so does Miss Foster. If we don't find her soon, you know Jack will hurt her." He paused and tried again. "Where did you take her? Was it near where we found you?"

His head rolled side to side. "No." He fixed his unswollen eye on Drake. "Old... warehouse."

"Which one, Mason? There are several in that area."

His face squeezed up, and he swallowed. "Boo."

"Boo?" Dark brows drew together across his forehead. "Boo? Do you mean blue? Is the building blue?"

His eye closed, and he didn't reply.

"Mason? Is the building blue?"

"...not boo."

Seth stopped pacing and glared. "What the hell is he talking about?"

"I don't know." Drake studied the injured man. "Mason? Is the building blue?

He didn't answer, and Drake tried again. "Mason? Can you hear me?"

Nothing.

He focused on the nurse monitoring his vital signs, and she shook her head. "He's passed out again."

Frustration mounted, and Seth wanted to hit something. Anything. "I'll never find her in time." Anguish tore at his soul. He was going to lose her.

"We'll just have to look for any warehouse with blue on it," said Drake as he pulled out his phone. "At least it's something."

"Detective?"

Seth turned to the first nurse.

"I don't know if this will help or not, but my grandfather worked at this sheet metal place back in the day. It's on old Acme Road about five miles from here." She glanced at Mason then back to Seth. "It was called Blue Steel Sheet Metal."

The hair on the nape of his neck tingled as a whisper floated through his mind.

I love you, Seth.

☙

Jess didn't waste time considering options since she only had two: escape or die. She braced her feet.

He stood three feet away; the Berretta pointed at her chest. "Finally, Detective. The party is about to start." He motioned with the gun. "Move."

His posture said he had the upper hand, so her attack caught him by surprise. She lunged at him with the razor-sharp knife extended and sliced it across his chest.

Surprise and fury filled his voice. "You bitch."

Momentum carried her into him, and the impact sent the flashlight to the floor as he staggered backward. His flailing arm hit the knife, and it clattered to the floor.

"I'll kill you!"

He swung wildly, and the butt of the gun skimmed the side of her temple. They tumbled to the floor, and his head banged against the concrete. She rolled away and something on the floor sliced into her thigh.

The flashlight lay against the corner of the office wall, offering minimal illumination. She didn't waste time looking for the knife. She must get away. A piece of curved metal about five inches long rested near her hand, and she grabbed that and stood. Before she took a step, Jack grabbed her foot and pulled. She barely had time to brace for the fall.

"I'll kill you," he shouted.

She kicked at his hands, then twisted and kicked at his face, but he didn't let go.

Suddenly, he rolled to his knees and sprang forward. She twisted, and he pinned her arm underneath her when he landed on top, his forearm across her throat. "I'm going to enjoy killing you the most." The blade of a knife gleamed in the dim light. "I'll cut you into so many pieces they'll never find them all."

All the air left her lungs.

"What's the matter, Detective? Cat got your tongue. Or maybe you're only a smart ass when you think you're in control."

Jess never knew fear, genuine fear, until this moment. The fanatical gleam in his eyes told her he spoke the truth. He would kill her slowly. And enjoy every minute of it.

But she would not go down without a fight.

Her body went limp beneath him. "You're so dramatic, Jack," she taunted.

"Shut up."

"Lottie said you talked big, but when it came to action, well, she wasn't impressed."

The tip of the knife pushed against her cheek, and his elbow dug into her throat. "I think I'll start with your face." He slid the point downward, and a trickle of blood followed its path. "Women hate having their faces disfigured. Even dead ones."

His sinister chuckle sent a chill through her. The weight of his body, coupled with the elbow at her throat, made each breath a challenge.

"What? Giving up already? I'm so disappointed. I expected more of a fight from you."

"Works for me."

Suddenly, she bucked upward and sliced his face with the metal fragment. Off-balance, he fell to the side, one hand pressed to his cheek, screaming obscenities.

She stood, grabbed the flashlight, and limped forward only to trip and land on her bad knee. Pain exploded and sucked air from her lungs.

Momentarily stunned, Jack surprised her when he plowed into her side and they went down.

He ducked when she swung the flashlight at his head and easily pinned her arm between them, the light wedged under his chin creating a horrifying vision.

He snarled and raised the gun. "I've had it with you, bitch. Now you die."

CHAPTER THIRTY-THREE

Siren's blaring, Seth weaved in out of traffic at break-neck speed while Drake maintained contact with officers at the location. The ten-minute drive to Blue Steel seemed like hours. "Do they have a visual yet?"

"No," answered Drake. "But they heard sounds of a struggle and are about to make entrance…almost there."

Three minutes later, they were parked and out of the car, rushing toward the front of the building.

Seth's heart stopped when a single gunshot rang out. "No," he roared and ran faster.

The officer covering the door didn't look away.

"Who fired?" Seth was afraid of the answer.

"Rollins," said the officer. "Waiting for an all-clear."

Just then, a deep voice sounded from inside. "Clear."

Seth pushed him aside and rushed forward, his eyes scanning the room, locking on a Maglite's beam thirty feet away.

Jess lay on her back, panting, arms outstretched. Blood covered her face and upper body. Fear and panic seized him as he dropped to her side. "Jess? Babe? Speak to me. How bad are you hurt?"

"Seth?"

"I'm here, Tex. I'm here." He pushed the hair away from her face and lightly fingered the cut on her cheek. "Where are you hit?"

"Not hit."

He raked his hands over her blood-coated body, looking for the source. "Where the hell is all this coming from?" He couldn't keep the fear from his voice.

"Not mine."

His hands stopped searching, and his racing heart slowed.

"Knife in my pocket. Used it on him."

The steel around his chest disappeared, and he drew a deep breath. "That's my girl." He smiled and stroked her face again, unable to believe they reached her in time. "Are you sure you're okay?"

She cupped his face with one hand. "I'm okay, Seth. Really. I am."

He gently pulled her to him. "Oh God, Jess. I'm so sorry. I should never have left you alone."

"He would have found a way sooner or later."

"Maybe." Weak with relief, he held her tighter, her cheek resting against his hammering heart. "God, I love you, Jess." Rocking her back and forth, he whispered. "I thought I'd lost you."

She nestled against him and inhaled deeply. "I love you more." After a moment, she craned her face up to him. "How did you find me?"

"We'll talk about it later. Right now, I just want to hold you."

"Works for me."

Drake walked up, and she turned to him. "Is he dead?"

"Yeah." He nodded toward the officer still standing over Walls' body. "Rollins was a Marine sniper. He doesn't miss."

"I'm glad," said Jess. "Though I would have loved to see him get the needle."

Drake's expression didn't change. "EMTs need to check you over. I'll get a statement later."

"Okay."

Seth never left her side while the medics went to work.

Her wounds were superficial, but they suggested evaluation at the hospital because of her previous injuries. Jess, however, insisted on going home, and they agreed after securing Seth's promise to have her examined by a doctor tomorrow.

Once she gave her statement to Drake, Seth helped her to the car. Inside, he buckled her in and got behind the wheel.

She reached for his hand and smiled. "I never did get to try that dessert you made."

"Whenever you feel up to eating, I'll bring it to you."

"I think I like being waited on."

He brought her fingers to his lips and kissed them. "Good. Cause I like doing the waiting on."

Her eyes shimmered in the flashing lights of the crime scene. "I love you, Seth."

His heart thumped. "I love you more."

She sighed and closed her eyes as he started the car. Before the turn onto the highway, she murmured, "A dolphin sleeps with his eyes open."

It took him several heartbeats to respond. "Camels have three eyelids."

"Madame Curie's notebooks are still radioactive."

"Black widow spiders eat their mate during sex."

She chuckled. "Be glad you're not a spider."

He held her hand all the way home, afraid to let go. The thought of how close he came to losing her made the blood freeze in his veins. She was his world, and life without her meant nothing.

But what if she can't work through the emotional baggage deposited by her family and trust our love?

He glanced at her from the corner of his eye. Her head rested on the back of the seat, and her eyes were closed.

Beautiful, vulnerable, and worth the risk to find out.

∞

Jess and Esther sat side-by-side on the couch, a blanket over their laps. Each sported bandages and bruises, but they were alive.

"So, how is it between you and Tony?" asked Jess. "Y'all have been attached at the hip since we got home."

Ess picked at lint on the blanket. "I'm hopeful." One shoulder lifted in a slight shrug. "Long-distance romances rarely work out, but…he's going to be home soon. So…" Voice steady and low, she faced Jess. "I'm not letting go this time."

"I'd jump up and down if I could," gushed Jess as she took Esther's hand and squeezed. "I'm thrilled for you both."

Esther smiled and changed the subject. "I'm glad you didn't take that job with the feds. So not for you."

Jess sighed. "It seemed like a good idea at the time, but yeah. I'm glad, too."

Esther leaned her head on Jess's shoulder as Seth and Tony entered from the kitchen. "I'd say we are two very lucky women."

"Absolutely."

"I think we're the lucky ones," said Seth as he perched on the arm of the couch and pressed a kiss to the top of Jess's head.

He couldn't seem to be near and not touch her in some fashion. He tended to hover and ask if she needed anything, but even that didn't bother her because she truly knew what it meant to be cherished.

She leaned against him and sighed. The danger was over, and everyone was safe. Her brother and her best friend may finally get together. Could life be any sweeter?

"How are Coach and Mason?" asked Esther. "Are they still in the hospital?"

"Mason is. They thought his spleen ruptured, but it's just badly bruised. He'll be fine."

"What's going to happen to him?" Jess tilted her head to face Seth. "Mason, I mean. He did help me get away. Sort of."

"It's up to the DA. If Jack were still alive, he could turn state's evidence and maybe work out a plea bargain."

"What about testifying against Koslow?"

"Like I said, up to the DA, but I think they'll work something out."

"And the DUI against Coach? Think it will stand?"

"I don't know. We'll see." He shifted on the couch and took her hand in his. "I don't want to talk about them right now."

She blinked and stared. "Oh. Okay."

"I thought I'd lost you, Tex. Those hours of not knowing…"

She pressed a finger to his lips. "Shh. It's over. He's gone, and I'm safe."

He took her hand and pressed it to his lips. "You're my world, Texas. I love you. I'm nothing without you."

Happy tears filled her eyes. "Oh, Seth. I—."

"I'm not done."

The intensity of his expression robbed her of speech.

"I never want to wake up without you by my side." He paused. "I don't have a ring…all I have is my heart and my love, which I give to you."

Her heart stampeded, and she swallowed hard. "Are you…"

"How do you feel about a beach honeymoon?"

EPILOGUE

Three days later

SUNSET PAINTED THE WESTERN SKY WITH BREATHTAKING shades of orange, blue and red as Jess eyed the lush backyard now filled with colorful baskets, greenery and twinkling lights. Friends and family stood in groups or sat at dining tables covered in white cloths and colorful spring flower centerpieces. The delicate scent of roses and snapdragons wafted by on the evening breeze linking the gathering to the joy of the celebration. White tulle draped the gazebo, and beautiful arrangements of yellow and white roses accented the arches. The table underneath became a cloth-draped altar, complete with a unity candle. Flickering torches and clear sparkling lights added a soft, romantic glow to the scene.

Tony managed a short leave extension and was there to escort Jess down the torch-lit walkway. Her knee was still sore, but she refused to use a crutch at her wedding and limped through the pain toward her future.

The ceremony was simple but heartfelt. Tears of joy sprang to their eyes as the flame of the unity candle joined them as one.

And then the celebration began.

Since she didn't want to wait for Tony's release from the Army to get married, his extension only left three days to arrange the event. Thanks to Seth's family, though, everything went off without a hitch. The final effect was more beautiful than she could have ever imagined, and Jess would be forever grateful to them.

When she commented last night about their willingness to plan a wedding with no notice, he shocked her with his reply. "I told them a month ago you were the one for me, and I just needed time to convince you we were meant to be together." He had laughed before pulling her tight against him. "I think Mother started planning things then."

A month ago—about the same time I decided I wanted more than friendship from him.

His mother and sisters took care of everything from minister to flowers to food, even her simple ivory gown. They arrived early this morning and spent the day ensuring everything was perfect for a sunset wedding. Their efforts would always hold a special place in her heart.

Her mother and sister arrived in time to make a grand entrance.

The warmth and acceptance from Seth's family more than made up for what her own were incapable of providing.

Jess finally accepted the fact that Ivy would never change. Insecure and self-centered, she needed constant attention to function. Later, she would find a way to make things work with her mother, but today belonged only to Jess, and she refused to let anything negative spoil it.

Fading sunlight glinted off the modest ring around her finger, and tears of joy clogged her throat. Seth wanted her to have something more elaborate, but she opted for a simple band of gold symbolizing their unbroken circle of love for each other.

Surrounded by well-wishers, she sat at a table near the porch and scanned the yard. Her mother and sister stood at the head of the food table, happily explaining the variety of fare Seth and his family provided, while his sisters smiled and passed out slices of wedding cake.

Esther and Tony sat at a table off to the side, heads close together as though in deep conversation. Maybe Bitsy catching the bouquet was a good omen for them.

Seth's parents stood arm in arm near the pavilion. Mrs. Hamilton held a glass of champagne in her hand, a look of such joy on her face it made Jess's breath catch.

She caught Jess staring and smiled, a warm, genuine smile that touched her like an embrace, then lifted her glass in a silent tribute.

Jess smiled back and nodded before movement caught her eye, and she saw Lucy dart up the steps back through the open kitchen door. The loveable feline was never far away from them and even rested on Seth's shoulder during the ceremony. When it came time for the kiss, Lucy moved to Jess's shoulder, much to the delight of everyone present.

She couldn't stop smiling as she sipped champagne. For the first time in her life, she was blissfully happy and fully alive.

Coach handled the music table and announced it was time for the bride and groom's first dance.

As the opening notes of Rod Stewarts *Have I Told You Lately* filled the air, she found Seth standing with Drake and two other Rangers a few feet away. Their gazes met, and his sparkling brown eyes glowed with love. His smile, intimate as a kiss, was captivating. Her pulse quickened in anticipation when he handed Drake his glass and moved toward her. No shadows clouded her mind as she cherished this moment. Everything she ever wanted or needed reached for her hand.

The world around them faded away as she rose and touched her happily ever after.

THE END

UNVEILING BEULAH

CHAPTER ONE

East Texas, Late February 1879

RAIN-SLEET MIXTURE PELTED THE GRIME-COATED WINDOW of the train car, leaving a trail of muddy streaks puddled at the bottom. Beulah Mae Lockhart considered this less-than-auspicious welcome to Texas a good omen. Start bad end well was her philosophy. At least, she tried to make it so.

She pulled the oft folded piece of paper from her handbag and smoothed it over her lap. A newly awakened sense of strength bolstered her spirits, and her body vibrated with new life as she reread it. *I, Frank Barker, owner of Bakersville General Store, Bakersville, Texas, do hereby sell said business, building, and all contents to B.M. Lockhart of New York City. Sale includes the inventory listed below, the house located behind the store, and any items left behind.*

Bea scanned the list already committed to memory, which was nothing like the items stocked by her father's upscale mercantile in New York. Basic frontier supplies: farm tools, flour, sugar, lard, seed. No silk or satin. No crystal or silver service. Nothing extravagant. Nothing special.

But it was hers. And one day, it would be special.

She returned the treasured document to her bag and shivered as frigid air seeped around the edge of the window. The heavy wool coat was no match for the deep chill ingrained into the wooden floor that leached into her feet despite her leather boots and thick stockings. *Only another hour or so. I can stand it that long.*

A woman seated across the aisle ducked her head when Bea

caught her staring at the jagged scar on her right cheek. Bea didn't bother to adjust the hat's veil to cover it. She refused to hide anymore. People would accept her as is, disfigurement and all, or they could go to, well, they could go away and leave her be.

Bea sat up straighter and addressed the woman. "Are you from Bakersville?"

Startled, the woman flinched and looked at the scar again rather than meeting Bea's gaze. "Um, yes. We live in town." She shifted in the seat, eyes finally making contact. "I've not seen you around before."

"I recently purchased some property there."

The woman's eyes lit up. "I'm Eunice Martin. My Jeb runs the post office and telegraph. The only thing I know for sale around here is the mercantile, but I heard someone named B.M. Lockhart from New York bought it. Is that your husband?"

Bea countered the question with one of her own. "How long have you lived there?"

The look of disappointment on her companion's face was so acute, Bea almost felt sorry for her.

"About six years." The woman cocked her head to one side. "You're not from around here, are you?"

"New York."

Mrs. Martin's eyes lingered over the scar, and Bea struggled to stifle the angry retort hovering on the tip of her tongue. She refused to explain it to anyone, especially someone so noticeably rude. "I understand there is a rather nice hotel in town."

"There is." She blustered and sat up straighter, gloved hands clasped over an expansive waistline. One bushy brow arched upward. "If you don't mind associating with…well, her kind."

Bea's protective instinct kicked in with a vengeance. A victim of unwarranted bias because of the scar, she had no tolerance for discrimination or prejudice. "And just what kind is that, Mrs. Martin?" She made no effort to temper the iciness in her voice.

Seemingly unaware of Bea's disapproval, the woman's face became infused with what appeared to be misguided happiness.

"She's not married." She leaned forward, and her voice dropped though no other passengers were close enough to hear. "And has a child." She straightened and sucked in a self-righteous breath. "And you know what that means."

It took Bea a moment to regain her composure. "No, I don't know." Before the nasty woman could say more, she cut her off. "And neither do you."

Mrs. Martin sputtered and sat back in the seat, blinking rapidly. "I'm merely trying to help."

"Are you now? By implying the owner of the hotel is somehow unworthy of my patronage simply because she has a child?"

"She doesn't have a husband," snapped Mrs. Martin, "and no one knows why."

"Meaning *you* don't know, and for that reason alone, you supposed the worst-case scenario." Bea sat up straighter. "I do not listen to gossip and prefer to evaluate people based on how they treat me. And others." With that stiff reprimand, she turned and looked out the window, effectively ending the conversation.

Unfairly shunned by her family and society as well, Bea quickly related to the unknown woman's plight. Ever since the accident when Bea was thirteen, she stoically endured her mother's declaration that the scar somehow made her unworthy of love or even affection. Tutors and other household staff tried to fill the emotional void caused by her parents' coldness.

But, thanks to her grandmother's steadfast love and support, Bea managed to grow up relatively well-adjusted but painfully shy. Her sudden death eight years ago left Bea inconsolable for weeks.

Until that surprise visit from Granny's lawyer. The sizeable and unexpected inheritance provided a much-needed boost of self-confidence and initiated a series of long-overdue changes. The first one being her refusal to relinquish control of the money to her father, who believed women in general, were ill-suited for such things.

Thanks to the guidance and support of her late grandmother's lawyer and banker, Bea discovered she possessed a shrewd head for business. Using her beloved grandmother as inspiration, Bea began to consider a future away from New York and her parents.

Still, after years of being told she was somehow defective, it took time to gain the confidence to not only venture outside the home but convince her father to teach her how to run his fashionable mercantile, albeit from the back rooms. The only reason he relented was her mother's declaration that since Bea was completely unmarriageable, "She may as well make herself useful." Under Bea's leadership, Lockhart's quickly became *the* place for the social elite to purchase whatever the most current rage happened to be.

Until disaster struck in the form of one Edmund Wilshire Abernathy III. Surprised and flattered by the handsome aristocrat's attention, Bea fell hard and fast. Three months later, they became engaged.

Even now, her face burned with shame as she recalled the debacle. *One would think a woman thirty years of age would be smart enough to see past the smooth-talking Englishman to the scoundrel lurking beneath the surface.*

Thankfully, Bea ignored her mother's insistence she grant Edmond control of her finances before they married. Otherwise, he would have likely squandered it all on his worthless schemes before his real character became known. Some of her parents' friends and her father were not so lucky.

Image was everything to her parents, and the subsequent scandal rocked their world. They placed full blame on Bea for the debacle, despite the fact it was her father who brought Edmond into their home and encouraged their relationship and subsequent engagement.

That disastrous event set her feet on the path she now trod.

She wasn't surprised when her parents' first concern upon hearing of her plan to leave was if she intended to replace the money Edmond swindled from them.

She suffered no qualms in refusing their request.

The screech of the train's whistle interrupted her musings. She stiffened her back and inhaled. *The past is gone. My future starts today.*

The steam engine's dirty window and swirling smoke obscured her view as the train rolled to a stop.

She allowed herself only a moment's hesitation before rising to meet her future.

"Can I help you, Miss?"

Bea turned to the gruff voice behind the counter to her right.

An older gentleman, reed thin and slightly stooped, squinted at her with faded blue eyes. A thick wool overcoat hung on his wiry frame, and a scraggly beard covered a weathered face.

"I'm looking for the station manager or someone who can assist me."

"Well, depending on what you need, I reckon that'd be me."

She took a step toward him and deliberately let the veil slip to show the scar.

His gaze never wavered.

"Name's Silas Upton, ma'am. How can I help you?"

She stepped closer and turned her head to inspect the small space. "Mr. Upton, I wonder if I might temporarily store my things here. Or is there someplace else I should take them?"

"How much stuff you talking about?"

"A couple of large trunks and some boxes."

"How long is temporary?" His toothy grin was charming.

She returned the smile. "Just until I get set up in town. Shouldn't be more than a couple of days."

His finger made a raspy sound as it raked against his bearded cheek. "I reckon that'd be all right."

"Perhaps you could see that the smaller trunk is taken to the hotel." She paused, and one gloved finger tapped her chin. "Or maybe I should check to see if they have a room first."

"Miss Lizzie will have room. Ain't nothing going on this time of year. I'll get it sent over for you. What name do I give her?"

"Bea Lockhart, please. And thank you for your assistance, Mr. Upton." She turned for the door and stopped. "Oh, can you direct me to the general store, please?"

"Turn right and go down past Doc Morton's office. The store will be on the other side of the road across from The Hanging Tree."

"The Hanging Tree?"

He nodded. "The big oak in the middle of the road. Used to be for hangin's, but we ain't had one of them in years."

It took a moment to mask her surprise before Bea thanked him again and stepped out on the rough plank walkway. The rain and sleet were gone, but an icy wind remained. Though cold, it was nothing like winter in New York, and the heavy wool traveling coat protected against the chill. However, she doubted her feet would ever be warm again.

She straightened her shoulders and looked around. The train station marked the southern edge of town. Across the street stood an empty wood-frame building, its weathered exterior badly in need of repair. Next to it was a wooden barbershop and bathhouse, its faded sign boasting a hot bath and shave for twenty-five cents. A narrow alley separated that establishment from the two-story Broken Spur Saloon that covered the block. An outside staircase led upstairs, and a simple balcony wrapped around the three sides visible from her vantage point. Movement from an open door drew her eye, and she watched as a cowboy exited one of the rooms, a scantily clad young woman hanging on his arm.

Face flaming, Bea jerked her gaze away and continued to survey her new home.

Further down, she saw the oak Mr. Upton mentioned. Squarely in the middle of the muddy boulevard, it towered at least fifty feet in the air. Gnarled, massive branches, barren of leaves, stretched over the road on either side. Easily three feet in diameter, the trunk was surrounded by twisted roots and patchy dead grass.

One could easily imagine it providing shade during the hot summer months for buildings in its shadow, one of which was the general store. *Mother would have a heart attack if I told her shade came from The Hanging Tree.* Thoughts of her mother dampened Bea's rising euphoria. She would no doubt have little good to say about any of it.

Shaking off the encroaching melancholy, Bea looked around. Worlds apart from New York, Bakersville sported an eclectic mix of structures. A brick-and-mortar bank sat next to a wooden apothecary. The hotel boasted a white stone façade and a large oak door, its glass heavily etched with an intricate design she could not determine at this distance and accented by dark blue trim. Another building was connected to the hotel, its bright yellow exterior shining in the drab, grey morning. Horses waited at scattered hitching posts, and an assortment of the town's inhabitants hurried about their business, no doubt anxious to get out of the weather.

On this side of the street, the telegraph office sat next to the station. A small alley on either side separated the blacksmith shop and livery stable from other buildings in the block. A sign hanging from the roof indicated the jail was up ahead, though she could see no further details from this angle.

She took a breath and headed in the direction of her new venture. At the end of the boardwalk, she stifled a groan. There was no walkway again until she got past the blacksmith shop.

She sighed and debated options. *Walking through the muck in the alley will ruin my shoes and my skirt.* She looked around, expecting to see a coach for hire. She sighed deeply and reminded herself she was no longer in the big city where carriages were the norm.

"Something wrong, ma'am?"

The deep voice came from a bear of a man standing in front of the smithy.

By his attire, a long leather apron and gloves, she assumed he was the proprietor and quickly pasted on a polite smile. "I don't suppose there is a carriage or something I could rent to get me to the general store?"

When he didn't reply right away, she wondered if he heard her question.

His slow, patronizing smile said he did. "No point in hitching up a carriage just to go there."

His voice, low-pitched and clear, held the faintest accent. French maybe? And more than a hint of disdain.

Miffed, Bea fixed him with her coldest glare. "I see. Well, thank you anyway." She bunched up her skirts and prepared to step into the muck.

"Hold up." He tossed his gloves onto a shelf behind him and walked toward her.

When he stopped at the foot of the single step, she found herself transfixed by sky-blue eyes framed by long, sooty lashes. The shadow of a beard on sun-bronzed skin added a rakish aura. Ebony hair was secured at the nape by a strip of leather while one wayward curl fell casually across his forehead, and masculine wisps coiled against the open V of his homespun shirt. Despite the cold air, perspiration hovered above full, sensual lips. She was acutely conscious of a broad, muscular chest and shoulders that appeared a yard wide. A quick inhale brought heady traces of sweat, leather, manure, and something she couldn't identify. It was rude to stare, but she couldn't help it.

He was the most handsome man she had ever seen in her life.

"Je vous donne une semaine, jolie dame."

Thanks to a determined nanny, Bea spoke fluent French and taught herself German as well. His French was smooth, refined, and totally out of place with his surroundings, so it took a moment for her surprised brain to translate the slight. Spine rigid, she looked down at him. "You give me a week for what, sir?"

Eyes wide, his head tilted back. "You speak French." The terse statement carried no hint of apology.

"Oui Monsieur. Couramment."

The sexy smile appeared slowly, and she sucked in a breath only to have it lodge in her throat when he scooped her up in his arms as though she weighed nothing and started across the street.

"What are you doing? Put me down this instant!" Even as she protested, she grabbed his apron for balance with one hand while the other remained pinned against a rock-solid chest.

He didn't stop. "You really want to walk in this muck?"

She jerked her head around, saw they were in the middle of the road, and bit her lip. "No. I don't."

They reached the other side in silence, and he set her feet on the boardwalk past the saloon. Face burning, she forced herself to meet his gaze. "Thank you."

He tipped his head slightly, murmured, *"Mon plaisir, Madame,"* and turned back to his shop.

Heart racing, she watched until he picked up his gloves and disappeared into the smithy.

Just then, Bea noticed Mrs. Martin gaping at her from the doorway of the telegraph office. The firm set of her mouth said the smithy was someone else of whom she disapproved.

CHAPTER TWO

L UCIAN CAUGHT THE GLARE OF LITTLE MOLE AS HE CROSSED the muddy street back to his shop. He smiled inwardly at the secret name he gave Mrs. Martin some time ago. She talked without thinking and made no apologies when the gossip she spread at will turned out to be false, nor did she cease her constant meddling. He shook his head, unable to understand a behavior he'd witnessed most of his life.

He entered the livery and picked up the gloves he'd tossed aside when the woman appeared. His first thought was Bakersville was no place for her. Mature, but not so much so, she carried herself with all the grace and elegance of any European aristocrat. The wintry wind whipped color into pale cheeks, and there was both delicacy and strength in her face. Dark hair glistening like polished mahogany peeked under the stylish bonnet, and rich, hazel eyes gleamed with purpose. He found himself intrigued at first glance. When she responded to his comment in French without the slightest hint of insult, his interest grew.

He didn't notice the scar at first. Though visible, it didn't detract from her beauty. Some people wore their marks on the outside. Others carried them deep in their core.

Despite his determination not to think about it, his mind drifted to the crumpled letter resting atop his dresser. It arrived two weeks ago and sat on the table another week before he opened it. He had no idea his grandfather even knew where he was. Not that

Luc tried to hide his trek to Texas. He simply thought the old man had written him off for good this time.

Apparently not. He would arrive mid-March and expected Luc to return to New York with him and assume control of the vast shipping empire that was the Moreau legacy. He even hinted that his broken engagement should proceed as planned.

"Not bloody likely," he murmured as his trip down memory lane continued.

Luc's father was a trapper, taking to the trade during an expedition to buy furs. During his second winter running traps, he met and fell in love with a Choctaw woman, and they eventually married. Luc remembered his father as a happy, smiling man who adored his wife and son. They did everything together. His father taught him to hunt, trap, fish, and his mother instilled in him the belief that family was everything.

While his grandfather never entirely accepted Luc's mother, he was civil when they visited him in New York. On such a visit when Luc was twelve, an outbreak of cholera robbed him of both parents and forced him into his grandfather's care.

A stern, taciturn man, Henry Moreau had no time for a grieving child and immediately sent him to a boarding school, followed by college and trips abroad.

Visits with his mother's people faded to a cherished memory as Luc traveled the world and rubbed elbows with nobles and the social elite.

It wasn't until his near engagement to Annabelle Blankenship two years ago that he finally realized something was missing from his life. And it wasn't marriage to a spoiled socialite.

Things came to a head at his grandfather's seventy-fifth birthday party, where the older Moreau planned to announce Luc's betrothal to Annabelle, a marriage arranged and agreed to by both families.

Luc didn't love her, wasn't sure he ever would, but she was

beautiful and sophisticated, and they got on well enough. Plus, she came from a wealthy family with connections, a necessity in the world he traveled.

And he was thirty-three years old. He wanted to settle down with a wife and family of his own. He wasn't particularly interested in the shipping business but felt obligated to his grandfather. Reluctantly, he resigned himself to a life in which he had little voice in planning.

Until he overheard a conversation between Annabelle and her best friend, Charlotte Ambrose, which revealed her true character and told him exactly how big a mistake he was about to make.

Even now, her cruel words sent anger coursing through his veins.

"You know his mother was a red savage," said Charlotte. "How can you bear to, you know, bed him."

Annabelle's laugh was cold and callous. "Darling, I'd bed the devil himself to get my hands on the Moreau fortune."

"What if you get with child?"

"Trust me," she murmured, "there will be no child in this marriage."

Luc barely heard their sharp gasps as he walked toward them from the shadows where he'd caught the conversation. "It is fortunate I found this out now." He couldn't keep the anger from his voice. Just this morning, she pledged to give him a child as soon as possible. But it was all a lie.

"Lucian, darling," she stammered, momentarily abashed, one gloved hand reaching for his arm. "I did not mean that the way it sounded."

He pushed her hand away. "And what way did you mean it, Belle?" He deliberately used the nickname she hated. "What else can one infer from it?" He took a step toward her, his steady voice filled with cold contempt. "You want my money. I've always known that. But you would deny me a child in return?"

"I-I, no, of course not." Face flaming, she glanced at Charlotte. "I merely meant I might not be able to conceive. My mother had great difficulty, you know, and I might as well."

Tension coiled around them like a snake, its bands growing tighter by the second as startled hurt turned to white-hot anger. "You are quite the liar, Belle."

He left her standing there, a protest dying on trembling lips.

Luc found his grandfather, told him the engagement was off, and walked out, leaving him to explain things to her family.

Their conversation the next day quickly escalated into a shouting match. His grandfather didn't care about what Annabelle said. He wanted the power that merging his empire with the Blankenship's lessor one would bring.

Luc's happiness meant nothing. And that hurt most of all.

When his grandfather calmly suggested Luc get a mistress, he walked out and never looked back.

Now, for whatever reason, he'd tracked him down and expected things to pick up where they left off.

Luc snapped tongs around a horseshoe and plunged it into the hot coals, working the bellows with his other hand. "Like bloody hell."

"You get that shoe any hotter you gonna ruin it."

The comment from Amos Bigelow, his friend and previous owner of the smithy, brought Luc up with a start. "I didn't hear you walk in."

"Some injun you are." He spit brown liquid toward a bucket in the corner. It hit the top and rolled down the side. "Thought you could hear a pin drop." Amos shuffled into the livery and lowered himself onto his favorite perch—an upturned barrel and sighed. "What's her name?"

Luc tapped the edge of the horseshoe with his hammer. "Who?"

"Don't play dumb with me, boy," he snipped. "The woman I seen you totin' across the road."

"No idea."

"What?"

He stuck the shoe back in the coals. "She came in on the train, needed to get to the other side. Couldn't let her walk through the mud."

"And you didn't ask her name? What's wrong with you?"

He ignored the dig.

Amos sighed. "I bet she smelled real good."

Like roses and honeysuckle.

"Well, did she?"

Amos's croaky voice drew him out of his reflections. "Did she what?"

"Hell, boy, ain't you listenin'? Did she smell good?"

He pulled the shoe out and pounded the edges again. "Fine."

"Fine? That's all I get? Fine?"

Luc stopped and looked at his friend. "Yes." He threw the shoe in a bucket of water beside him. "That's all you get."

Amos smacked his lips. "I seen her go into the general store. Mable said some man from New York bought it. Wonder if she's his wife?" He leaned over to look out the door. "Did you see him?"

It never occurred to Luc she might be married since she appeared to travel alone. Now, he found the thought rather disheartening. "Only folks who got off were her and Mrs. Martin."

"Hmm."

"Hey, Frenchy," came a gravelly voice from the doorway. "Can you do me a favor?"

He turned toward the voice. "Sure, Silas. What do you need?"

"That lady who came in on the train today, Miss Lockhart, needs a trunk taken to the hotel. It's a mite heavy for me. Would you mind taking it over?"

"No problem. She need it right away?"

"Well, now, she didn't say. She was headed to the general store. That's all I know."

"Give me an hour or so. I have to finish two shoes, then feed the stock."

"Thanks, Frenchy."

"If you find out she needs it sooner, let me know."

"I will. I sent that Martin boy over to tell Miss Lizzie she was gonna need a room, so she'll be expecting the trunk."

Luc watched him shuffle off, wondering not for the first time, why the gusty wind didn't topple him end over end.

"He's got rocks in his pockets."

Amos's comment drew Luc's gaze.

"To keep him from blowing away." Amos slapped his knee and cackled, the sound bordering on a hen's cluck.

"You're a fine one to talk, Old Man," teased Luc.

The cackle ceased abruptly. "She's a fine lookin' woman, though, ain't she?"

A grunt sufficed for a reply. This wasn't a conversation he wanted to get into at the moment.

"I watched her walk up the street, struttin' like a queen." He smacked his lips again. "Think I'll mosey over to the store and see what she smells like." He grimaced as he pushed himself up from the barrel. "These old bones are just gonna stop working one day."

He hobbled out, and Luc swallowed past the lump in his throat. Despite all his bluster and sass, Amos was the salt of the earth and the closest thing to family he had now.

Except for a grandfather who expected him to return to a place he hated and marry a woman he could never love. Or trust.

Unveiling Beulah is available now!

ACKNOWLEDGMENTS

There are many people to whom I owe a debt of gratitude for the completion of this book. First, to God for giving me the talent and making it possible to pursue my dreams.

Thank you to my wonderful husband, Boudreaux. Bless his heart. He has listened patiently to my rants when my 'imaginary friends' aren't speaking to me; given endless advice on covers, plot twists, and problem scenes; eaten take-out and leftovers more times than I can count, and never once complained. Thank you, Sweetie. I couldn't do this without you.

My mentor and friend, Patty Wiseman, will always tell me the truth, even when I don't want to hear it. My critique partners Beth Howlett, Phyllis Still, and Mike Clifton each provide a unique perspective that helps me stay grounded. You guys rock.

And a special thank you to Investigator Roxanne Warren, UPSO Retired, for answering my endless law enforcement questions on procedures, what-ifs, and stuff in general. Your patience, knowledge, and humor are appreciated.

This is a work of fiction, so any errors in procedure or process for the sake of the story are mine alone.

You know I love to include recipes at the end of my books. Usually, it's something one of the main characters cooked for the other one. In this case, it's the steaks Seth cooked for Jess and the dessert they didn't get to that night. My parents gifted us with triple-trimmed filets from Omaha Steaks over thirty years ago, and I've used them ever since. Any good filet will do. And this light, refreshing dessert is super easy and quick to make. I've made it with peach, lemon, and key lime, all of which are delicious. Use your favorite gelatin/yogurt combination. AND when using the sugar-free/fat-free/low-fat options, it's only 3 WW Points ☺. You're welcome!

Filet Mignon with Red Wine Reduction

2 (6 oz) Filet Mignon steaks, 1" thick
Salt and pepper to Taste
Herb Butter—softened (or regular butter if you prefer) (I love the parmesan, basil, garlic-flavored butter found at Walmart)
¼ cup chopped green onions (plain will do)
2 cloves garlic, minced
¼ cup beef stock (can use beef base mixed with water instead of stock)
¼ cup dry red wine
2 Tbsp chopped parsley

NOTE: Steaks are best when allowed to come to room temperature before cooking (thank you, Food Network). You can also omit the red wine reduction and just enjoy the steak as-is, but I like the addition. DIRECTIONS: Salt and pepper both sides of the steaks to taste. Place about 2 Tbsp of butter on top of each steak, smooth over the surface, and pat it down. Turn and repeat. Cover and allow to rest at room temperature for half an hour before cooking. Heat a heavy sauté pan over medium-high heat. Add steaks and cook to preferred level of doneness (about 4 minutes per side for medium, depending on thickness.) Turn, repeat. Once you turn the steaks, baste with the melted butter in the pan; transfer to a serving platter when done. Set aside to rest. Add additional Tbsp butter to the pan. Reduce heat to medium. Add onions and garlic and cook for one minute. Don't let it get brown. Add wine, stir well, add beef stock, stir well, and bring to boil. Reduce heat to simmer. Cook until most of the moisture evaporates and the sauce glazes to deep brown— about 1-2 minutes. Pour sauce over filets, top with chopped parsley, and serve.

You can also season and add butter to the steaks, then refrigerate, even overnight. Just allow to reach room temperature before cooking, and the butter will help to flavor and tenderize the meat.

LIGHT AND EASY CREAM PIE

1 (4 oz) pkg sugar-free peach-flavored gelatin
¼ cup boiling water
1 (8oz) carton fat-free whipped topping
1(6oz) carton peach flavored light yogurt
1 reduced-fat graham cracker crust.

Mix yogurt and whipped topping together in a large bowl. Set aside. Dissolve gelatin in boiling water. Once dissolved, add to whipped topping mixture and gently stir until well mixed. Pour into graham cracker crust. Cover and chill until set.

This recipe can be made with any gelatin/yogurt combination. I prefer the peach, but strawberry banana is good, too. Just match the gelatin with the yogurt, and you are good to go.
You can also use regular gelatin instead of sugar-free.

ABOUT THE AUTHOR

 Dana Wayne is a sixth-generation Texan, admitted die-hard romantic, and a lover of good food, good wine, and good company. She routinely speaks to book clubs, writers' groups, and other organizations and is a frequent guest on numerous writing blogs. A strong advocate for new authors, she started a podcast in 2020 called A Writer's Life where she shares her experiences on the road from writer wanna be to award-winning romance author. Her romantic stories are filled with strong women, second chances, and happily ever after.

She published her first book in 2016 and never looked back. Among her accolades are two first-place wins, one-second place, three RONE Award Nominations, Scéal Award Finalist, Top 50 Indie Authors You Need to Read, Reviewers Top Pick, and Five Star reviews from Readers Favorite, InD'tale Magazine and Books, and Benches Magazine.

"I am all about the romance and strive for real in my books. They are entertaining and heartwarming with a splash of humor and suspense. My stories are character-driven with a lot of emotion. They are steamy and typically have one or two love scenes toward the end because I believe romance is about emotion, not sex, and the journey is more important than the destination."

She is a long-time member of Writers League of Texas; Authors Marketing Guild, LLC; East Texas Writers Association; Northeast Texas Writers Organization; and East Texas Writers Guild.

www.danawayne.com

www.instagram.com/danawayne423

www.facebook.com/danawayne423

www.twitter.com/danawayne423

https://anchor.fm/dana-wayne

CPSIA information can be obtained
at www.ICGtesting.com
Printed in the USA
LVHW100706030423
743272LV00001BA/158